FIRE IN THE SKY

Acclaim for Radclyffe's Fiction

Finders Keepers "is a delightful slow-burn, enemies-to-lovers romance...It also has puppies—six adorable, bright eyed, floppy eared, soft and cuddly puppies. I admit it. I'm an absolute sucker for sweet, furry baby animals. Add them to a romantic couple in a story, and I'm hooked."—*Rainbow Reflections*

Only This Summer "is an absolute must-read for anyone who enjoys a well-written lesbian romance novel...A law enforcement officer with a penchant for trouble meets a doctor who is desperate to get away and find some modicum of peace...What I've found is typical in Radclyffe's storytelling is the depth and complexity of the characters. They are richly drawn and fully realized, making it easy to invest in their journeys and root for their happy endings." —*station12reads*

"Radclyffe writes fantastic books. They are easy to read, well-paced, with relatable and realistic characters. I find [the *PMC Hospital Romance*] series particularly fun to read because Radclyffe was a practicing surgeon before turning full time to writing, so the medical storyline reads so well. Her stories tend to be a slow burn with lots of flirting and tension building and a spicy, well-written, realistic payoff at the end...I really enjoyed that the 'rivalry' [in *Perfect Rivalry*] was more of an ambitious respect for another—so, not enemies to lovers but more cranky to inseparable."—*rubiareads*

"After seven books [in the *Rivers Community Romance* series] about the lives and loves in this small town, I do admit that I am starting to wonder if there may be some pheromone that lures unsuspecting, brilliant, handsome/gorgeous, brooding/plucky lesbians into town where they get sucked into the Rivers hospital community...All that [in *Pathway to Love*] with smoldering chemistry between the mains as well as lots of action in the ER/OR and the bedroom. But, hey... these are Radclyffe novels. And I get sucked into each and every one of them."—*MEC for TBR Reviews*

"Medical drama, gossipy lesbian romance, and angsty backstory all get equal time in [*Unrivaled*], Radclyffe's fifth PMC Hospital Romance...[F]ans of small community dynamics and workplace romance without ethical complications will find this hits the spot." —*Publishers Weekly*

Praise for Julie Cannon

Shut Up and Kiss Me

"A feel good, tingly romance."—*Best Lesfic Reviews*

"Fast-paced, sexy, and fun with a bit of an insta-love plot (a trope I love!) I thoroughly enjoyed this read."—*JK's Blog*

"Great story, and I will definitely read this author again!"—*Janice Best, Librarian (Albion District Library)*

Wishing On a Dream—Lambda Literary Award Finalist

"[The main characters] are well-rounded, flawed and with backstories that fascinated me. Their relationship grows slowly and with bumps along the way but it is never boring. At times it is sweet, tender, and emotional, at other times downright hot. I love how Julie Cannon chose to tell it from each point of view in the first person. It gave greater insight into the characters and drew me into the story more. A really enjoyable read."—*Kitty Kat's Book Review Blog*

"This book pulls you in from the moment you pick it up. Keirsten and Tobin are very different, but from the moment they get together, the heat and sexual tension are there. Together they must work through their fears in order to have a magical relationship." —*RT Book Reviews*

Smoke and Fire

"Cannon skillfully draws out the honest emotion and growing chemistry between her heroines, a slow burn that feels like constant foreplay leading to a spectacular climax. Though Brady is almost too good to be true, she's the perfect match for Nicole. Every scene they share leaps off the page, making this a sweet, hot, memorable read."—*Publishers Weekly*

"This book is more than a romance. It is uplifting in a very down-to-earth way and inspires hope through hard-won battles where neither woman is prepared to give up."—*Rainbow Book Reviews*

By Radclyffe

Innocent Hearts

Promising Hearts

Love's Melody Lost

Love's Tender Warriors

Tomorrow's Promise

Love's Masquerade

shadowland

Turn Back Time

When Dreams Tremble

The Lonely Hearts Club

Secrets in the Stone

Desire by Starlight

Homestead

The Color of Love

Secret Hearts

Only This Summer

First Responders Novels

The Honor Series

The Justice Series

Midnight Hunters (writing as L.L. Raand)

PMC Hospitals Romances

Provincetown Tales

Rivers Community Romances

Visit us at www.boldstrokesbooks.com

FIRE IN THE SKY

by

RADCLY*f*FE AND
JULIE CANNON

2023

ISBN 13: 978-1-63679-573-7

THIS TRADE PAPERBACK ORIGINAL IS PUBLISHED BY
BOLD STROKES BOOKS, INC.
P.O. BOX 249
VALLEY FALLS, NY 12185

FIRST EDITION: DECEMBER 2023

CREDITS
EDITOR: STACIA SEAMAN
PRODUCTION DESIGN: STACIA SEAMAN
COVER DESIGN BY TAMMY SEIDICK

Acknowledgments

With thanks to Sandy Lowe for suggesting that after 70 novels, I try something new: writing a book with another author. When we discussed it, the obvious first question was who? We both answered instantly—Julie Cannon. The whys are many: Julie is an experienced, skilled, and professional writer as well as being personally confident, good-natured, and goal-oriented (as in the final product is the priority). Our goal was to write the best book we could in a way that worked for both of us. After all, writing should be fun. This was an adventure whose destination was unknown at the beginning, and a process I enjoyed from beginning to end. The product of our collaboration is one I enjoyed working on immensely and am delighted to bring to all our readers. Thank you, Julie, for the trust, camaraderie, and fine work.

—Radclyffe

When Radclyffe asked me if I'd like to write a book with her, I was stunned, flattered, scared to death, and everything in between. It was the first time collaborating on a book for both of us, and I hope you enjoy the happenings at the Red Sky Ranch as much as we did writing them for you.

—Julie Cannon

Dedication

Special, heartfelt thanks to Stacia Seaman for the care and attention she gave this work during a personally difficult time.
—Radclyffe

For my family.
—Julie Cannon

AUTHOR'S NOTE

The location of the Red Sky Ranch was inspired by a recent visit to Wickenburg, Arizona, a small town located northeast of Phoenix. As an author I've exercised a bit of creative license to describe the town, surrounding area, the weather and terrain. What is not fiction is the residents of Wickenburg and their warm, welcoming smiles and conversations with visitors. Come visit, you'll love it.

—Julie Cannon

CHAPTER ONE

Wickenburg, Arizona
April

Kelsey Brunel propped her dusty boots on the wooden rail, sipped her last mug of coffee for the day, and watched the two-year-old midnight black colt in the corral opposite the ranch house snort and fuss. She could swear he was glaring at her.

"Still put out, are you?"

She'd spent most of the morning trying to convince Rebel, so named for his contrary nature, that a saddle was not a torture device. She smiled and rubbed the sore spot on her thigh where she'd landed on a rock, courtesy of His Highness out there.

"You can carry on all you want. I'm a lot more stubborn than you."

"More than any animal or person, I'll wager," a gravelly voice behind her said as the screen door swung open with a screech before slamming shut.

"I've been meaning to fix that damn door," Kelsey said.

Her father appeared beside her and leaned against the porch post, his hands shoved into the pockets of his worn tan canvas work pants. A lifetime of hard work under the Arizona sky had aged him past his sixty-eight years. His hair had once been the color of hers, jet black and just as unruly. But now tufts of gray stuck out from under his sweat-stained cowboy hat. Her stomach tightened. The set look of his squared-off jaw, another feature they shared, indicated he was chewing over something he wished he didn't have to talk about. The first time she'd seen that look had been the day he'd delivered the worst news she could ever imagine.

She steeled herself for some kind of bad news now. Was he sick? Had one of the hands been in an accident? Had they lost one of their irreplaceable stock? "What's going on?"

"I don't know any way to say this but straight out," he said with a hint of heat. "Kelsey—I sold the ranch."

Kelsey heard the words but couldn't make sense of them. "You did what?"

"I sold the ranch. To some developers." His words were choppy, as if he wished they'd disappear into the air. "A resort owned by some people with more money than brains. A lot of money. They're gonna turn it into a spa or something."

Kelsey shot out of her chair so fast it almost tipped over. The sound of her boots on the wooden porch floor echoed like rifle shots in the quiet late afternoon. "Are you out of your mind?"

When her father didn't answer, Kelsey stopped dead. "You made some kind of deal for our *ranch* without talking to me about it?"

"Now, Kel honey, let me explain."

Kel. He only ever called her that when he was trying to railroad her into believing something or hoping to get her to see his way.

You won't even miss her in a few weeks, Kel honey.

Don't you worry, Kel, I'm done with the drinking.

We'll have that little loan paid off before you know it, Kel.

A wave of fury nearly choked off her voice. She'd heard that tone from him before, too. The one that said he was sorry he'd missed her birthday or her first competition ride or some other first because he'd been busy working. Busy drunk, was what he hadn't said. She took a long breath. Those days were behind them. But this?

"Explain?" she said through a clenched jaw. She'd never get

anything out of him if she lost her temper, but holding back a flood of curses took all her willpower. "There is no explanation that makes what you did right. Just—tell me why."

"Kelsey."

She ignored the look on his face. The one that said she was about to step across the line. The line of respect she never crossed, not even when she despaired that he'd ever keep his word when he claimed to have had his last drink. "How could you do this behind my back? This is my home, my *life*, we're talking about."

Her father looked away. "I needed the money."

"For what?" Kelsey snapped, the anger and fear more than she could contain. The Red Sky Ranch had to be worth tens of millions of dollars. What had he done that he needed that kind of money? "Dad. Answer me."

"It's none of your business."

"The hell it's not!" Kelsey balled her fists to hide the trembling. This couldn't be happening.

"Don't talk to me like that," he said, annoyance replacing the conciliation in his tone.

"What do you expect?" Kelsey replied. "You've cut my legs right out from under me. Did you expect me to just say, *Yes, sir, it's fine by me that you've just destroyed my whole life?*"

"It wasn't your decision."

"Well, it's pretty damn obvious that *you* think so. And how it affects me didn't cross your mind either."

"Of course it did."

"Bullshit." Kelsey was as surprised as her father by the outburst. She rarely ever swore in front of him and never *at* him. But she'd never been in this position before. Everything she loved, everything that mattered to her, was suddenly coming apart, and she was helpless.

"You blindsided me, Dad. Like a damn coward."

"Kelsey," her father began, a pleading note replacing the anger in his voice, but she didn't want to hear any more.

"When do we have to be out?" She sounded on the edge of

dangerous, and that was how she felt. The thought of leaving the ranch behind tore her soul apart.

"The fifteenth."

"What? That's less than a month. Deals like this don't happen that fast."

"They had cash. No need to get the banks involved to slow things up."

"They paid cash?" Kelsey did a quick calculation in her head. There had better have been a lot of zeros in the purchase price. Not expecting an answer, she asked anyway. "How much did they pay?"

"None of your business."

"You didn't give it away, did you?"

"None of your business." His tone was much harsher this time.

"It is my business," she snapped. Or at least she'd thought it was. "Did you at least get Harrison involved?"

"I don't need an attorney—or you—telling me what I can and can't do."

"You didn't, did you? What the hell is going on? You owe me an explanation."

"I don't owe you anything. I didn't ask you to come back here."

Kelsey staggered at her father's words, the pain worse than if he'd actually struck her. She'd returned after college because this was her home, because she loved this land, this ranch…him.

"And don't think you're getting any money from the sale."

"The money—" Kelsey stopped midsentence. Another blow from the man she loved, and who she thought loved her. This bad dream had turned into a nightmare.

She turned her back on him, jumped down from the porch, and stormed across the yard to the barn. She needed to get away. To… think. There had to be some way to change what couldn't possibly be true. First, she needed to put distance between her temper and the man who had completely changed her life.

The hinge on the barn door squeaked as she pulled it open and stepped inside. The late afternoon sun slanted across the hard-packed earth floor, leaving the stalls and rafters in comforting shadows. The smell of horse, hay, and leather was familiar and calming. Several horses stuck their heads out over their stall doors, curious about their unexpected visitor, their ears perked and alert.

Kelsey walked past Zippy, a twenty-two-year-old paint, followed by Hope, a Belgium draft, then Apache, Moody, and Sugar. There were nine other horses in this barn and an additional nine in the adjacent one. During a typical week, they used six to eight of the animals for guests for the horseback riding activities. Staff rode four others while supervising the events. That allowed ample time for all the horses to be well rested between outings. Kelsey knew the personality and temperament of every horse and was personally responsible for matching horse and rider.

She stopped in front of Adira, a seventeen-year-old Belgium draft, and pulled a peppermint from her pocket. She was still amazed how a simple treat or piece of a carrot could make a horse feel special and loved. She took the halter off the hook to the left of her stall, unlatched the door, and stepped inside.

"Hey, baby girl, how was your day?" Kelsey moved slowly, keeping her voice calm and soothing. Horses could detect a fly landing on their bare back and just as easily sensed the mood of those around them. Just now, she simmered inside—a combination of anger, hurt, and betrayal—but she wasn't about to inflict those feelings on her horse.

Adira deserved nothing but love and affection—just like all the others at the ranch—but Kelsey had a soft spot for her. She'd been rescued from a kill pen eighteen months earlier and had been Kelsey's baby ever since the transport truck had dropped her and another frightened, malnourished horse, Angus, off by the side of the road in the middle of the night. Adira had numerous medical issues and had almost died twice, but after a dozen visits by the vet, solid nutrition, and months of patience, she was thriving. Now she was Kelsey's horse. Or maybe it was the other way around.

Kelsey continued talking to Adira in a soft voice about nothing much as she buckled the leather halter with Adira's name embossed on a brass plate on the side. The familiar motions and aimless conversation helped quiet the roaring in Kelsey's head and eased the constriction in her chest. After leading Adira outside and giving her a quick but thorough brushing, Kelsey saddled her, mounted, and with a slight click in her throat and a nudge of her boots, walked her out of the paddock area toward the south gate.

In the coolness of the April afternoon, with the sun on the downside of the day and shadows creeping in, she was glad for the duster she'd grabbed from a peg on her way out of the tack room. The sky flamed in breathtaking shades of orange and purple against the Black Hills mountains. Some might take the heart-stopping sunsets for granted after a lifetime in the desert, but Kelsey never would. No wonder countless artists and songwriters had attempted to catch the magnificence of the fire in the sky. The Red Sky Ranch lay in the heart of those spectacular mountains, peaks, buttes, and plateaus. Kelsey couldn't imagine living anywhere else. Her throat tightened at the thought of the unimaginable, and she pulled her focus back to the beauty around her.

As she rode deeper into the desert, her boots and jeans brushed against the prickly pear and ocotillo cactus, and their needles made their way onto her legs.

"Should have worn my chaps," she grumbled. "Tenderfoot mistake."

Her mind had not been on what she was about, still reeling from her father's announcement. Pronouncement, more like it. As if her opinion about her own damn life didn't matter. And what did he expect her—*them*—to do without the ranch? Move to town? She snorted. Not damn likely.

There had to be a way to undo what he'd done—she *had* to find it.

Adira picked up her pace, sensing where they were headed, where Kelsey needed to be. It was her place. Where she went to think, to empty her mind, and to heal. More than a few times she'd traveled this way with tears threatening to stream down her cheeks. The first time had been when her mother had left and her father had gruffly said she was never coming back. Kelsey'd been seven. There'd been other heartaches—girlfriends and lovers she'd lost or left before she'd figured out relationships weren't for her—that she'd healed on this well-worn path. But nothing like this pain.

"Whoa, girl."

Adira halted instantly, and Kelsey swiveled in the saddle, the creak of leather the only sound as she took in the land around her. Red Sky Ranch land as far as she could see. The ranch itself was just visible on the horizon—the main house with eight guest rooms on the second floor, two bunkhouses holding a maximum of eight guests each off to the left, and spreading out over two acres in the rear, six casitas, one of them hers. Other guest amenities included a pool, clay tennis courts, and the critical features, at least in Kelsey's view—the four open air corrals, tack room, and two barns housing their trail horses. A dozen or more wranglers depending on the season—several of whom doubled as blacksmiths and farriers— three cooks, and Kelsey and her father made up the staff.

Twenty thousand acres that had been in her family for five generations. Her great-great-great-grandfather had settled on land thought to be uninhabitable, but he'd seen the potential and built a thriving cattle ranch. The generations after him expanded the enterprise. When economics made running cattle unprofitable, her grandfather had seen the future and transformed the ranch into one of the most highly successful dude ranches in the country. Reservations at the Red Sky were often booked a year in advance by people coming from all over the world. What was the plan now? Would those reservations be canceled with little to no notice? Would the Red Sky Ranch even *be* a ranch by the end of the year?

Had her father given any thought to their reputation? And what about the people who counted on them? Many of the staff had been at the ranch since before Kelsey was born, and they, too, were impacted by her father's decision. How did a fifty-six-year-old cowboy like Rubin, their lead trail hand, build another life?

The tears she'd been fighting streaked her cheeks, and she swiped at them impatiently. She ignored the pain that made every breath an agony. She wasn't about to let everything she cared about just slip away.

"God damn it, Dad. Why did you sell the ranch? And how the hell do I undo this disaster?"

Chapter Two

The Sutton Building, Manhattan, New York
May

Elizabeth Sutton's phone vibrated, signaling an incoming message. Frowning, she picked it up off her desk to check the screen. She studied the message…just a few words and numbers. The image icon was clear enough—her father. That made the intent clearer. She took a breath. *Meeting my office. 600*

"Isn't it just about six?" she asked as she set the phone down. She had a very good internal sense of time and rarely needed to check, but this time minutes mattered.

"Mm, a couple minutes to," Olivia said.

"We'll have to call it a day," Elizabeth said. "We can finish this up tomorrow."

Olivia cocked her head. "Why? We've only got another section to go." She laughed, her deep brown eyes sparkling. "And I don't have any exciting plans tonight."

"I've got a meeting."

"What? There's nothing on the schedule."

Olivia would know. Her best friend and longtime admin managed Elizabeth's schedule, knew the topics of every meeting, provided a summary for those she couldn't attend, and through the rumor mill and her keen insight, knew as much about what was going on at Sutton as anyone other than Elizabeth's father.

Elizabeth gestured to the phone. "A summons."

Grimacing, Olivia stood, all five-feet-nothing of her graceful and elegant in sand-colored heels, tapered beige pants, and a burnt orange fitted silk shirt. As she crossed the expanse of Elizabeth's office to the credenza and poured a glass of water, she said casually, "And he just now texted you? Not a voice message."

"It's fine," Elizabeth said gently. "Save your energy for the real battles."

Olivia grinned, a dangerous grin if you knew her well. And Elizabeth did. "Power move."

"I know."

"You want me to go with?"

Elizabeth shook her head. Whatever this was about, her father had arranged it so she'd be off-balance. No need to let him know she was. "I'll be fine. Go home."

Olivia pursed her lips. "I don't like it. But all right. Call me soonest."

"I will."

" 'Night," Elizabeth called as they parted in the hall outside her office. She hurried across the wide expanse of carpeted lobby, past the imposing chest-high, curved walnut reception desk, and through the equally imposing wide, dark cherry doors into her father's office suite.

His admin nodded. "In his office."

"Yes," Elizabeth said and walked through the open door to the chief executive's—aka her father's—imposing corner office. Her father, tanned, fit, and looking a decade or two younger than his early sixties. Strangers often remarked on their resemblance, but her father's thick hair appeared leonine in tone and hers had always been described as honeyed. His eyes were more on the ice-blue side while hers were a warmer azure. They both had the same faint dent in their chins. Daily trips to the gym, regular visits to the back room of his barber shop for a touch-up, and four times a year Botox injections often had him mistaken for her brother.

Today he was behind his desk, his back to the two walls of floor-to-ceiling windows with Manhattan spread out below him, as she expected. What she didn't expect was the other occupant sprawled in the club chair in front of the desk. The chief financial officer of Sutton Properties, Michael Wyland. Only a few years older than her, his thinning brown hair and sharp, pinched features made him look forty-nine rather than late thirties.

"You're late," Michael said with a smirk. "Have trouble with the message?"

Elizabeth ignored him. She'd had a lifetime of practice disregarding the subtle digs and not-so-subtle comments of people using her dyslexia to belittle her. Michael only knew of her challenges because her father had told him—a slip her father had dismissed as unimportant. That betrayal had cut deep at the time, but she'd buried it with all the others. She'd given up trying to understand why people tended to pick on those they perceived as different about the time she was ten years old, too.

She took the other chair and glanced at her father, letting Michael know who she saw as having the power. "Something come up?"

Her father smiled thinly. "I'll let Michael fill you in on a new project I'm sure you'll find interesting."

Michael handed her a thick prospectus. "It's all in here, but I'll lay it out for you—so you won't have to spend too much time with the details."

"Thank you," Elizabeth said flatly and rested the prospectus on the corner of her father's desk. She'd have everything in it memorized within twenty-four hours. She schooled her expression as Michael spoke and the very unsavory details emerged.

"And that's pretty much the big picture," Michael said after a few minutes. "Any...questions?"

So, you're sending me to bum-fuck nowhere? was what she wanted to ask, but if she did, she'd find herself at an even greater disadvantage than she already was. Michael, the weasel, had obviously run to her father with the story he thought would give him the upper hand in all of this.

"Where is *Wickenburg*?" she asked, hoping she sounded more eager for the assignment than she really was. She had earned better than this project. She'd paid her dues. She was on her fifth passport and had successfully overseen the production of twelve of the thirty-eight Sutton Properties resorts around the world. And now they were sending her to some backwater hole as punishment? This could only be coming from one thing. One momentary—and rare—lapse in judgement.

How was she to know the woman she'd met over a late drink in the lounge at the Grill and allowed herself to be seduced by the admittedly very attractive brunette's interest in her was the chief financial officer's baby sister? Allison Wyland was like no baby Elizabeth had ever known. And she was certainly not innocent when she skillfully maneuvered her tongue on Elizabeth's intimate parts. How was she to know the woman wasn't out of the closet to her family? The final surprise came when baby sister pointed her finger at Elizabeth as the instigator of the lip-lock big brother Michael stumbled upon in the office parking garage one morning after a dinner date turned into an all-nighter.

"Wickenburg?" Michael said, as if anyone else would know where it was. "It's about ninety minutes outside Phoenix. Red Sky Ranch is currently a dude ranch owned by a man named Red Brunel. He had a string of bad luck at cards, so local sources say, and was looking for a quick sale. I lowballed him, and he jumped on it. We close next week. We're getting twenty thousand acres, the main house, several bunkhouses, a couple of barns, and a bunch of horses."

"Horses," Elizabeth said. What kind of modern resort had horses? Well, they'd have to go along with the rest of the probable quaint kitsch during the remodel.

"Yep," Michael said, clearly enjoying himself. "They have confirmed reservations for the next eight months, so we need to keep the present staff on to run the place. Who stays after that will be up to you once you get there and sort things out."

Elizabeth flipped through the prospectus for Sutton Properties' latest spa and retreat and scanned the photos of the existing resort. Sutton Properties was a global company with high-end resorts, wellness centers, and spas, and now she was building what looked like the back lot of an old western movie. "So, the plan is to keep most of the buildings. I guess we can work with that. The architecture has a Southwestern theme at least. What's the timeline?"

"It needs to be ready to open November first."

"*This* November?" She'd been given difficult projects in the past, but transforming a dude ranch into a five-star resort and spa in six months was next to impossible. She didn't know anything about a dude ranch other than that it was probably nothing but dirt and cow patties. She made a note to stop at an outdoor recreation store. She wasn't going to ruin her Loro Piana boots by stepping in piles of horse shit. She didn't often splurge on designer wear, but she loved those damn boots.

"I know it's a short timeline, but we fully expect that you'll get it done." Michael gave her his patented grin-fuck again. God, she loathed him.

She held his gaze until he looked away.

"Summer is the slow season for everything in Arizona when their temperatures climb above one hundred and five degrees," her father put in. "Their guest reservations reflect that, so they won't be in the way too much."

"It gets hotter than hell in July and August. My *older* sister lives in Phoenix, and it's like stepping out of your house and into a furnace," Michael commented.

"Yes, well," her father hurriedly added, "the winter months are the high tourist season when all the snowbirds start coming to town. Even the locals want to get away and relax, so you can count on occupancy accelerating then."

They'd done their homework. Just how long had they known about this? Obviously much longer than her five fucking minutes. Her father's part in blindsiding her hurt, but why she was still surprised by his lack of support was the more surprising thing. More fool she for hoping anything would change. He insisted on calling her the heir to Sutton, but he'd given Michael Wyland more and more power every year, to the point that Michael was closing deals for him now. Michael had obviously had a major hand in this one.

"It makes sense to have it open before the holidays," Elizabeth commented, her natural business instinct overriding her anger at being kept in the dark. "It does look like there's plenty of potential."

One aerial view showcased the white buildings under pale-pink tiled roofs. A nearby pool with a large, covered patio adjoining it looked inviting. The wood and timber structures appeared to be in good shape, but who knew how long ago the pictures were taken. If Brunel was having money trouble, he probably hadn't kept up regular maintenance. Several other glossy photos featured smiling people on horses riding through the desert—*not on your life*, others sitting on the ground around a roaring campfire—*I refuse to sit on the ground*, trying to throw a rope over a cow—*great, more shit to step in*, a woman shooting some type of rifle—*great, I'm going to be stuck in the wild west*, and Jeeps kicking up dust on a dirt trail—*nope, not getting grit under my contacts.*

"Brunel is expecting you on Sunday."

Elizabeth pressed her hands to her thighs to keep from clenching her fists. Her father expected her to stop her life and pick up and relocate to Nowhereville, Arizona, in three days? Of course he did.

"Well, since we've got that settled," Michael said with one last non-smile in Elizabeth's direction, "I'm meeting my *other* sister for dinner."

"Ellie," her father said as Michael strolled out and Elizabeth rose to follow, "can you stay for a few minutes?"

Elizabeth gritted her teeth. *Can* was a word her father never meant. To other people *can* meant *are you able to*. For her father it meant *you* will *stay for as long as I want you to*.

She said, "Dad, I've asked you many times to call me Elizabeth, especially in the office. It's just more professional."

"You don't need to be bothered by that BS." He waved her off. "You've proven yourself to everyone."

But not to you. Her oldest brother, a neurosurgeon, lived in Connecticut and rarely communicated with anyone in the family. Her next brother was the attorney general of the state of Illinois. Neither one of them had shown any interest in following in her father's footsteps, but she had. For the longest time, her father had never taken her seriously. Partly because she was a woman and would never compare to her brothers in his eyes. And partly—mostly—because he and everyone else had never believed her capable of the skills and intelligence required to excel in business. Or anything academic. She'd finally discovered a way to show her teachers and him that she was far more competent than anyone realized. She wasn't sure she'd ever really convinced her father, and she often wondered why she continued to try.

Today was one of those days. She didn't harbor any illusions about him, which made her desire to please him even more aggravating. Jonas Sutton was a legend in the business world. He was a gentleman in the office and a crude, bigoted asshole when not. He was a ruthless competitor, a subtle womanizer, and proudly defined by his successes. Elizabeth, in the vulnerable place inside that wants to be loved by a parent, still wished to be one of those successes.

"And you're Elizabeth Helene Sutton," he said, like it was a name that had come down from God. "Anyone disrespects you disrespects me."

Hell, he sounds like a don in one of those mafioso movies he likes.

"Sit," he commanded, leaning back behind his enormous, gleaming dark walnut desk. Another move she was well used to. He always used his position behind the massive desk as a power play.

Elizabeth sat. The sooner this conversation was over, the sooner she could get started on the ten million things she had to do before she had to leave.

"I had an interesting conversation with Michael a week ago," he said.

And there it was. The real reason for this whole charade.

"About?" She wasn't going to make this easy for him. Why should she? She was well beyond the age when her private business was any of his, and Allison—Michael's *baby* sister—was well into her twenties. Her father had never approved of what he insisted on calling her *lifestyle*, as if she had chosen to love women like she'd decided to live in Manhattan.

"Come now. I think you know."

"Michael has a lot of things he talks to you about."

Her father's eyes sparked with temper and Elizabeth secretly smiled. She was his daughter, after all, and he knew exactly what she was doing. Irritating him was petty, perhaps, but she didn't appreciate being ambushed by the likes of Michael Wyland and called into account by her father as if she was twelve years old.

"The incident with Allison." He emphasized the word *incident* as if she'd committed a crime.

"When he walked up on us kissing, you mean," Elizabeth said blandly.

Her father flushed. "Michael claims that you'd forced yourself on her."

"Did he?"

"Allison told him she wasn't like *that* and had asked you on several occasions to leave her alone. She said she'd told you to stop pursuing her."

Elizabeth rose and picked up the prospectus of her next project. Like it or not, she had a job to do, and she'd damn well do it better than anyone else in this company or any other could do. She looked across the desk at her father, whose surprise showed. "The only time Allison ever told me to stop was when it followed the word *don't*."

It took a moment before he shot to his feet.

"For fuck's sake. He wanted me to fire you."

"Is that why he's in such a sour mood? Or is it because *I've* said no to *him* more times than I can count?" She shook her head. "So, sending me to BF Nowhere is to appease Michael?"

Her father didn't answer her questions. If he cared that Michael had hit on her, to put it nicely, he didn't show it. "Just don't embarrass Sutton Properties and me."

"I'd never do anything to intentionally embarrass Sutton or you. But I'm not going to live in the proverbial closet. Not for you. Not for anyone."

Elizabeth's heart was pounding, but she refused to break eye contact.

The ticking of the antique Howard Miller clock on the corner of his desk was the only sound in the room.

"Get out of here and keep me in the loop," he finally said, dismissing her as he sat down and picked up his tablet.

"I always do." Elizabeth didn't hurry as she walked back to her office. She was surprised, when she saw her reflection in the glass wall separating the reception area from the hallway, that steam wasn't puffing out of her ears. Lately every conversation with her father turned into a battle, and she hated to lose.

As she walked into the empty anteroom of her smaller suite, she instructed her phone's AI to call Olivia.

"Pack your bags, we've got a new project."

"What? Where? When did this come up? Wait—don't tell me—the mystery meeting."

"Still ahead of the curve," Elizabeth said, not bothering to hide the bitterness in her voice. Olivia would know the frustration wasn't aimed at her. "It will all be in the prospectus Michael dropped on me."

"That rat bastard," Olivia muttered.

"I thought weasel, but they're similar." Elizabeth laughed. Thank heavens for Olivia. Her best friend kept her sane, as well as saved her butt a dozen times a day. They'd met in grade school, and although their backgrounds were very different, they'd become instant friends. Maybe because neither of them really wanted to be at the exclusive school or because they shared a love of sports. With her petite build, Olivia had been a natural at gymnastics, and Elizabeth had already discovered the bliss of being alone in the water. Swimming was her escape. Olivia had also been the first one to recognize that Elizabeth's problems in school stemmed from her difficulty reading and not, as everyone assumed, because she wasn't intelligent.

"You like math a lot more than reading, don't you?" Olivia had said one day.

"Maybe, why?" Elizabeth asked cautiously, having learned already not to speak of this. She'd been seven when she'd realized the other kids were reading while she was struggling to understand what she was seeing. The one and only time she told anyone was the day she said to her mother, "The other kids are learning the words in the storybooks, and I can't do it."

Her mother had looked at her expressionlessly and said, "Elizabeth, *can't* is not a word we use in this family. You will learn, and you will be the best at it."

There had been no encouragement or offer of assistance—only silence, and Elizabeth had never spoken of it again until the day Olivia finally offered her a lifeline.

Olivia said, "You always finish the math problems way ahead of everyone else."

"Math is easier," Elizabeth said.

"Easier than what?" Olivia's tone had been curious, but not mocking or critical, and her directness had made Elizabeth feel safe.

Because she needed so much not to keep carrying the secret, she'd said, "Than trying to figure out what the words mean."

"You don't know the words?" Olivia frowned.

"No. I know the words, but when they're all together I... don't." She took a breath. How could she explain what she didn't understand? "When I hear the words...like someone reads out loud? I understand. But seeing them...I...it's like they don't mean anything."

Olivia held out her hand. "Show me what you're reading. I'll read it out loud, and you follow the words on the page."

"Why?"

"Why not?"

From then on, when they weren't practicing for their respective sports, Olivia was helping Elizabeth read. Eventually, at Olivia's prompting, Elizabeth had been able to explain her difficulty to her teachers and finally her family—who had always treated her as if she'd been incapable of meeting their high standards. She and Olivia still worked through extensive documents together, since Elizabeth had excellent auditory recall and could commit data to memory with no effort.

"What exactly are we doing?" Olivia asked suspiciously.

"It's a long, dusty story," Elizabeth replied. This assignment was likely to be harder on Olivia than her. Olivia Martinez was the daughter of Guatemalan immigrants but a child of the city. Her parents had moved to Manhattan when Olivia was just a baby. Olivia loved fine dining, getting a mani-pedi twice a month, and gyms with personal fitness trainers to keep her trim frame toned and her looking twenty-five. How in the hell was she going to adapt to the wild west?

"What?" Olivia asked.

"We need to be in Arizona in three days."

"I'll come back in," Olivia said instantly.

"No need. Everything will be in the prospectus, and I've got the general details already."

"I'm not going to like this, am I."

"I doubt it," Elizabeth said. "Not unless you've lost your mind in the last few hours. It appears my father bought a dude ranch and has developed plans to make it our first resort west of the Mississippi or the Mason-Dixon line or the Rockies or wherever."

"Where?"

"Wickenburg, Arizona."

"Where the hell is Wickenburg, Arizona?"

"We're about to find out. Google it."

"Wait."

Elizabeth could practically see Olivia's fingers fly over the keyboard.

"Okay," Olivia said. "This is what I've got. Wickenburg, Arizona, was founded in 1863 and is about sixty miles northwest of Phoenix. Population 7,500. Damn, concerts in Central Park draw a bigger crowd than the population of the entire town. Ranchers and farmers came to the area…who knows why…and built homes along the fertile plain of the Hassayampa River." She paused. "I wonder if that's right?"

She had pronounced it Hass-AYAMP-a.

"How in the hell would I know?"

Olivia continued. "Wickenburg was a supply point for the mines and army posts in the interior of Arizona Territory and presently occupies a total area of 26.5 square miles."

"That sounds…small," Elizabeth muttered.

"This sounds like my worst nightmare," Olivia said.

"Yours and mine both, babe. Saddle up. We leave at dawn day after tomorrow."

CHAPTER THREE

Wickenburg, Arizona
May

Kelsey knew it was too dark to be riding. The sun had disappeared over an hour ago, revealing thousands of twinkling stars in an almost jet black sky. Adira could stumble and toss Kelsey over her head. Not that she'd mind all that much for herself, but she didn't want Adira getting injured because she couldn't stand to be at the ranch on what might be her last night there. The last night her home would be her own. She set Adira to graze by a natural spring, built a small fire, and sat with her back against a mesquite tree. She wasn't sure there'd be many more chances to spend a night like this. The new owners—God, that word hurt—were on their way.

The attorney she'd contacted had made things crystal clear— *even if you had a hundred thousand dollars or so to fight an international conglomerate like Sutton Properties, it wouldn't do any good. Contract law is pretty cut and dried. Red signed the contract, and you might think he was crazy to do it, but he made the decision. You'll have to honor it.*

She hadn't even thought about her next move—all she could do was remember. Her first time on top of a horse when she was four years old. The time when she got too cocky on the dirt bike she got for Christmas when she was eleven. She must have spit sand out of her mouth for days. The cut on her elbow from the rock she landed on, leaving an impressive scar that still itched.

The crushing feeling when she finally realized her mother was not coming back. Over thirty years with not one word from Lois Brunel. Not a letter, birthday card, or phone call. At least as far as Kelsey knew. Several times she thought about finding her mother. She practiced what she would say if she ever saw her again. She'd tell her that her leaving was selfish, cowardly, and unforgivable. How everyone in town looked at Kelsey with pity in their eyes. *There goes the little Brunel girl. Her mother left, so sad.* In her twenties, she'd even gone as far as hiring a private detective, but when he'd called to tell her he had located her mother, she told him she was no longer interested. If Lois didn't want to see her, then the feeling was mutual.

And now what? She could work for the state or the Bureau of Land Management. She had some university chums who worked at the Department of the Interior in Washington, DC, but she'd go nuts in a big city. She loved this harsh, beautiful land. The ranch, this land, was her life, it was in her blood. She couldn't see herself leaving again, and when dawn broke, she still couldn't imagine another option.

She rode up to the main house and took it and the other buildings in with a critical eye. What would an outsider see? The paint was still pretty good, the roof not too bad, but the bushes could use a trim. The barns and bunkhouses were in perfect order. Why wouldn't they be? That was where their livelihood was centered. The corrals were weed-free, and she'd applied a fresh coat of paint on the metal fencing and gates a few weeks ago. The horses were well fed and shod, and the all-terrain vehicles that shuttled guests around the resort were sparkling clean. Several of the rocks that flanked the walkway to the front door had shifted, and Kelsey made a mental note to straighten them after taking care of Adira.

"Hell, what's the point?" Kelsey muttered. "It's not like we're trying to impress a potential buyer."

A middle-aged couple in matching shorts and polo shirts exited the front door, the clicking of their golf shoes a clear indication of their plans to visit the course in the nearby town. Laughter from the pool area indicated the family with six-year-old triplets had hit the pool early this morning. The lead trail hand, Ruben Elliot, was scheduled to take four riders out later that morning, and Josie had a Jeep tour for a couple from Spain. Kelsey's life might be over, but life continued on the ranch. Stock needed tending, weeds pulling, and guests made happy. No matter the circumstances, the reputation of Red Sky Ranch was her legacy, and she was not going to let it be sullied.

As if she would really have anything to say about the ranch's future. She couldn't even envision her own.

❖

Phoenix, Arizona

"That was the flight from hell." Elizabeth raised her voice and leaned close to Olivia to be heard over the powerful engines of the Airbus A320 powering down to stop the multiton airliner. A baby had cried for almost the entire four-plus hours from New York to Phoenix. Even though she and Olivia were seated in first class, the thin privacy curtain was certainly not an effective sound barrier.

"That is only one of the reasons why I'm never having kids," Olivia replied, pulling her Tumi leather briefcase from under the seat in front of her.

"That ship has long since departed from my dock," Elizabeth commented. There was a time she'd thought seriously about motherhood. She'd even gone as far as visiting a sperm donor clinic. Not because she'd felt the clock ticking or some internal cry to nurture a new little being, but because she'd thought it was the thing to do. The next step in her journey through adulthood. Go to college, work for her father, get married, have kids, and live happily ever after. And of course, have a career along the way. The kids and marriage didn't necessarily need to be in that order. She'd been twenty-eight and, with no marriage in sight, had the resources to go it alone.

Elizabeth had lost track of how many drinks with little umbrellas she'd consumed while sitting on a pristine white beach in the Caribbean celebrating—or mourning—her last vacation before what would be an arduous journey into motherhood. The setting sun had just touched the horizon when, with absolute clarity, she'd realized that she really had no desire to be a mother. She'd never followed the rules—if she had, she wouldn't be her father's presumed successor at Sutton—and didn't know why she would do so now. She canceled her appointment at the clinic and never gave it another thought.

And look how well her plans had turned out. Here she was at yet another airport, waiting for luggage before taxiing off to yet another hotel. She'd gotten what she'd wanted—Wickenburg, Arizona, notwithstanding. This place would soon be a disappearing stoplight in her rearview mirror.

Elizabeth gritted her teeth. She hated waiting for her luggage after a flight. She never understood how people couldn't recognize their own suitcase. They elbowed through the crowd to retrieve their bag the instant it came off the conveyor belt. For some indecipherable reason, everyone bought black suitcases, and they ended up chasing after them, stepping on toes while they tried to read the paper name tag. Her suitcase was red and immediately recognizable as it slid down the conveyor belt and onto the gleaming carousel. Again, unlike her fellow passengers, she waited for it to get to her and not the other way around.

She was almost run over by a woman cradling her phone between her shoulder and her ear because her hand was holding a Starbucks iced something or another, her large purse in the crook of her elbow. She carried on an inane conversation and reached for the handle of her oversize suitcase. She wasn't able to pull it off the conveyor belt and ran into several passengers, including Elizabeth, as it dragged her around the carousel. All the while she was laughing at whatever the person on the other end of the wireless said.

"Do you think you could get off the damn phone and pay attention," Elizabeth snapped, loud enough for the people around her to hear, after the third time the woman careened into her. Several muttered in agreement.

"What a zoo." Olivia set her Louis Vuitton bag between them. "Why did I think this place would be saner than New York?"

Elizabeth's exasperation matched hers. She had been uncharacteristically short-tempered since getting this assignment, her patience having flown the coop. Good God, now she was even yelling at strangers as if she'd been raised on a farm—or a ranch or…whatever.

Elizabeth pulled up the handle on her bag. "Get me the fuck out of here."

Unfortunately, an hour later they still didn't have their rental car. There was a mix-up at the counter, and the man in the sloppy uniform with the rental car agency patch on his sleeve was a complete incompetent. He had no idea what to do when the car Elizabeth had reserved was not on the lot. He tried to give her something else, with the associated upcharge, and that was the end of her dwindling-to-nothing patience.

"Absolutely not. You will provide us with the vehicle we reserved, or another of a grade above, *at the same rate*."

"Well, I…" He visibly cringed when trying to meet her eye while mumbling, "I don't think I can do tha—"

"I'm sure your supervisor can. Please call them right now." She had the money, lots of it as a matter of fact, but not paying for things that she hadn't received helped her keep it.

The manager, if that's what he was, had at least ironed his shirt, although he wasn't much better at customer service. Finally, they were driving out of the rental lot in a gleaming new black Cadillac Escalade.

"Google maps says we won't get there until after dark," Olivia said as Elizabeth drove. "We won't see much tonight."

"We probably won't see much more in daylight," Elizabeth muttered. Damn, she really needed to get her control back before she had to deal with whatever she was going to find at the site.

Unhappy people, to be sure. "Let's stay in Phoenix and get an early start tomorrow. Can you find—"

"Two blocks up on the right—a Marriott. Two king rooms reserved."

Elizabeth laughed, and some of the churning in her midsection settled. "Why haven't I married you yet? Oh wait—I haven't got the right equipment."

"I never said that," Olivia said with unusual reserve.

"Have I missed something all these years?" Elizabeth asked.

"Not exactly."

Surprised, but sensing Olivia's reluctance, Elizabeth said, "One of these days, you'll have to tell me what that means."

"Mm, one day when I know," Olivia said.

After checking in and a quick shower, Elizabeth met Olivia in the lobby, and they headed across the street to the Mexican restaurant the concierge recommended for a late dinner. One pitcher of margaritas later, Elizabeth put her credit card back in her wallet.

"Let's meet in the lobby at eight tomorrow. I'm going out for a while."

"You're going out to get laid is more like it." Olivia chuckled when Elizabeth shot her a bogus glare.

"What?" Olivia said, pretending indignation. "It's your pattern. It's what you do before every big job."

Elizabeth couldn't argue. Olivia was mostly right about her looking for a fast encounter before a new job—maybe not before *every* job, but a lot of them. A good night's sleep after a mind-blowing orgasm always cleared her head for the next day. And she desperately needed both right now. Not having a steady relationship, her sex life was erratic. Working long hours and being away from home for months at a time were not conducive to a long-term thing. That, or maybe the women she chose didn't think she was worth waiting for.

Sex, she'd discovered, was a surefire way to clear her mind and leave her focused on what needed to be done for a successful project. She had a feeling she'd need that for this one. Stranger sex was the best solution. No worrying about morning-after awkwardness or the *how do I get out of here* dilemma. After a few awkward encounters in her twenties, she generally suggested they get a room—on her—so she could leave when she wanted to, which was usually less than five minutes after she caught her breath.

She shook her head and, despite their separate rooms, said as she usually did, "Don't wait up."

"Text me when you get in," Olivia said, as she always did.

"I will," Elizabeth replied, just like always.

❖

The navigation system in the SUV led Elizabeth to the destination she'd googled earlier. The Last Stop was tucked away in a nondescript strip mall flanked by a shoe repair store on the left and a doggie day care on the right. The perfect spot, as signs on both doors said the businesses closed at six, and the Last Stop didn't open till eight.

As it was already close to midnight, she parked between a tricked-out Ford truck and a Prius. From the outside, the bar didn't resemble the clubs she often frequented, but what mattered was on the inside. Women, many of whom would be looking for what she was looking for: fun, adventure, pleasure—escape. Maybe all those things. Just thinking about who she might find waiting made her pulse race. She didn't normally have a type. She thought all women were beautiful, and sexy came from within. Age, body type, butch-femme-androgenous—what mattered to her was the sexual energy coming her way. The vibes that said *I want you tonight* and *I want you to make me come.*

She didn't question why she wanted—needed—this. That would come later in the middle of the night in some obscure hotel in some city she'd never visited. Tonight, however, was not for thinking. Tonight was all about pleasure.

Chapter Four

The beat of the music reached Elizabeth the instant she stepped out of her car. Pounding, hard and heavy, just like what her body craved when she needed to escape. Her pulse stuttered for a moment, then picked up the rhythm as she walked through the front door.

She'd been in bars like this more times than she could remember. In her baby-dyke late teens, she and the queer crowd she'd discovered in college had tried to outdrink and outscrew each other. Friday and Saturday nights they'd carouse and cruise, looking for Ms. Tonight. The demands of college, even when *finally* text-to-voice software made courses more manageable, along with the challenge of carving out a place at Sutton soon replaced scotch and scoring. She still met those of her old friends who were still around for happy hour on the rare occasions she was in town and free, but she always went out alone when she was looking for sex. And that was all she was looking for tonight—a few hours with nothing in her thoughts but pure physical release.

Giving her eyes a chance to adjust to the low lights, she slowly edged her way through the long, narrow room, packed with bodies, to the bar. The scent of beer, sweat, sex, and a hint of desperation in the air felt familiar, and if she paused to think about it, sad. Wasn't there a line in some country music song about how all the girls get prettier at closing time? She'd seen it happen over and over, when alcohol and desperation fueled the need to fill a few long, lonely hours with the comfort of a body in the night. She didn't let the pangs of loneliness linger. She knew why she was here and what she wanted.

Half a cocktail later, Elizabeth sensed eyes on her. Ever since she was a little girl, she'd had what she'd called Spidey sense—a feeling when something was off or something good was about to happen. Hopefully tonight would be one of those favorable times.

Using the cover of stepping around a couple who really needed to go home to fight, she casually surveyed the room, suddenly feeling very old. She was probably only ten years older than most of the women here, but the difference seemed like a lifetime. When had her life become more about winning than enjoying her successes? And when the hell had she gotten to feeling so sorry for herself? She had everything she'd worked for, everything she'd ever wanted. And tonight what she wanted was here, waiting for her.

She made eye contact with a blonde, two brunettes, and one woman who was more than a little bit scary. None of them pinged her come-and-get-me button until she saw the tall, dark-haired woman across the room who cocked an eyebrow as if to say *hello there.* The hazy light did nothing to hide a smile that almost stopped Elizabeth's heart. God, she was good-looking—her face all sweeping angles and planes framed by unruly collar-length midnight waves and a wide mouth that promised pleasure. All the blood raced through Elizabeth's veins and shot between her legs, leaving her truly shaky. Even from across the room, the sparks of interest in her eyes glittered. Elizabeth knew, even without the familiar tingle. She was the one for tonight.

Unfortunately, when Elizabeth's brain started working again, she realized an equally gorgeous woman with long black hair flowing around her slim shoulders stood with an arm draped over the woman's shoulders. When she leaned in close to say something to her, a pang of jealousy took Elizabeth by surprise. WTF was that? She didn't even *know* this woman, let alone have any sort of claim on her, and she sure as hell was not interested in someone who was already hooked up.

So much for her Spidey sense.

She turned away and took several long swallows of her drink.

She must be more keyed up than she realized. Finishing her Crown Royal and Coke, she switched to water. Two was her limit when she was driving. She didn't mind. She didn't need to be drunk to get laid. All she needed was a willing participant who knew exactly what they were doing and what they weren't going to do, as in get into a relationship. Or exchange personal info, for that matter.

She turned down several offers to dance and, surprisingly, shot down two obvious hook-ups. And what was that all about? Wasn't that what she was there for? What made even less sense was that her attention kept drifting back to the dark-haired woman, and the longer that went on, the more her body kicked from simmer to boil. She surreptitiously watched her dance a few times, although she seemed to deliberately stay away from the woman who'd been touching her earlier.

Abruptly, the woman dropped her beer off with a waitress and headed directly toward Elizabeth. Yes indeed, she filled out her jeans nicely. A wide leather belt with a silver buckle glinting in the lights circled straight hips, and her short-sleeved white T-shirt accentuated the muscles in her arms and the shape of her breasts. Elizabeth's mouth went dry, which was the only part of her that was. This woman was walking sensuality and sex. Elizabeth's body hummed in anticipation. The woman held Elizabeth's gaze as she drew closer, the move another big turn-on. Too often women wouldn't maintain eye contact, especially in bed. Like, they would let her put her mouth on their clit, but not look her in the eye? Ridiculous.

When finally, at last, she stood a foot away, Elizabeth was swallowed up by the raw desire in her eyes. As she leaned toward her, for a crazy second, Elizabeth thought she was going to kiss her. Wanted her to. Public sex wasn't her thing, but at that moment, she didn't care. Every cell screamed *touch me.*

"Would you like to dance?"

Low, husky, direct, and sure. More than sexy. Off the charts hot.

And how stupid of me to think she was leaning in for a kiss. With the almost deafening mix of music and conversation, she was just getting closer to be heard.

"What about her?" Elizabeth motioned to the table of women the stranger had just left. The last thing she needed was more drama in her life. She might have casual sex, but she never knowingly poached another woman's woman. "The little brunette you were with earlier?"

"Oh, you noticed?"

"I don't have many rules," Elizabeth said, "but not getting in the middle of someone's thing is top of the list."

A flicker of understanding followed by an intrigued grin flashed across the woman's face. "We're all just friends, including her. We haven't seen each other for a while."

Elizabeth studied her. The direct gaze, and the interest in them, never wavered. "In that case, I'd love to dance."

"How about names? Is there a rule there, too?" the woman asked, offering Elizabeth her hand to lead her to the dance floor.

Another plus in Elizabeth's book. She hated it when she was asked to dance and then the woman would turn her back and walk toward the dance floor, expecting her to follow. Often, she didn't, much to the confusion of her prospective dance partner when she got to the dance floor and Elizabeth wasn't behind her. Elizabeth liked a lot about this woman already. She wasn't all just good looks. Maybe that was why she answered. "Ellie."

"Ellie. Nice. I'm Sky."

Elizabeth smiled. Of course she was Sky. From her cowboy boots and jeans to her tight white T-shirt and very, very nice body, this one was all cowgirl. Or maybe cowboi, with an *i*.

"Hello, Sky. Let's dance." Elizabeth placed her hand in Sky's larger, not unpleasantly rougher one, and a jolt of heat shot from her fingertips directly to her crotch. She might have just grabbed a live wire—and that was exactly what she wanted for the night. Her very own live wire. Sky must have felt it, too, because she looked at their joined hands and smiled that devastating smile.

The beat was fast, and Sky moved like she'd been dancing to this song her entire life. She held Elizabeth's gaze while they danced, another tick in Elizabeth's *I want to have sex with you* column. Most women barely looked at her when they were dancing, even when they'd been the ones to make the first move. Like they just needed a partner to be socially acceptable to be on the dance floor. As if anyone would do. Elizabeth wasn't looking for a forever date, but she did want to feel like she was noticed.

Three fast songs shifted into a slow one, and by some unspoken agreement, Elizabeth stepped into Sky's arms. Her body was as firm and enticing as it had looked—muscles that moved beneath her hands and long, sensuous curves that fit with hers as if they'd been dancing together forever. Sky smelled like citrusy cologne and something startlingly earthy and unexpectedly erotic.

"What is that you're wearing?" Elizabeth asked, her cheek turned to Sky's shoulder.

"What? My shirt?"

Enchanted, Elizabeth laughed. "No—the scent. Your cologne."

"Oh." Sky laughed. "That would be Horse and Hay."

Elizabeth laughed again. Just as she'd surmised. Cowgirl. "Nice."

Sky was a fabulous dancer, and song after song, they glided across the floor, each move more sensuous than the one before. Sky's leg snugged between hers, pressing on all the right parts. What Elizabeth wanted was to be somewhere naked with that leg between hers so she could rock into the orgasm that was building inside her. Her hunger must have shown because Sky slid a hand down to the base of her spine and pulled her in even more tightly.

"You're a wonderful dancer," Elizabeth said stupidly, since saying *I really want you to fuck me* seemed a little premature.

"Thank you, you too." Sky's gaze on Elizabeth's face felt like a caress. "At the risk of having you walk away, I think you're the most beautiful woman in the room. And the hottest."

"Why would I walk away after such a nice compliment?"

"Because it sounds like a practiced hook-up line."

"Is it?" At this point, Elizabeth didn't care. Talk about foreplay. Between the dancing, the focus that never left her, and the mutual attraction, she was supercharged already. Any more of this and she might come just from this conversation. "A hook-up line, I mean?"

"Do you want it to be?"

"I think we're well past that, don't you?"

Desire flared again in Sky's eyes, and Elizabeth suddenly had trouble standing up.

"Yes, we are." Her voice was confident, sexy, and smooth. Exactly like she'd be in bed. "If you'd like…"

Elizabeth silenced her with a searing kiss.

Sky hesitated for a nanosecond before kissing her back. Her lips were soft and demanding, and as the kiss drew out, she angled her head just enough to cover Elizabeth's mouth while playing her tongue over the inner surface of her lower lip. Elizabeth almost forgot they were in a public place. She was on fire, every sense alert, and Sky had barely touched her. When they got naked—and they *would* get naked, or she was very, very badly out of practice—she'd likely come in seconds. When she broke the kiss, she whispered, "That's what I'd like—more of that."

"Do you want to get out of here? I want to be alone with you."

"What about your friends?"

"They have their own ride home." Sky shot her another devastating smile, the one that said she knew exactly what Elizabeth needed and would give it to her.

Elizabeth's knees threatened to buckle, but she managed to say calmly, "Then we should definitely leave. The sooner the better."

Sky tossed a small wave to her table and headed to the front door, her grip tightening on Elizabeth's hand as she led her through the crowd.

Chapter Five

The fresh air that hit Elizabeth the moment she stepped outside did nothing to cool her lust. She'd never actually believed anyone could be so turned on their skin burned, but she could now swear to it. The Southwest night might be an oven temperature-wise, but her body was an inferno. Somewhere in her far-distant thinking mind, little warning bells clanged, but she had no intention of stopping or even slowing down. Sky had held her captive with magnetic force the instant their eyes had met. Sky must have been feeling some of the same urgency, as she rapidly tugged Elizabeth into the shadows at the rear of the parking lot. Elizabeth hustled to keep up, matching her step by step.

As soon as they were out of sight of the bar—the only place open in the entire strip mall—Elizabeth stopped beside an enormous pickup and pulled Sky around to face her. "I can't go another step without kissing you."

The words had barely passed her lips when Sky's mouth met hers. Hot, hard, and demanding, and a very good start to exactly what she needed.

Right then what she needed was more. Elizabeth dragged her mouth away and kissed a path down Sky's neck to the pulse point bounding just below the skin. She bit lightly and sucked the place she'd just tormented, making Sky groan. The sound shot through her, igniting the fire between her legs. Sky slid both hands down her back, cupped her ass, and pushed her thigh between Elizabeth's. The jolt of pressure pushed her so close to the edge, she couldn't hold back a moan.

More, more, more ricocheted through her awareness, and Elizabeth tugged at Sky's T-shirt until she could slide her hands over her abdomen. Finding warm skin and taut muscles, she pushed the shirt higher, along with the tank beneath it, and took a nipple in her mouth. Sky jerked and grabbed the back of her head, her body arching into Elizabeth's.

"Fuck," Sky exclaimed, her fingers trembling against Elizabeth's neck. Elizabeth finally straightened, dazed and momentarily disoriented. She blinked and saw them as if from a distance—their clothes half-off, breathless, and looking damned near wild. She felt wild. Wild and out of control. She didn't even recognize herself, and she didn't care. She couldn't stop, not without losing what remained of her mind. "I want you."

"Are we going to do this here?" Sky asked, her voice raspy and breathless.

Elizabeth glanced around, not so far gone she'd risk someone walking up on them. No one in sight. She might be in a public place, but at that moment, with that woman, she didn't care.

"Yes." She made it both a statement and a question, giving Sky the power to decide. Elizabeth already had.

Elizabeth held her breath and, even though she wasn't a religious person, mentally whispered a silent prayer that Sky would agree. She'd never been this reckless, this overwhelmed with need, as much out of her mind for someone as she was with this stranger. The mutual desire was powerful, exhilarating, and all-consuming. She feared any interruption and the connection would be lost forever.

Sky hesitated, and the disappointment was like a blow. Crushed, Elizabeth backed away on shaky limbs.

"Stop." Sky jerked Elizabeth hard against her and kissed her with such force every cell in Elizabeth's body kicked into overdrive. Sky fumbled with the snap on Elizabeth's pants, pulled the zipper down, and slipped her hand between Elizabeth's legs. "This?"

"Yes, God, yes," Elizabeth gasped. And then Sky was inside her. Her mouth covered Elizabeth's again, smothering her cry.

Elizabeth lifted up on her toes to press her clit harder to Sky's palm. "I need you to make me come."

"Fuck, you feel good," Sky groaned, her mouth against Elizabeth's neck.

"I'm…close," Elizabeth managed to get out. She spread her legs as far as she could, giving Sky room to go deeper, faster. Almost there. Please, God, soon. When Sky flicked her finger back and forth, Elizabeth just about lost it instantly.

"Yes, yes." Elizabeth's breath came in gasps. "God, touch me like that again. You'll make me come."

"Not…stopping," Sky said, her voice stark and tight.

The orgasm unfurled as Elizabeth mindlessly whispered, "Fuck me. Fuck me. Please, fuck me."

When the orgasm ripped through her—flung her beyond sensibility—Elizabeth wrapped her arms around Sky's neck and just held on.

A kaleidoscope of colors flashed behind her eyelids. Raging tremors crashed through her. For long moments she was deaf, blind, and incapable of words. Shuddering, struggling to breathe, she finally opened her eyes.

Sky's smug look of complete satisfaction reignited Elizabeth's lust. Turnabout was fair play.

"We're not done." Elizabeth struggled with the damn belt buckle on Sky's jeans but finally succeeded in getting it open and yanked Sky's zipper down. She riveted her gaze to Sky's, smiling to herself at the look of shock as she found Sky's clit. She was warm, wet, and just what Elizabeth needed. Sky's lids flickered as Elizabeth stroked her clit. "Good?"

"Hell, yeah," Sky muttered. "Don't you fucking stop."

"Don't worry—you feel too amazing." The first instant Elizabeth touched a woman was always like this, like the first time ever. The silky glide of her fingers over warm, welcoming flesh nearly stopped her heart.

"Damn, damn, you're going to make me come."

Elizabeth laughed, heady with power and wonder. "Isn't that the point?"

"Faster," Sky gasped, and Elizabeth complied.

Elizabeth always followed directions.

"Oh yeah, that's it, just like that."

An instant later, Sky buried her face in Elizabeth's neck and shuddered. Her body quaked, and Elizabeth cupped her warm, wet sex, speechless, mindless with the incredible beauty of the moment. Never—*never* had she experienced such pleasure.

"That was…" Elizabeth croaked, her throat dry. She didn't have the words to describe what had just passed between them.

"Yes, it was," Sky muttered, equally breathless.

Elizabeth's clit twitched as Sky gently, slowly slid out of her. Sky must have felt it, because she grinned and started to stroke Elizabeth again. Everything came crashing back into focus, including their location, and Elizabeth gently pushed against her, putting a little space between them. Sky gave her a questioning look.

"What's wrong?"

Elizabeth's hands were shaking so badly she could barely straighten her clothes and zip her pants. Finally, she succeeded and, stepping farther away, ran both hands through her hair. Whatever this was—whatever the hell had just happened—she needed to end it. Now. "I have to go."

"Can we…I'd like to—"

"No." Elizabeth covered Sky's lips with her fingers, the fingers that had just been inside her, and the heat flared in Sky's eyes again.

"Let's get out of here—get a motel room or—"

"No, I can't. I have to go."

Elizabeth turned away and hurried to get to her SUV. She knew Sky was watching her and prayed she wouldn't follow. She yanked open the driver's door, climbed into the seat, and pushed the start button. Without taking even two seconds to fasten her seat belt, she pulled out of the parking lot without looking back.

CHAPTER SIX

Red Sky Ranch
Early morning

The sun rose early in May in the desert, but the first rays hadn't even broken through the clouds when Kelsey's phone rang. She rolled over, grabbed it, and groaned. Sophia. Damn it. For ten seconds she considered ignoring it. And then imagined it ringing every minute until she answered.

"Hel—"

"Was she as hot as she looked? Did you sleep with her? Did she rock your world?"

"Soph, jeez, give me a minute." Kelsey kicked off the covers, the cool morning air hitting her naked skin. She'd been awake most of the night thinking about the mysterious woman who had, in fact, rocked her world. She normally slept like a rock after a mind-numbing orgasm, but a cascade of images, each one sexier than the last, kept her brain on overdrive—long, silky blond hair, hungry blue eyes, and demanding hands. Damn talented hands that had made her come faster and harder than anyone she could ever remember.

"Is she there?" Sophia whispered.

"Who?"

"Don't *who* me. The woman you left with last night."

"No."

"Did you just get home?"

"No."

"Did you sleep with her?"

Kelsey pulled on a pair of shorts and a T-shirt from the ever-present pile of clean clothes on the dresser she kept meaning to put away, stumbled into her kitchen, and pushed a pod into her Keurig. "We got together, yes."

Even in the bright sunlight, what they did would not be called sleeping together. Stupid phrase.

"Well?"

"I'm not going to give you details, even if you are my best friend." Kelsey closed her eyes, rubbed her forehead, and told the drip to hurry up.

"If you can't tell me, who can you tell?"

"Nobody, that's the point." Kelsey could picture Soph scowling on the other end of the line.

"Come on. You have never, and I repeat, never left the bar with someone. She must have been really something, or you were really horny."

Her best friend didn't know everything about her, but Kelsey didn't correct her since it *had* been a damn long time—like years. She tamped down a flash of anger. Soph's questions made last night sound torrid and cheap, and location and circumstances aside, it felt anything but. She carried the mug into the front room—the focal point of the house with its big stone fireplace, vaulted ceiling, and wide windows overlooking the ranch—sat down on the couch, and cradled her coffee mug in both hands. She propped her feet on the stone-topped coffee table.

"Look, we just connected," Kelsey said, remembering the nearly instantaneous attraction she'd felt the moment she'd seen Ellie across the bar. Not something she wanted to try to explain to Sophie when she didn't understand it herself. "We were on the same wavelength, you know?"

"I'll say," Sophia agreed. "You two were about to combust on the dance floor. The entire bar was watching. Half the women wanted to be you, and the other half wanted to be her."

Kelsey blinked at the unexpected flash of jealousy imagining someone else touching Ellie the way she had—and just as quickly discounted it. Jealousy wasn't her thing. Right?

"So, come on—who is she? What's her name? Where's she from, what does she do? I need some frame of reference here."

Kelsey sighed. No kidding. So did she. "Ellie."

After a beat of silence, Sophia prodded, "Okay. And...what else?"

"I don't know."

"What?" Sophia shouted. "Shit, I dropped my glass in the sink. You don't know any more about her than that? Maybe that's not even her name!"

"No, I don't, and what difference does it make." Kelsey snorted. Now what had seemed perfectly natural probably sounded bizarre. "I had my hands down her pants, and that's all I know about her. End of story."

"Not a chance. Did you tell her yours?"

"Look—it's complicated."

"Holy fuck. Did you two say *anything*?"

Kelsey remembered the sound of Ellie's voice when she told her just how she wanted to be fucked. "Not much, no."

"How do you plan on reaching her again?"

Kelsey had no reply. If she wanted to track her down, that was going to be a problem. If. "I don't know."

"Did you go back to her place? You said she's not there with you."

"No."

"A hotel?"

"No."

"What is with the one-word answers? Do I have to drag it out of you minute by minute?"

"I already told you—I'm not saying."

"If you had sex in your truck, I'm driving from now on."

Kelsey closed her eyes. Her head throbbed. No sleep and Sophia's incessant pestering and the steady thrum of arousal that would *not* quit were wearing on her. "No, we did not have sex in my truck."

"Hers?"

"No."

"Oh. My. God. You did not have sex in the parking lot."

Kelsey's silence was her answer.

"That is…hot. Hot and so totally not you."

Absolutely correct. And that was what was so troubling. She'd had sex in a variety of places that were not a bedroom, the advantages of living and working outside.

"Were you out of your mind?"

Completely.

"You could have been arrested."

Kelsey realized that now, but then she hadn't cared.

"What were you thinking?"

"Obviously nothing rational in the moment," Kelsey admitted. That was an understatement. All she'd wanted was to touch her, be inside her, make her come screaming all over her.

"This is so unlike you." Sophia sounded oddly solemn.

"Tell me about it." She'd been trying to get her head around the whole thing since she'd driven away and still couldn't get any of it— Ellie most of all—out of her mind. "I don't know how it happened, and I was there. It was the most exciting, erotic experience I've ever had. It might seem sordid, but it wasn't. Just pure, raw, and hot."

"Does she have a sister? I sound like a broken record, but wow. I mean, what do you say after that? Thanks, I'll call you?"

"I didn't get a chance to say anything. She just said she had to go, got in her car, and drove off."

"What will you say if you see her again?"

"I have no idea." She only knew what she wanted again—to breathe in her scent, taste her, hear her moan, and make her come again.

"Did you get her number? No, wait," Sophia said before Kelsey could answer. "If she didn't tell you anything except her *maybe* first name, she wasn't going to give out her number."

"Yeah, well…" Kelsey sighed. "I guess it wasn't meant to be anything except one night."

Sophia laughed. "Give me one of those! All I can say is you go, girl. It's about time you had some fun. You've done nothing but work for years."

They'd been having the same conversation for months. Kelsey's personal life had been moved far down the to-do list with everything she needed to do at the ranch, and she was okay with that. Or at least she'd been okay until last night when some switch had been flipped inside her and all she'd wanted was Ellie.

"Well, I certainly jumped right back in."

"I still feel like you're holding out on me," Sophia said, "but I'll let that go for now. And listen—hang in there today."

Kelsey's throat tightened. "Thanks. I will."

"Call me whenever, you know—you know something."

"Yeah." What else could Kelsey say? She had no idea what the rest of the day would bring, only that it couldn't possibly be good.

And as to what had happened the night before? She had no explanation that made sense. She'd had no choice from the moment she'd seen Ellie walk in. She hadn't been able to see any other woman after that—and was very afraid she never would again.

❖

"Where in the hell is this place?" Olivia grumbled. "I thought the brochure said they were forty-five minutes from Phoenix."

They'd been driving for over an hour and, according to Google Maps, still had another forty minutes to go. They'd exited the interstate and were now on a bumpy two-lane road that could stand resurfacing. The navigation system on the large screen in the console indicated thirty-three miles to their destination.

"Phoenix is a big city," Elizabeth said absently. Cacti of all shapes and sizes dotted the landscape. Some she recognized, but far more she didn't. They hadn't passed another car in the last ten miles. The land was barren, yet captivating in its stark beauty. The contrast to Manhattan was so extreme, she almost felt transported to a completely different world. "I think there's almost five million people in the urban area, and by what we saw of downtown, they obviously scattered out instead of up. It's probably forty-five minutes from the city limit boundary closest to the resort. Not from downtown."

"We'll need to keep that in mind with our marketing materials," Olivia said, inputting something in her tablet. "Right now, it feels like a huge bait and switch."

"Isn't there a regional airport closer than the main one in Phoenix?" Elizabeth asked.

"Hold on—let me ask my good friend Google again." After a minute, she said, "There is a Wickenburg Municipal Airport located three and a half miles from downtown."

"It's probably cost-prohibitive to fly from Phoenix. Maybe a limo service," Elizabeth mused.

"I'll check into it. It'll be expensive either way." Olivia looked out her window. "Did the old man even come out here to see this place?"

Elizabeth snorted. "Jonas Sutton does not make first contact—or these days, much contact at all. And that's getting to be a problem."

"So why buy this place in the middle of nowhere? Why would anyone want to come out here? It's the desert, for God's sake. Don't people die in the desert?" Olivia shook her head. "I'd die of boredom in half a day. There is absolutely nothing out there to look at but scraggly cactus and dirt."

"Okay, I get the message. You hate everything about the place so far. Tell me more about the area. We have to find the positives."

If she was going to call this place home for the next six months and, more importantly, make the Sutton resort a success, she needed more intel. She relied on Olivia to synthesize stacks of information that would take her weeks to read in short, bite-sized chunks or spend hours listening to sections she didn't need to know anything about because she couldn't effectively skim the material. Olivia was one of the few people at Sutton, other than her father and unfortunately

Michael Wyland, who even knew about her reading challenges. She owed much of her success to Olivia.

Olivia swiped at her iPad. "According to one blog—"

"Do you get all your info from the Internet?" Elizabeth asked. "You know those articles are not always accurate."

"I know, but it works in a pinch. And we are definitely between a rock and a hard place on this one." Olivia shot her a look over the top of her Dolce & Gabbana sunglasses before continuing, "Phoenix is the anchor of the metropolitan area, also known as the Valley of the Sun. The metropolitan area is the eleventh largest city in the U.S." She paused, looking around. "Looks to me like we're two feet from hell and forty feet from water, as my daddy would say."

Elizabeth snorted. "Your father is a New Yorker. Five years or whatever it was they lived in Texas when you were an infant does not a Texan make."

"Thank goodness for that," Olivia echoed. "Okay. Phoenix became the capital of Arizona Territory in 1889 and has a hot desert climate." Olivia tapped the temperature reading on the dash with a red-polished nail. "Ya think? It's the middle of May and already ninety-eight degrees outside, *and* it isn't even noon yet."

Elizabeth reached over and lowered the air-conditioning temperature setting on the dash. "There. Keep reading."

"Phoenix receives the most sunshine of any major city on Earth. I'm glad I brought plenty of sunscreen," Olivia muttered. "The average high temperatures in summer are the hottest of any major city in the United States. On average, there are one hundred eleven days annually with a high of at least one hundred degrees. Oh, lucky us. Highs top one hundred ten degrees an average of twenty-one days during the year. God help me, I am going to shrivel up and die like a raisin."

She scowled at Elizabeth. "Remind me *again* why you didn't say no to this project. You've got plenty of seniority. You don't have to take—"

"Allison Wyland."

"Oh. Well, shit."

"Yes, exactly. So, we get in, we get it done, and we get the hell out of Dodge. Or Phoenix—or Wickenburg."

Olivia continued to read as Elizabeth kept one eye on the road and the other on the surrounding area. Surprisingly, there was something about the harsh barren landscape that struck her as beautiful. She'd seen pictures of the desert, but none had captured the sheer magnitude of this branch of Mother Nature's tree.

"It's pronounced sa-wa-ro, not sag-u-are-o. And choy-a, not cho-la," Elizabeth said, correcting Olivia's pronunciation of the cactus surrounding them.

"Well, that's just stupid. Why don't they spell it like its pronounced?"

Elizabeth chuckled. "Like Marine Corps and island?"

"My point exactly." Olivia emphasized her opinion with a point of her finger at Elizabeth.

"All right. We've done geography and—what, flora? So what are the animals around here?" Elizabeth asked.

"Um…lots of native species, some of which we'd rather not have our guests encounter—coyotes, javelina…don't ask me what that is…mountain lions and smaller dangerous felines like bobcats, jackrabbits…okay, bunnies will work, mule deer and coati…again, no clue, and bald eagles." She turned to Elizabeth. "What is a coati?"

"Beats the hell out of me," she answered. "Add it to your assignment list."

"Holy crap," Olivia exclaimed, sounding truly frightened.

"What?"

"Snakes…many, many kinds of snakes. Rattlesnakes, several varieties because one kind isn't enough, Western Sonoran sidewinder, and others unnamed."

"That sounds…unpleasant."

"Wait," Olivia said. "It gets worse. Gila monster, desert spiny lizard, and a bunch of other things I don't even want to think about. And let's not forget about the Arizona bark scorpion, giant desert hairy scorpion, Arizona blond tarantula, Sonoran Desert centipede, tarantula hawk wasp, camel spider, and tailless whip scorpion."

Olivia looked at Elizabeth, wide-eyed. "Desert hairy scorpion? Turn this car around and get me the hell out of here."

Elizabeth echoed her unease but couldn't show it. Actually, the idea of running into any of those things scared her shitless. She was a city girl, and seeing a garden-variety cockroach gave her the willies. "I'm sure they have adequate pest control in place to assure no guests are harmed. No way could they be successful if their guests were stung or eaten by what was it? The desert spiny lizard? I don't even want to imagine how big a giant desert hairy scorpion is, or what an Arizona blond tarantula feasts on." She shuddered. "There's a reason I hated going to the zoo when I was a kid, and creepy, crawly things are it."

"Don't look now, but you've been in the middle of one for the last hour." Olivia pointed out the window. "Look. What are all those RVs and campers doing out there? People are riding motorcycles and driving those golf carts-on-steroid things."

Elizabeth chuckled. "Those golf cart things are called off-road side-by-sides."

"Well, aren't you little miss drive in the dirt."

"Research, my dear assistant. I may have trouble reading, but I excel at YouTube." Elizabeth mentally shook her head, surprised. She rarely mentioned her dyslexia to Olivia, who'd known before she had, and never to anyone else. That she had just now highlighted how off-stride this whole project had thrown her. Which probably explained why she'd been so out of sorts and out of control the last few days. And *that* thought brought back the events of the previous night she'd been working very hard not to revisit since she'd awakened. That woman who'd instigated—no other word for it, unfortunately—down and dirty sex in a freaking parking lot couldn't have been her. *She* had casual sex—not mindless fucks in dark corners.

For the tenth time, she shut down the images of her and Sky, although her body took a while to get with the program. Damn it, she could not spend the rest of the day being ambushed by persistent horniness.

"What?" Olivia asked.

"What what?" Elizabeth said.

"You got quiet, and then you grumbled."

"Nothing," Elizabeth said quickly. "Just…trying to get a read on this place. It's so…foreign."

"Well, this might help," Olivia said, sounding genuinely excited. "Look, there's a lake out there!"

"A lake? In the middle of the desert?"

"That's what the sign says. Lake Pleasant Regional Park."

Elizabeth slowed as they came up behind a huge pickup with a raised bed sitting on four oversized tires, two a side, pulling an even larger boat, that turned onto the dirt road by the sign. "Obviously it's not a lake in name only."

"Maybe we can rent a boat or Jet Skis and catch some sun one day?"

"We have six months to get this place ready to open. I doubt we'll even have time to hit the pool." And to maintain her sanity, she planned to be in the pool before dawn every morning.

"Right," Olivia said, slumping a bit and falling silent. The road got rougher as the miles to their destination decreased.

"This road…being generous here…will rattle your fillings," Olivia complained after the third time Elizabeth couldn't avoid several potholes.

Elizabeth gripped the wheel harder and tried to make out the depressions in the road before she drove through them. With the sun's glare, the endless unrelenting brown, and the heat shimmering off the surface of the ground, she had trouble making out details. Or she was going blind? Damn it. Would they never arrive?

"We need to find out the status of repairing this road," Elizabeth said. "This will kill us if guests leave a review and rag on how bad the road is and what a miserable drive it is to get here."

"Yes, but it's pretty," Olivia said with false cheer.

Bright yellow and blue wildflowers in full bloom flanked the road. They must be nearing some kind of civilization, too. Road signs declared Vulture Mine Road, Calamity Wash, and Dead Horse

Trail, and there, miraculously, a sign declaring they were entering the town of Wickenburg. Elizabeth wanted to cheer.

Adobe houses dotted the land on either side of the road, their distinctive red trim and roofs a welcome splash of color on the monotonal landscape. A pack of Harleys with their patented tailpipes rumbled past them going in the opposite direction. The engine roar drowned out most of Olivia's less than enthusiastic comments about a gun range.

More buildings appeared on what might be the main street—a paved two-lane too narrow for a car to get around a double-parked vehicle—with brick and clapboard buildings fronting on both sides for several blocks. A Ford dealer on the left sprawled next to a Quick Mart that shared a parking lot with a Motel 6. Across from this, a feed store appropriately named Feed Stop, and the Cowboy Cookin' restaurant.

"Oh my God," Olivia said. "Where are we? *Why* are we wherever we are?"

Elizabeth was thinking the same thing. Olivia was the yin to her yang—Olivia vented her emotions to feel more in control, while she buried them. They had a job to do, and just like the other dozens of times she'd had to prove herself to her father, she'd get it done. And Olivia would be by her side.

"Hey!" Olivia pointed to another road sign. "This road takes us to Las Vegas. Can we just keep going?"

"You and I wish." Elizabeth smiled. "Not today."

"Spoilsport." Olivia sighed. "Turn left at the next cross-street. We're almost there."

Chapter Seven

Red Sky Ranch

Kelsey stood on the porch with her third cup of coffee of the morning in much the same place she'd been standing when Red had come out behind her and made his big announcement. She'd been thinking of him as Red since that night—a man she'd thought she'd known and been very wrong about. Today was the day the buyers—she couldn't say owners yet—were arriving, and she didn't know any more now than she had the night he'd told her he'd just torpedoed her whole damn life. For weeks, she'd tried to get him to tell her why he'd sold their ranch. His response consisted of the same answer: None of your business. She'd kept pushing, and she'd finally gotten some details about what he'd done, if not the why. The sale included the land, all the buildings, the livestock, and everything else on the Red Sky Ranch. Whenever Red crossed her mind, anger boiled inside, threatening to bring up what little breakfast she'd managed to choke down. She had no appetite, and she'd had to tighten her belt buckle one more notch to keep her Wranglers up. Even her hat seemed almost too big.

She still had no plans for what came next. She lived on the ranch, so her expenses were minimal. Red Sky paid her a salary, and she had money in the bank, but nothing could prepare her for this. She'd started half-heartedly searching for a new job, but the pickings were slim for a ranch manager. She'd finally come around to accepting she would have to move to another state to find work.

Her bags were packed and, along with a few other personal items, stored in her casita. She had a hotel room in town reserved for a few days. If she didn't get the answers she was looking for when the new management arrived, or they tossed her out...well, she'd cross that dry gully when she got there.

A familiar trail of dust in the distance signaled a vehicle coming down the approach road. She hadn't seen Red that morning, and because she was standing on the front porch, it fell on her to welcome her visitors. Alone, but why not. She was, after all, alone now in every way. Kelsey wondered how many more times she'd even get to talk with guests. She wasn't a natural extrovert like Red, who could talk to anyone about anything, but she liked passing time with interesting people. At least she'd changed into a plain white shirt and jeans that didn't have worn spots, which was as far as she planned to go to present a professional image to whatever hatchet men Sutton Properties had sent to upend her life.

A big, black SUV with tinted windows stopped in the center of the circle drive and was quickly enveloped in a cloud of dust. If the occupants had any sense, they'd wait a minute or two for the dust to settle before getting out. Somewhere in the middle, the driver's door opened.

One tony-looking, silk pants-clad, booted leg hit the ground followed by another. Not cowboy boots—some fancy, expensive leather items definitely not suited to desert walking. The door closed and the most beautiful woman Kelsey had ever seen stepped forward. Except, holy hell, that's exactly the same thing she'd thought the *first* time she'd seen her, less than twelve hours before. And every time she'd thought of her since then—Ellie of the mind-blowing sex. Ellie who'd walked—no—run away without a backward glance. Ellie who'd populated her feverish, restless mind all damn night.

Holy hell. Again.

Images of their encounter flashed through her mind, and her body joined the parade. Her pulse raced, and she was instantly aroused. Ellie—who should not, *could* not, be standing there—squinted up at the bright sun, then leaned back inside the SUV, the angle clearly outlining her ass. Kelsey's palms twitched at the memory of how that part of her had fit perfectly in her hands.

The sound of boots crunching on the gravel brought Kelsey back into focus.

Ellie covered her long blond hair with the hat in her hand and walked toward Kelsey. She started to speak, then stopped, all color draining from her face. Recognition was clear in her eyes, along with more than a little shock. Kelsey watched her swallow and stand a little straighter. Steel shutters dropped over her eyes, and Kelsey could no longer read the emotion, if there was any, behind them. Ellie took a few steps closer as a petite brunette with skin the color of desert sand and eyes with a sharp appraising edge joined her. Her jeans, boots, and shirt, like Ellie's, looked starched, pressed, and new.

Kelsey gritted her teeth. Perfect. Another couple of wannabe cowgirls. She waited silently for Ellie to make the first move—she wasn't about to make any part of this easy.

"Good morning," Ellie said, her tone cool and her expression remote. "I'm Elizabeth Sutton. I'm here to see Red Brunel."

Chapter Eight

Kelsey couldn't reply, could barely think. She wasn't sure if she was even breathing. The woman's—Elizabeth's—voice beneath the ice was as smooth and sultry as she remembered from the whispers, pleas, and urgent demands they'd shared the night before. She'd dated her share of women and slept with quite a few, but no one had done—was still doing—what Elizabeth had managed. Elizabeth's crystal blue eyes that echoed the color of a cloudless Arizona sky continued to bore into her, taking her back to the night before, and like then, her knees weakened and her mind blanked. In the anonymity of last night, those eyes had appeared dark and smoldering, but then both of them had been on fire then, with only one thing on their minds—sex, fast and hot.

"Is this the Red Sky Ranch?"

The name of the only true place she had ever belonged slapped Kelsey out of her lustful stupor back to reality. Standing in front of her was the woman who was here to take it all away.

"Yes, it is."

"Is Mr. Brunel here?"

"Not at the moment."

"Do you know when he'll be back?" Elizabeth asked.

"No." Kelsey was not going to do anything to speed along this change of control.

"I'm sorry," Elizabeth said, "and you are?"

"Kelsey Brunel." *If I'd told you that last night, would you still have begged me to fuck you?*

Elizabeth appeared unfazed by Kelsey's lack of communication. "And Mr. Brunel is...?"

"My father."

"Ms. Brunel, your father was expecting us today." Elizabeth glanced at what looked to be a very expensive watch. "About this time, as a matter of fact."

"I'm not my father's keeper." Kelsey surprised herself at the venom in her voice. "As I wasn't part of...whatever the hell this is, I can't help you."

"Ms. Brunel—"

"Kelsey." Kelsey bit off the word. If they were going to continue this charade of not knowing each other, she was at least going to make Elizabeth use her damn first name. She wasn't about to be erased that easily.

"Kelsey, then. I represent Sutton Properties, the new owner of—"

"I know who you are." Kelsey figured she knew a lot more about her than Elizabeth Sutton wished she did, but that wasn't her problem.

"Then you know why I'm here."

"How much?"

"Excuse me?"

"How much did you pay my father for Red Sky?"

A cross between confusion and anger flashed across Elizabeth's face. "I'm afraid those negotiations are between him and my father."

"*Your* father?"

"Yes."

"And he sent you here to do his dirty work?"

"No, I'm here to turn this..." Elizabeth looked around. "This *ranch* into a five-star resort and spa."

"If you took advantage of—"

"Ms. Brunel," Elizabeth's companion said, her tone carrying just an edge of warning, "while we appreciate a transition like this is difficult—"

"Transition?" Kelsey snorted. "From where I'm standing, it looks like highway robbery."

"Your insinuations—"

"It's okay," Elizabeth said, placing a hand on her friend's arm. "This looks like a massive case of miscommunication." She glanced up at Kelsey. "I can assure you, your father was offered a fair price for this property, and he accepted. If you were not included in all the negotiations, that's unfortunate, but that is an issue between you and your father."

"Ms. Sutton." Kelsey paused, finding that the name did not fit anything at all that she knew about this woman. And wasn't that just exactly what was stoking her temper as much as what her father had done. "I don't know you from the local tax collector, and I wouldn't trust what he said about money either."

Elizabeth held Kelsey's stare for so long, Kelsey started to get nervous. Even though there was no point, this had somehow become a battle of wills, and she did not want to back down. Pointlessly stubborn, perhaps, but damn it, Elizabeth Sutton—the woman who'd shaken her world the night before—was about to destroy it. How much was she expected to take with a smile?

"The deal is done," Elizabeth said softly, her tone in direct contrast to Kelsey's heated one. "If your attorney has not provided you with all the details of the sale, I'm sure your father will. And as we are here, I'd like to have a look around."

"Meaning what?"

"Meaning you know who I am and why I'm here, and I'd like to have a look around. Since your father is not here at the moment, it looks like you're my tour guide."

CHAPTER NINE

Kelsey relaxed her hands on the steering wheel. She wasn't sure if her death grip was to keep her hands from shaking or to keep from strangling Elizabeth.

The last few minutes had been surreal. The woman from last night—Elizabeth—was the last person she expected to see this morning. Had she wanted to see her again? Absolutely. Even if she had to drive back and forth to Phoenix, she would have. Elizabeth had been captivating—and not just the way she'd responded in her arms, although that had been pretty damn unforgettable—but more than that, she'd exuded passion and energy and a magnetic pull that had grabbed Kelsey and wouldn't let go. She wanted to have sex with her again, oh yes, but more than that, she wanted to know about her. She almost laughed at that. Maybe that was past tense. When she'd woken up that morning with *Ellie* on her mind, she'd wanted to know everything about her. Who was she, beyond the sexiest woman she'd ever touch? What made her tick, what did she do for a living, what did she think about poverty, gun violence, and who would win the Oscar this year for best actress? She'd wanted to know what made her eyes sparkle and whether her passion for life burned as brightly as the passion they'd shared.

Now what the hell? What the holy hell?

That same woman was now sitting beside her in the cart they used to ferry guests around the resort. It was a glorified golf cart designed to hold six people comfortably. Elizabeth's perfume drifted over to Kelsey, and a flashback of the night before clouded her vision. Arousing, confusing, and infuriating.

"Tell me about the property," Elizabeth said, and the illusion of who Kelsey'd imagined Elizabeth to be disappeared.

"You bought something without knowing anything about it?" Kelsey shook her head. She shouldn't be surprised at how rich people spent their money, considering most of their clientele, but this whole story was beyond belief.

"I didn't buy it, as I already explained, my father did."

"And you're here to turn his vision into reality."

Elizabeth's jaw tightened before she answered. "Something like that."

"What are your plans?" Kelsey asked as they drove down the narrow road toward one of the bunkhouses. She didn't want Elizabeth to know she was completely in the dark. Elizabeth already knew more about her than she wanted her to. The most intimate things.

"In terms of?" Elizabeth asked. "There are a great many details and layers of development to be undertaken."

"The ranch," Kelsey said, as if there was anything else that mattered. "The current staff? The animals?"

Silently, she added *Me*.

"It's my understanding guests are booked out several months."

"We're booked into the fall. Red Sky has a great reputation in the industry." Kelsey doubted Elizabeth cared anything about the past, only what the Red Sky name would give her in the future.

"The priority, of course," Elizabeth said, "is to ensure Sutton's commitment to our clients is fulfilled."

Sutton's? Kelsey stared ahead so long without blinking, her eyes watered from the grit. That one sentence brought it all home like a kick to the gut. The Red Sky Ranch was a Sutton property now. She finally asked, "Which means what?"

"That we give them the five-star experience they're expecting. That's all spelled out in the T's and C's of the contract."

"T's and C's?"

"Terms and conditions," Elizabeth clarified. "We have six

months to transform this property into the Sutton Southwest flagship wellness resort."

"But what about the people?"

"People?"

"The ranch doesn't run itself." From memory, Kelsey listed the names and tenure of the year-round staff. "This ranch is the only work some of the staff have ever done. And Wickenburg is not a hub of alternative employment options. You'll put a lot of locals out of work if these people lose their jobs."

"What is this building used for?" Elizabeth asked, pointing to one of the bunkhouses.

Kelsey noted that she didn't answer the question, irritating her even more. "It's the Wilcox bunkhouse."

"I'd like to look inside."

Kelsey gritted her teeth at Elizabeth's statement. It wasn't a request. She hit the brakes a little harder than she needed to.

"Whoa, there, cowgirl," the woman in the back seat said.

What did Elizabeth say her name was? Olivia? She was so small, the large seat practically swallowed her. "Sorry."

The two women trailed behind her as they approached the front porch. The sunbaked adobe brick building featured prominently on the front of the Red Sky Ranch brochure. Kelsey flipped on the lights.

Olivia said, "There are eight separate bedrooms upstairs, each having a private bathroom with whirlpool tub. The central area here connects to a kitchen and an all-season room in the back."

Kelsey stared. "How do you know that?"

"It's in the prospectus," Olivia replied as if Kelsey should know that.

"Right. The prospectus." Kelsey pointed across the large room where a wide-screen TV nestled into a bookcase custom-made for it next to two wide French doors. "Patio through there with a Jacuzzi, sauna, and cold tub beside that."

"Not my idea of real ranch experience," Olivia muttered.

"We have a variety of lodgings to suit any style here at Red Sky," Kelsey said. What had they expected? Outhouses? By the looks of Olivia's perfectly tailored, fashionably short pants and ankle boots, how would she know what a ranch experience was all about? "Along with the Wilcox, we have the Stoneman bunkhouse that has eight single bunks, three bathrooms without the whirlpool tubs, and is far less extravagant. We also have separate casitas that will each house two to four guests. For the more adventurous that want an even closer experience, we offer guided off-site camping accommodations."

"And of the suites in the main house?" Elizabeth asked. "How many have en suite baths?"

"All of them." Kelsey vacillated between being impressed and annoyed. Someone had done a lot of research on the ranch. These two were a lot better informed than she expected. But then, she hadn't really known what to expect. Certainly not Elizabeth Sutton, on any level.

Once outside, Elizabeth eyed the property, frowning. What was she thinking? Was she envisioning the end result? Did she think the ranch was broken down and hokey? Was she reliving their episode in the parking lot?

"What about the desert creatures?" Olivia asked.

"Desert creatures?"

"Snakes and tarantulas and all that." Olivia made it sound as if they were about to be attacked at any second.

Kelsey almost laughed. The Red Sky was on the outskirts of town, not in the middle of bumfuck nowhere. But then again, this probably seemed like the wilderness to someone so obviously city bred as to show up looking like she'd just stepped out of a salon.

"I think you might mean scorpions. If I told you they were everywhere, would you void the sale and go back to wherever you came from?"

Olivia arched a brow, and damn if she didn't grin. "I *came* from New York City. We have our own versions of vermin there. I'm just not likely to step on any of them or find them in my room."

"I'm afraid, Ms. Brunel," Elizabeth said with an edge of impatience, "this is a done deal for all concerned. It might be better if you accepted that so we can all get on with what must be done."

"You didn't buy *me*, Ms. Sutton," Kelsey snapped.

"I can see we need to clarify some things." Elizabeth's eyes hardened. "As you haven't reviewed the contract, I'll summarize. All critical employees are to be retained at salaries to be set by Sutton Properties until the end of the official opening of the new center. As interim manager, it will be your responsibility to see that they do."

"Interim manager," Kelsey repeated, sounding poleaxed even to herself. What the hell did that mean? Was that why Red had forbidden her to tell any of the staff about the sale? "And if I don't care to stay on to do your bidding?"

Elizabeth shrugged. "If we have to bring in our own management people and train them to do what the present staff are already doing, we will incur significant expenditures and loss of production time. As a result, your father forfeits fifty percent of the sale price. And let me assure you, that is a lot of money to blow away in the wind because of your obstructive attitude."

"My *obstructive* attitude?" Kelsey secretly applauded at the irritation in Elizabeth's tone. At least she was getting some little bit of payback by annoying her. Petty, yeah, maybe. But she had a lot of reasons to be hurt and angry, starting with losing her home and ending with still wanting to kiss a woman who clearly couldn't give a damn about her. Or anyone else at the Red Sky, it seemed. Elizabeth Sutton hadn't blinked when discussing people's lives and livelihoods reduced to costs and expenditures. As if Kelsey would care about Sutton's bottom line. But she did care about the people who'd been loyal to the Red Sky for more than thirty years. No way was she walking out on them.

"You've been nothing but argumentative since we got here," Elizabeth said tersely. "None of this should be news to you. If Mr. Brunel did not inform you of the final terms of sale, that is not our doing. This is your new reality, so the sooner you get on board, the sooner we can all get this project finished. Any other questions?"

CHAPTER TEN

"Let her go," Elizabeth said to Olivia as Kelsey Brunel stalked away. Maybe a few minutes would cool the anger brewing in Kelsey's hot dark eyes. Hot as in furious, and hot as in sexy. Kelsey Brunel—who she would not think of as Sky or in any other way associate with the previous night—was more than a little hot in a rough-and-tumble cowgirl way. If Elizabeth was interested in getting down and dirty, with emphasis on the dirty. Which she was not. She only liked to sweat in the gym or in the bedroom. The former was unavailable, and the latter out of the question. Oh wait, she hadn't even needed the bedroom, had she? Oh no—she'd been happy to get sweaty and a lot of other things in a parking lot in the middle of nowhere. Something she'd like to forget and hadn't been able to stop thinking about since tearing out of the parking lot.

So unlike her to do anything so reckless. Risky on multiple levels, not to mention she could have been arrested, for God's sake. She could not begin to imagine what her father's reaction would have been, and it definitely was not something she wanted to think about. She'd spent her entire life proving to him she was worthy—of being a Sutton, of being loved. Of not being an embarrassment to her image-conscious family because she was different.

Elizabeth shook off the cold chill the memories brought with them. She was not that desperate child any longer—even if she'd been desperate last night. Her heart had begun hammering the instant she'd seen Sky—Kelsey Brunel—standing on the porch of the property she, as the embodiment of Sutton Properties, now owned and was responsible for transforming. The woman she had fucked in the dark shadows of a parking lot. A woman she never expected to see again. The woman who instantly stirred the same visceral reaction as she had the first time Elizabeth had seen her— arousal that spread through her like hot lava.

There was nothing to be done about the whole mess now. She, for one, planned to treat it exactly as it was—an almost anonymous casual encounter. What else could she do? What could she say? *Sorry your father sold your home out from under you? Really a shame he didn't bother to tell you about the fine print? Sorry I accepted your offer for a quick screw and then turned out to be the last person you wanted to see again?*

God, what would Kelsey say when they came face-to-face without an audience?

Elizabeth could just imagine it. *Hi, remember me? I picked you up at the Last Stop, we dirty-danced, then fucked in the back parking lot. Want to take a tumble in the hay barn this time?*

"Are you all right?" Olivia asked too quietly for her words to carry the thirty feet to where Kelsey now leaned against the ATV, arms folded over her chest, staring back at them.

Elizabeth forced a smile. "Of course. I've dealt with much more difficult people than a pissed-off rancher. Remember Istanbul?"

Olivia rolled her eyes. "Don't remind me. I'm just surprised you're being so reasonable when she's got no grounds to complain. Or resist getting on board."

"Apparently she's been left out of the loop," Elizabeth said, knowing just how painful that could be. She took a breath. "But you're right. I need to get her cooperation or get her out of the way."

But first she needed to stop seeing Kelsey and immediately thinking about their encounter. Or, worse, remembering the sensation of Kelsey's hands on her body when they danced, the heat of her fingers as they caressed her bare skin, and her warm breath on her neck when she climaxed. Only, God, she was beautiful. Even without her lust-filled haze and the flattering lights of the bar, Kelsey was stunning. She had that fresh-air look and a body honed by hard, physical work. Elizabeth's fingers tingled as she recalled the firm muscles under smooth skin and the texture of her short, silky curls running through her fingers. Like last night, Kelsey's gaze was direct, her eyes as green as fresh cut grass.

Elizabeth's skin burned as Kelsey, still staring, looked her over from the top of her boots to the flat brim of her gaucho hat. Somehow, Elizabeth managed to keep her breathing relatively normal and summoned the composure she'd spent a lifetime honing. She didn't intend to let Kelsey know how much her presence made her heart pound—made everything inside her pound. And she certainly wasn't going to let Kelsey's attitude interfere with business.

"Give me a minute," Elizabeth said to Olivia and walked over to Kelsey, who straightened with a wary look as she approached. Elizabeth met her gaze, unperturbed by the heat directed her way. "I'm not sure what your problem is with this, but your father advertised this property for sale, and my father bought it. Simple as that."

"There is nothing simple about it."

Damn, but Kelsey was hot when she was, well, hot. Fierce and passionate. Just the way she fu—

Elizabeth focused. "You didn't know about any of this this, did you?"

Kelsey hesitated a moment too long before answering. "Of course I did."

"Don't bullshit me, Kelsey. I can smell it like I just stepped in it."

"Eww," Olivia said from beside her.

"After the fact," Kelsey finally admitted.

Elizabeth sighed. "Well, that makes two of us who had no idea what their fathers were up to."

Olivia coughed, a subtle reminder not to give anything away. Information was power.

Elizabeth usually agreed, but not this time. "But here we are, and we have to make the best of it."

Kelsey took one step closer and stopped abruptly, emanating controlled fury. "We are not in the same place. Not even close.

You're going to make a lot of money, which you probably don't need, and I got fucked. It's as simple as *that*."

Elizabeth said nothing as Kelsey climbed into the ATV and started the engine. At least she didn't drive off without them.

And I got fucked. Her words brought every minute back in living color, and Elizabeth wanted to do it again. And several more times after that. She was in trouble if she didn't get hold of this situation.

"Let's go," she said to Olivia. "We have a tour to finish."

"You've got your hands full with this one," Olivia muttered.

This was one of those rare times Olivia didn't know the half of it.

CHAPTER ELEVEN

A tall, thin, tired-looking man in worn jeans, boots, and a long-sleeve green button-down shirt stood on the porch of the main house when they returned. The brim of his hat hid his eyes. Elizabeth climbed out of the ATV and walked over to him, hand extended. She didn't really need an introduction. Kelsey looked just like her father, although a far less world-weary version.

"Mr. Brunel, I'm Elizabeth Sutton."

"Ma'am." He didn't shake her hand but tipped his hat in greeting instead.

Elizabeth recognized the signs of a long-term drinker in the pallor of his skin, unlike the golden brown from the Arizona sun of his daughter, and the broken blood vessels across his nose. The dullness in his eyes told his story. Whereas Kelsey stood tall, defiant, and proud, this man was stooped and defeated.

"My associate, Olivia Martinez. We've been touring the ranch with your daughter."

Red Brunel still hadn't said anything. The only acknowledgment was another slight nod toward Olivia.

"Mr. Brunel, may we step inside? We have a lot of ground to cover."

"Out here is fine."

Like father like daughter. Stubborn.

"All right, Mr. Brunel." Elizabeth stepped onto the porch

uninvited. She was tired of taking the low-key approach and being met with one roadblock after the other. And though she wouldn't admit it, she was hot, thirsty, and more than a little off-stride from seeing Kelsey again. But all that would have to wait. She was done with diplomacy. "Are you going to be staying on during the transition?"

"Won't be staying. I've already cleared out."

"You did what?" Kelsey asked, hustling onto the porch.

"Stay out of it, Kelsey. This isn't about you."

Elizabeth saw the look of shock cross Kelsey's face. How could a man be so heartless?

"Mr. Brunel, there is no reason—"

"Do you have any questions for me?"

Elizabeth had dozens, but she wouldn't get any answers from this man. "Your daughter was kind enough to show us around, but—"

"Then she can answer anything else." He headed toward a blue truck parked nearby. A small pile of boxes thrown into a haphazard jumble filled the bed. Kelsey hurried after him.

"Dad, what are you doing? You're just leaving?"

"You have a college degree, and you can't figure it out?"

Elizabeth and Olivia exchanged looks. What the hell was happening here? Her understanding had been that Kelsey was intimately involved in every aspect of running the Red Sky. She assumed that included the sale. It certainly didn't look like that by this conversation. No wonder Kelsey was furious.

Olivia whistled softly behind her. "What a jerk."

The tension was thick as summer in the South when Kelsey returned to the porch. She was pale, and Elizabeth thought she saw tears in her eyes. Her father was an arrogant, self-serving ass at times, but he stopped short of outright cruelty. Red Brunel was in a class by himself.

"Excuse me, Kelsey." A stout, middle-aged woman with beauty parlor hair and a baby-blue apron with voluminous pockets covering a calico dress hovered in the doorway. "Should I be making any changes in the dinner schedule?"

Kelsey took a deep breath and straightened her shoulders. She turned to Elizabeth, her face void of any emotion, her eyes cold steel. "Ms. Sutton, our head cook and house manager, Charmaine Duval. Charmaine, Ms. Sutton is the new owner of the Red Sky."

A look of complete shock crossed Charmaine's face, then she forced a smile and said, "Ms. Sutton, a pleasure to meet you."

"And you as well, Ms. Duval. This is Olivia Martinez." From an early age, Elizabeth had vowed she'd be very different than her parents. They would not have given Charmaine the time of day other than to answer her question. They never would have introduced any of the help to a visitor. Elizabeth hated it when her parents called their house staff *the help*. The staff were people hired to do a specific job, and they did it with the same pride, dedication, and effort as any worker employed by Sutton Properties. Just because they worked in and around their house did not make them any less important. With a glance at Kelsey, she added, "I'm sure Kelsey will explain the changes to you and the rest of the staff as soon as she can. In the meantime, please consider everything to be business as usual."

A look of relief passed over Charmaine's face as she nodded to Olivia, then looked back and forth between Elizabeth and Kelsey.

"Will you be staying for lunch, then? All the other guests will be out," Charmaine added.

Elizabeth looked at Kelsey. Typically, she would have stepped in and answered, but she deferred to Kelsey instead. Instincts told her she couldn't bulldoze her way into getting Kelsey to cooperate. Not her usual style, but where Kelsey was concerned, nothing appeared to be usual for her. Olivia gave her another raised eyebrow, what-are-you-doing look, but she just smiled.

"Yes, thank you, Charmaine," Kelsey answered. "I'll be back to talk to you in a bit. We'll get everything sorted soon."

Charmaine hurried back inside, probably thankful to leave. Elizabeth wished she could disappear as well, but the day's business was far from done. She followed Kelsey inside.

The cool air conditioning was a relief, and it took a moment for her eyes to adjust from the bright midday sun.

"This is lovely," Olivia commented.

Elizabeth had been watching Kelsey's ass as she strode across the room. Her jeans weren't designer, or even all that tight. But she filled them out in a way that said the body inside was built for hard work. She already knew how good those legs felt between hers.

With supreme effort, she looked away and focused on her surroundings. She took in the worn but gleaming hardwood floors, scuffed from what she assumed were hundreds of pairs of boots over the years. The furnishings were desert Southwest, the dark leather furniture sturdy and functional. The couch was flanked by solid end tables and two large recliners that faced a matching loveseat. A massive fireplace dominated one wall, the large river stones climbing from the hearth to the tall ceiling. Dark, almost black beams ran the length of the large room. Several rugs gave the room a warm, comfortable feeling. A set of wide stairs led to the second floor. At the far end opposite the entry, a massive dining room table with seating for at least twelve sat under a large chandelier. Off to one side, five smaller round tables each provided seating for two to four people and a little more privacy. The room looked like it belonged in an old western TV show her father had watched when she was a child. She wondered for an instant if that was why he'd bought this place, but then discounted it. Her father was not the nostalgic type.

"Thank you," Kelsey finally said to Olivia's compliment. "Charmaine takes care of everything inside the house. Marie is Charmaine's daughter—she's probably in the kitchen now—and she helps with the cooking for major meals. Buck is the outside cook."

"Outside cook?"

"When we do overnighters."

"Like a chuck wagon?" Olivia asked.

"Something like that, yes." Kelsey smiled although she looked like she didn't want to. "The suites are this way."

Kelsey stopped in front of the first closed door to their right. She pulled a card key out of her back pocket, flashed it over the lock, and opened the heavy wooden door. "Right now, this is the only room that's not occupied."

Elizabeth had never seen anything like it other than in pictures. The room was twice the size of a king suite in a luxury New York hotel, with a fireplace holding stacked logs fronting a sitting area at one end. A sand-colored leather couch and matching chair atop a large rug with earth-toned geometric designs defined the open seating area. Pillows covered in Southwestern fabrics added a splash of color. A round wooden coffee table stood in the center, a large candle in a red glass globe in the middle, waiting to be lit.

Despite the understated elegance and unique design choices, Elizabeth's attention immediately jumped to the four-poster king draped in a colorful Southwestern spread that dominated at the opposite end of the large space. Six accent pillows leaned against a large wooden headboard, with matching nightstands on either side. A six-drawer dresser sat against the wall with a larger mirror on the wall above it. Windows on either side provided a sweeping view of the desert and mountains beyond.

An image of her and Kelsey in the middle of the bed, covers in disarray, flashed in her head. She was on her back, Kelsey's mouth between her legs, their reflection captured in the mirror over Kelsey's shoulders.

"Beautiful," she murmured.

"We think so," Kelsey said.

A nudge from Olivia brought her out of her reverie, and she found Kelsey watching her curiously. Despite her best efforts, she felt color rise to her cheeks. "The bathroom?"

Kelsey waited another beat, her gaze still searching Elizabeth's, then turned and walked toward a door on the far side of the seating area. "Through here."

Mercifully, Elizabeth managed to make it through the rest of the facilities walk-through without another relapse into sexual fantasy. Not an easy chore with Kelsey nearby. She must radiate some kind of pheromone. Elizabeth had never before been so aware of another woman's presence, nor in such a constant state of arousal. Finally pulling her mind out of bedroom activities as they walked back downstairs, she asked, "What are the amenities and activities guests can select while they're here?"

"We have a range of packages that allow guests to choose their accommodations, meal plans, and resort activities according to their desire to have an adventure vacation or a relaxing, unstructured experience. They can select overnight camping, day hikes, or longer horseback excursions. Or they can choose from the spa facilities and stay poolside."

Elizabeth walked to the window. "What about golf?"

"What about it?" Kelsey asked.

"Where do the golfers go to golf?"

"There's a public course a half hour away," Kelsey said, looking uncomfortable for the first time.

"You've got the perfect terrain for one right out there," Elizabeth said, pointing out the window.

"Yeah, well," Kelsey said, "that takes a lot of money to build."

Elizabeth looked toward Olivia. "Add it to the plans. When will the construction crews arrive?"

"Done," Olivia muttered, entering something on a handheld device. "One week."

"I want a proposal by then," Elizabeth said.

"Done," Olivia repeated.

Kelsey stared. "Just like that?"

"That's what we do." Elizabeth met her gaze. "Is there anything else?"

Kelsey held her gaze. "We have the romance package."

"Consisting of?"

"We provide wine, chocolate-covered strawberries upon arrival. We give them a picnic basket with another bottle of wine, a couples massage, and a choice of a horseback ride at dusk or dawn, a Jeep tour, or a hot air balloon ride before a private dinner on the patio. With champagne, of course."

"Of course," Elizabeth murmured, her pulse beating faster.

What they'd shared could not be described as romance in anyone's imagination. However, she could easily envision them having a moonlight drink in a hot tub before moving into one of those enormous beds, where they would not get a minute's sleep. Imagining Kelsey's hands on her, in her, making her come over and over and over… She suppressed a shudder.

"I think that's enough of a tour for the moment," she finally said. "I'll want a look at the books after lunch."

"The books," Kelsey said flatly.

"Yes. Is that a problem?"

Kelsey shook her head. "Would it matter?"

Elizabeth smiled wryly. "I'm afraid not."

CHAPTER TWELVE

Lunch was worse than awkward, and the afternoon was about to get worse. Within the span of ninety minutes, Kelsey had met the woman who was taking over the ranch, been formally introduced to that same woman who just happened to have fucked her senseless the night before, and watched her father drive away to who knows where, leaving her stranded and swinging in the wind. She hadn't really seen him to notice if he'd been drinking that morning, but judging by the smell of him as he'd passed her on his sprint to his truck, he had apparently found his way back to the nearest bottle.

And next on this hit parade was an afternoon spent looking at finances with Elizabeth Sutton.

"Would you like some more lemonade, Ms. Sutton?" Marie asked.

"I'm fine, thanks, Marie—and just Elizabeth is fine."

Kelsey narrowed her eyes. What the hell was that? Elizabeth had no trouble asking a near stranger to use her first name. What was she expected to call her, seeing how Elizabeth seemed to reserve Ellie for her one-and-done fucks? Ms. Sutton? Elizabeth? Damned if she was going to ask.

"Am I to make up a room for you and Ms. Martinez?" Marie asked Elizabeth after shooting a quick glance at Kelsey.

Kelsey's heart skipped. She hadn't even thought about where Elizabeth and her sidekick would be staying. Who was Olivia, anyway? Elizabeth had yet to say exactly what her role was. Suddenly, another wave of nausea crashed into her. Was Olivia her girlfriend? Wife? She looked at Elizabeth's hand. No ring on the *I'm married* finger. Olivia's was bare as well. Not that that necessarily meant anything. Plenty of people didn't wear wedding rings, especially if they were going to fuck strangers in dark parking lots. The dull headache Kelsey had woken up with pounded harder.

"No, thank you, Marie. We have reservations in town."

"Actually, Ms. Sutton," Kelsey struggled to keep from choking on her words, "this is your home now. Any rooms you require can be made available."

"Actually, Ms. Brunel..." Elizabeth hesitated, slowly wiping her mouth with the napkin from her lap before folding it neatly on the table beside her plate. "It belongs to Sutton Properties."

"And you are Sutton Properties," Kelsey countered, making her point.

"Not precisely," Elizabeth replied with annoying composure. "On a personal level, we do not evict individuals from their homes. The transition is staged for precisely that reason. You should have adequate time to make alternate arrangements."

Alternate arrangements. Kelsey clenched her fists under the table. "Which doesn't change the fact that I have no choice, does it?"

Olivia rose abruptly as the atmosphere in the room sparked with all that wasn't being said. "I want to get a look at the stables."

"Barns," Kelsey corrected, holding Elizabeth's gaze. "We call them barns out here. Ask for Andrea, one of the wranglers. She'll show you around."

"Thank you. Elizabeth, text me if anything comes up."

"I will." Elizabeth sat back in her chair as Marie cleared the table. When they were alone, she said, "Ms. Brunel, I can understand your situation."

"You know nothing about my situation," Kelsey interrupted sharply. "And damn it, call me Kelsey."

"You're right. Kelsey. I do know that you're angry and looking for someone to blame. I can't do anything to change that." Elizabeth leaned forward. "I have a job to do here. So do you. You are now an employee of Sutton Properties."

"Yes, you have made that perfectly clear." Kelsey hadn't been anyone's *employee* for years. Technically, she supposed Red had been her boss, but she'd always thought of them as partners. She wouldn't make that kind of mistake again. With anyone.

"I would appreciate it, then," Elizabeth said, ignoring the sarcasm in Kelsey's tone, "if you could take me to the main office so we can get a look at the up-to-date finances."

"Main office." Kelsey rubbed her face with both hands. "That would be my fath—Red's room, I guess. He has a kind of office there."

"A kind of office." Elizabeth's eyebrows rose.

"Look, Ms. Sutton—"

"Oh, for God's sake…" Elizabeth shot a glance toward the open doorway to the kitchen. "Call me Elizabeth."

"Elizabeth," Kelsey said, "not Ellie."

Elizabeth's expression cooled. "No, not Ellie. Not now or in the future."

Kelsey stood. Well, that made things very clear. She worked for Elizabeth Sutton, and she would not be having mind-blowing sex with Ellie again. How she'd manage either, she had no idea.

She'd been on an emotional roller-coaster ride since the minute she'd recognized Elizabeth, veering between despising her and everything she represented to craving the passion and reckless desire Elizabeth had stirred in her. She wanted her gone, and she wanted to stroke her until *Ellie* pleaded with her to make her come again. She wanted the touch of Ellie's lips on her neck as Ellie teased her into another blinding orgasm. And worst of all, she didn't want to be feeling any of it.

"I'll take you to Red's room," Kelsey said. Maybe then Elizabeth would leave her in peace to run the ranch for the time she had left.

❖

Elizabeth squeezed the bridge of her nose. She'd been staring at jumbles of numbers for a good two hours. Jumble was the only word for it. Red Brunel had obviously never heard of something as simple as QuickBooks. He kept a ledger of sorts—an honest-to-God ledger in a big, green leather-bound book with lined pages, columns of figures, and chicken-scratched notations. Some of which were indecipherable.

"Can you make out what this is?" Elizabeth pointed to another scribble next to a number. Math was her forte. She'd always been able to recognize numbers, do complex calculations in her head, and remember rows of numbers without difficulty. Fortunately, most of the notations in Red's books were single words that she'd been able to recognize as names.

Kelsey, who sat on a stool next to her, leaned closer to look. "Where?"

They'd been at it the better part of the afternoon. And Elizabeth struggled through most of it, trying not to be aware of Kelsey so close. But she smelled good. Like sunshine on a hot day. "Here."

"Um," Kelsey muttered, then, "that looks like pay part… next…month?"

"I guess that's just his note to himself." Elizabeth leaned back and looked at Kelsey. "This isn't good news."

"Why aren't I surprised," Kelsey said, the usual edge in her voice missing.

Kelsey looked defeated, something Elizabeth hadn't seen in her before, and it pulled at her. She had no way of making any of this easier. What had been done was done. She had others to answer to, not just her father. Sutton crews would be arriving to start work on building new additions, upgrading those that existed, and expanding the outdoor facilities. All of that was in the works, or would be soon. There was no going back for any of them, her least of all.

She'd had a wild, unbridled, incredible few moments with Kelsey Brunel. And that was done as well. She couldn't see any way forward but to put that encounter firmly in the past. One not to be revisited.

"Well?" Kelsey said. "Are you going to tell me what all this means?"

"He didn't bring you in on any of the financial aspects of the ranch?"

"If he had, do you think I would have been so poleaxed by this takeover?" Kelsey said bitterly. "He was always in charge. I guess I never thought to question how things were going, but…"

"But what?"

Kelsey sighed. "There were little things. When I talked to him about expansion, things like that golf course you mentioned, he'd get this look—like there was something he didn't want to say. It was always *we'll see how things go* with him." She grimaced. "Maybe I should have pushed harder. Maybe then he would have told me about this crazy idea he had to sell the whole place to you."

For the first time, her rancor didn't seem directly aimed at Elizabeth, and Elizabeth didn't see any point in correcting her again that Red Brunel had sold the Red Sky Ranch to Sutton Properties, not to her. Instead, she said, "It probably wouldn't have made any difference. He wouldn't have told you about any of this."

"What," Kelsey said tightly, "has he done?"

Elizabeth leaned back and sighed. "To put it briefly, there's no money."

"Sorry? What?"

"The ranch accounts are empty and have been for a while."

"What about the sale money? The money to pay the employees?"

"As near as I can tell, and we'll need our forensic accountants to look over these books, whatever money your father got from the sale is gone. He's been running on a deficit for months—likely close to two years. He's been using all the profits after essential expenses for quite some time to pay off something else. Loans, perhaps?"

"Loan sharks, more like it," Kelsey said grimly. "I knew he gambled, but I never thought…"

She shot to her feet, shoving the stool back so hard it tipped over. "No wonder he made a quick sale. If I'd paid more attention, maybe I could have stopped this from happening."

"Kelsey—" Elizabeth began, but Kelsey was already gone.

❖

Kelsey needed a few minutes with Adira to settle her mind and ground her in what mattered most—taking care of the ranch. She set about grooming her, which Adira probably thought was odd, if she thought about it at all, and let the familiar motions soothe some of her pain and confusion. Her chest hurt with every breath, while the rest of her seethed with the restless energy that usually sent her looking for sex. Except she'd just left the woman she wanted to have sex with, and she really, really did not want to think about Elizabeth Sutton in any way at all.

Sure, okay, she'd been stunned when she'd first seen Elizabeth at the bar. She was gorgeous—and more than that, she radiated power. Why wouldn't she find her attractive? And they'd had incredible sex—lucky her—and so what? She didn't do commitment. Everything from college on had been casual and usually brief. Why the hell not this time?

She knew why and wished she didn't. They'd been strangers, but that hadn't prevented the lightning connection that flared between them from the moment they touched. They—*both* of them—had been exposed out there in the dark, physically and emotionally. She'd let Ellie see her need, and Ellie had bared her own vulnerabilities. She couldn't forget that—wouldn't have wanted to forget. Probably would have gone looking for her. Hell, for a couple of seconds after Elizabeth had stepped out of the car, she'd thought that somehow Ellie had found out who she was and where she lived and then tracked her down. Except Elizabeth Sutton had arrived, ripped a hole in her world, and finally burned it all down by telling her that her *father* was one short step away from being a liar and a crook.

Kelsey leaned her head against Adira's neck and closed her eyes. "God damn it, Red. God damn it, Elizabeth—why did it have to be you?"

"Kelsey?" Elizabeth said from somewhere behind her.

Kelsey quickly straightened and turned. Elizabeth stood just inside the partially open barn door. The sun was behind her, turning her image to shadows, an instant reminder of what they'd done in the shadows. Her stomach tightened and the pain in her chest spread.

"Are you lost?"

CHAPTER THIRTEEN

Elizabeth hadn't planned on following when she saw Kelsey walk toward the big red horse barn, but she couldn't just ignore what she'd seen in Kelsey's eyes—the hurt and betrayal that she recognized because she'd felt it herself when the person who was supposed to love you turned out to be someone very different. And no matter how old you were, the pain wasn't any less deep.

By the time she slipped through the half-open door, her pulse was racing, her hands sweaty, and her mind completely blank. She had no idea what she should say—only that she couldn't go on pretending they were strangers.

She saw Kelsey immediately at the far end of the long building, standing in the pale light provided by a series of skylights that illuminated the interior. A wide, wood-floored walkway divided the space between the horse stalls on either side. Several horses had stuck their heads over the stall gates and nickered as she passed. Kelsey watched her silent approach, her expression wary.

"I thought we should talk," Elizabeth said when she stopped a few feet from Kelsey and a beautiful mare who eyed her hopefully. "Sorry, sweetie, I didn't bring any treats."

"You ride?" Kelsey blurted, as if she'd suddenly discovered an alien creature capable of speech.

"Yes, I ride." Elizabeth took a breath, aware of her heart pounding even harder. That was the first personal information they'd actually exchanged.

"Could you tell me what it is you need," Kelsey said, the brief moment of connection severed, "and I'll see that one of the staff takes care of it. I'm done playing tour guide for the day."

"I wanted to talk to you about last night."

"That was a mistake," Kelsey said quickly. "Anything else?"

"It certainly didn't seem like it at the time," Elizabeth said.

A frown creased Kelsey's forehead. "Well, looks can often be deceiving."

"If it was a mistake, why did you do it?" Elizabeth didn't see Kelsey as the kind of woman who acted impulsively. And Kelsey *had* approached her. Was she wrong to think something more than sex had happened between them, or that Kelsey had been as affected as her? Did Kelsey relive every moment like she had? Did her body crave it again?

Kelsey blew out a breath and snapped, "I did it because a beautiful, sexy woman I was extremely attracted to asked me to fuck her."

Elizabeth lifted her chin. Blunt but true. "And that was a mistake how?"

"Which part? That I didn't even know the name of the complete stranger I hooked up with? That it was in a parking lot? Or the fact that you're my boss?"

"I wasn't your boss then." Elizabeth didn't know why she couldn't let this go. "And technically, I'm not now. Sutton Properties has contracted with you to oversee management of the ongoing activities of the ranch, which will at some point become Sutton's wellness center. We're basically sharing duties during this transition, since I wouldn't know a horse from, well...a horse's ass."

She was exaggerating, since she *did* know how to ride, but running a dude ranch was a far cry from stabling her horse where someone else took care of it for her. When she'd wanted to ride for pleasure or otherwise, a groom was always available to assist.

"That's putting a pretty fine point to the distinction," Kelsey muttered.

"And furthermore," Elizabeth said, undeterred, "we were both complicit in remaining anonymous, *Sky*. I don't recall you asking for any personal information before you escorted me to the parking lot."

"I don't give out my full name somewhere I might run into a potential guest without knowing it." Kelsey laughed, sharp and hard. "And *escorted*? You seem to have a different recollection of what went on than I do."

"Really? Do I? I remember two adults in full control of their faculties having hot consensual sex. I remember you fucking me, and I remember you coming all over me. Do I have that wrong?"

Kelsey rubbed a hand across her face. "What does it matter now?"

"It matters what we do about it." Elizabeth had intended to be rational and composed, and the longer they stood there, the more she watched the pulse beat in Kelsey's throat—exactly where she'd kissed her—the more she wanted her again and the less control she had.

"What we do about it." Kelsey's eyes smoldered and she stepped closer, so close they almost touched.

Elizabeth refused to back up, but when Kelsey jammed her hands on her hips in an arrogant challenge, Elizabeth caught sight of the same belt buckle she'd struggled with the night before. A rush of desire shot through her, which she was certain Kelsey saw.

"And what is it that we should do?" Kelsey almost whispered, her hot stare burning into Elizabeth's. "Do it again? Take another walk on the wild side? Here in the barn? In an empty stall? We have a couple."

If Elizabeth let her body answer, the response would be a resounding yes. Yes, anywhere right now would be fine. Just *do it again*. Elizabeth swallowed hard.

"It means we act like adults and accept that it happened, and it's over. We didn't know each other then, but we do now, and it can't happen again." Elizabeth looked Kelsey directly in the eyes. "It won't happen again."

The flame in Kelsey's eyes shifted from desire to anger. "If you think I would ever want to have sex with you again, you are not living in reality. Now if you will excuse me, I have work to do."

❖

Kelsey's hand shook as she removed her hat and wiped the sweat from her forehead. She'd let Elizabeth think she regretted their encounter—or at least thought no more of it than any other casual, one-time thing and had no desire to repeat it. None of that was true. Just the opposite. Those moments with Elizabeth had touched her, gripped some deep place in her and wouldn't let go. She'd told herself she'd have gotten her head around what happened, and the night would fade into a very pleasant memory. Maybe that would have happened—maybe, but all that changed when Elizabeth stepped out of the car. From that instant, she'd wanted her again, but she wasn't a naïve eighteen-year-old who believed every obstacle could be overcome. Considering the direction her life was headed, she could barely control her own future.

She stopped on the other side of the corral, not sure where she was headed. There were dozens of things that always needed to be done on a ranch like the Red Sky, especially with guests coming and going. Livestock needed tending to, not to mention the regular upkeep of the buildings and grounds. Except now, and for the foreseeable future, everywhere she went, Elizabeth would probably be there as well. That was something she dreaded and looked forward to at the same time.

CHAPTER FOURTEEN

"Yee doggie, she is full of spit and vinegar," Olivia said, mimicking an old western saying as they walked into the two-bedroom suite—the only one in the entire town of Wickenburg—they'd reserved for an indefinite period. Airbnbs had not yet arrived in the burg, apparently. Fortunately, the Sutton crews would be setting up air-conditioned trailers for living and working space during the transition out at the ranch. And space would never be a problem there. They could bring in a small city of trailers and not make a dent in the acreage.

"I think it's piss and vinegar," Elizabeth corrected. "And where did you pull that from?"

"Research," Olivia said smartly. "That too, apparently. You're going to have to work your charms on that one."

"I already did."

"Oh really? What did I miss, because from where I was sitting, you failed miserably."

"I'm always charming," Elizabeth replied, covering her gaffe. She really didn't want to get into the details with Olivia, who didn't miss anything. Olivia didn't judge, as best friends didn't, but somehow the retelling of her encounter with their now-employee lent a sordid tinge to it that couldn't be farther from the truth. Not for her, and she hoped not for Kelsey. "Let's get room service, pull out the blueprints, and get to work."

Olivia sighed. "Charming, right. I'll call the kitchen."

They spent the next several hours reviewing the design for the resort, discussing which of the existing buildings would stay and where new buildings would be constructed. Elizabeth had better than average facility with numbers, shapes, and designs and had excellent recall. She had a hard time concentrating and maintaining focus when absorbing content that required reading as well, particularly when she was tired or under stress. Kind of like now.

"What did I just say?"

"What?" Elizabeth asked.

"Have you even been listening to me?" Olivia leaned back in her chair, a frown creasing her perfectly smooth forehead, and sipped the mixed drink she'd had delivered with their meal. "That's not bad, actually."

"You can't go wrong with Crown Royal and Coke no matter what size town you're in," Elizabeth said. "And of course I've been listening."

"Don't lie to me. You've had half of your attention on the plans, the other half somewhere else. My guess is on our dear Ms. Brunel."

"Our *dear* Ms. Brunel?" Elizabeth hadn't thought she was so transparent. But then Olivia knew her too damn well.

"Or should I call her the *hot* Ms. Brunel?" Olivia narrowed her gaze.

"Hot?" Elizabeth completely agreed but wasn't about to say so. "She's not your type, unless there's something you want to tell me."

"Not on your life," Olivia replied, "but you think so."

"What? No, I don't." Not a lie, as hot was not even remotely descriptive of how Kelsey looked.

"Then you haven't been looking." Olivia pursed her lips. "But *she* has, in case you missed the way she looked at you."

"Of course she looked at me. I was talking to her. It was probably hate you saw on her face anyway."

"That's not what I mean, and you know it."

"She didn't look at me like that."

"Oh yes, she *definitely* looked at you like that, and if you weren't worried about establishing your professional creds with everyone out there, I bet it wouldn't be me you'd be having dinner with."

"You don't know what you're talking about. There's nothing happening between me and Kelsey." And if she repeated that enough, she might start believing it one day soon.

"Well, my guess is she'd be happy with absolutely *nothing* between you two." Olivia raised her eyebrows several times.

"Enough!" Elizabeth said, even as an image of being naked with Kelsey flashed in her mind. "We are done with this puerile conversation. It's…unprofessional."

Olivia leaned toward her. "I dare you to say that again without laughing."

Elizabeth laughed. "I am technically her boss."

"A slender technicality so remote as to be on another planet. As your best friend I'm hurt that you don't have faith and confidence enough to tell me. But as your best friend, I'll leave it alone for now." Olivia regarded her seriously. "So, what's got you so quiet tonight? Did you run into problems out at the ranch?"

"I'm just tired," Elizabeth offered, knowing Olivia would probably not buy her explanation.

"Bullshit. I've seen you fly halfway across the world through multiple time zones, and you exude energy at the start of every project." She pinned her with a no-nonsense stare. "You hardly said anything all afternoon. Now, what gives?"

"Nothing."

"I call BS on that again."

"Kelsey had no idea her father had sold the ranch. I don't think she even knew it was for sale." Imagining the betrayal Kelsey must have felt when she'd discovered that wasn't hard for her to imagine, and Elizabeth ached for her.

Olivia shook her head. "And then the minute we get here, he leaves, just like that. What an asshole."

"Unfortunately, it's worse than that." Elizabeth sipped her drink, welcoming the warmth as the liquor settled in her stomach. Telling Olivia about the state of the ranch finances left her cold inside. "This won't affect Sutton's plans, of course, but it's just another blow that Kelsey didn't see coming."

"That explains his quick exit this morning," Olivia said. "He's running from something."

"If I'd done to my daughter what he did to Kelsey, I'd run pretty damn fast, too," Elizabeth said, "although from the looks of those books, I suspect there's more to it than that."

"Not our problem, thankfully." Olivia pushed the room service cart toward the door. "So, what did you think of the place?"

"The ranch?" Elizabeth held the door open for her to wrangle the cart out into the hall. "I think it's beautiful."

"Really?"

"Yes, really, if you're into that sort of thing—the dust and dirt and barren landscape."

"Let's not forget desert stickers and crawling things that can kill you," Olivia said.

"I thought the whole place had a certain amount of character," Elizabeth said.

"Well, I must've flunked character in school because I don't see it. The financials absolutely support this project, but this is not the place that I would drop ten thousand dollars a week for a vacation. And you wouldn't either."

"Yeah, you're probably right."

"Probably has nothing to do with it. If it weren't for this project, you'd *never* be here."

In lieu of hitting a nail on the head, Olivia had poked her with a cactus needle. She was a city girl. She needed lights, action, restaurants, bars, and clubs. Not crickets and tumbleweeds. When she looked up, she wanted to see skyscrapers with blinking lights and five-star restaurants on the roof, not clear skies overflowing with twinkling stars.

There was nothing out there for her.

CHAPTER FIFTEEN

Kelsey wasn't up to having dinner with the guests, but since her father had abandoned the ranch, she didn't have a choice. In addition to her ranch manager responsibilities for the Red Sky, she guessed she was now spokesman and dinner host. After a quick shower and donning a fresh pair of jeans and a western style shirt with white pearl snap buttons—or at least what were supposed to look like flat pearls—she threaded her favorite belt through the loops. As she hooked the silver buckle, she saw Elizabeth impatiently tugging it open, as frantic to touch her as she was to be touched. Hot lust and an unfamiliar pang in her chest struck at once. Kelsey leaned against the dresser and closed her eyes. The Elizabeth of the parking lot was just a phantom—a woman she hadn't known and still didn't. But, God, she wanted that woman again—and very much feared that when she got to know Elizabeth Sutton, she'd find her.

"Sure," she muttered, pushing herself into motion. "And Red will come back with all the money, my mother will drive up in a fancy car, and I'll wake up tomorrow and this will all be a bad dream."

None of this was her doing, but she'd damn well do what needed to be done. Resolutely, she went down to the communal dining area to play her part.

Guests occupied ten of the twelve seats at the large table, having left the end ones unoccupied. Most of the other guests either made arrangements in town to eat out or were off on overnight or longer program excursions. Kelsey chose the seat her father typically sat at and tamped down her feelings about his absence. After a while, even anger and pain receded into a dull ache she'd have to get used to.

The retired couple from Minnesota who sat to her left spent every day on the nearby golf course, and listening to them recount every stroke on every hole to anyone who would listen, she thought of Elizabeth's plans to build a course on the ranch. She was right—they had the perfect terrain for it, and Sutton had the money to build it. The surge of curiosity as to what exactly Sutton places offered surprised her. She didn't want to care about what they had planned, but the ranch was in her blood. She couldn't abandon it just because she was no longer in charge.

She let the conversations around the table drift and didn't need to say much. Marie scowled when she removed her practically untouched dinner plate, but Kelsey pretended not to notice. Dinner and coffee finally over, the guests headed to the back patio for drinks and stargazing or back to their rooms, and Kelsey was finally able to escape to the porch. She drew in a long breath of the cool desert air and settled into a deep cushioned lounge chair in the shadows. The beer bottle she'd carried out with her sweated in the hot night air, and she rubbed it over her forehead. The beer was the same brand as she'd had last night, and just like that, she was back in the bar. She didn't go out to the bars very often. Honestly, the trip was too far, getting home before dawn too difficult if she ended up with someone. But every now and then she needed to see her friends, have a couple of beers, a dance or two, and sometimes find a woman to lose herself in for a few hours. She loved the ranch, but the nights could be long and lonely.

She uttered a curse and said, "Don't you have enough to worry about?"

Staring at the cloudless night sky, she made a solemn desperate vow not to relive the night with Elizabeth again. She might have kept the promise—with a lot of effort, but before she had a chance to find out, Sophia's image materialized on her phone screen. She didn't feel like talking to anyone, but Sophia had promised she'd call to find out about her day and offer moral support. She could probably use some of that and swiped to take the call.

"Hey, there," Kelsey said.

"How was your day? Who is the new owner? Is he nice? What kind of changes do they plan?"

Kelsey smiled. Just like Sophia, jumping right in with a dozen questions. She could never ask just one question, but she always made it sound as if she cared about the answers. That's probably what made her a good social worker.

"I'm doing okay. How are you?"

"Yeah, yeah, yeah. You're not sounding okay, and don't try to convince me otherwise."

Kelsey decided on the condensed version of her truly monumentally crappy day. She just wasn't ready to get into all of it with anyone, even Sophia.

"They showed up around ten in a black Cadillac Escalade."

"Talk about pissing on a tree and marking your territory as a first impression," Sophia said. "Just like a man. Probably overcompensating."

Kelsey would have thought the same thing, except she had a feeling the rental came from corporate, not Elizabeth. Who was most definitely not a man. And she had nothing to compensate for in addition to having the perfect body parts. Kelsey could testify to that. She'd had her hands all over those parts.

"He is a she."

Sophie hesitated a beat. "The new owner is a woman? Holy crap."

"No, the owner is a man. He sent his daughter to oversee the renovation, or whatever the hell is going to happen." She still had no idea.

"I don't know why I didn't expect that. What's she like? Is she some Madison Avenue *too good to get down and dirty in nature* type?"

Kelsey got hijacked at *down and dirty*. Because damn, yes, she was all that and then some more. "Uh…"

"Wait—was she bitchy to you? I'll hunt her down and—"

"No," Kelsey finally managed. She wanted to say yes but, in fact, any bitchiness was on her. "No, not really."

"Is she cute?"

Yes, Kelsey didn't say. And drop dead gorgeous even in her city ranch wear. And don't forget about hot. She was definitely hot. Or at least she made Kelsey hot. No, she'd make any woman who loved women hot. "She's the daughter of the owner. I'm not going there."

"So, she *is* cute."

Kelsey had to shut this conversation down before she went somewhere she didn't want to go with Sophia.

"Come on. I've got bigger things to deal with, and her hotness is nowhere on the list." At least the list she'd show anyone. Just because it was at the top, circled in red, and had four stars next to it didn't mean anything.

"Okay, okay." Sophia didn't try to hide her disappointment. "So, what happened?"

Kelsey gave Sophia the CliffNotes version of the day, leaving out what she'd learned about Red and the money and any of the parts about sex with Elizabeth and wishing she could do it again and her conversation with Elizabeth in the barn.

"So where did you leave it?"

"There was nothing to leave—they'll be back tomorrow, and I'll find out more. If Red knew anything, which I doubt, he didn't tell me."

"Who is they?"

"Elizabeth had her assistant with her. A woman named Olivia. She's as out of place as a roach in a punch bowl. Her hair is perfect, her nails are perfect, her clothes are perfect. She's five feet tall, if she's lucky, and from what I could tell, has a perfect body. She was probably an Olympic gymnast."

Sophia laughed. "This gets better and better. Well, not really better, but you know what I mean." She paused, the silence unnatural when talking to Sophia. "What's she really like? Elizabeth, I mean. Is she someone you can work some of this out with?"

Kelsey mentally stumbled to a halt. Who was Elizabeth Sutton, besides the woman who plagued her every thought? "I guess I really don't know."

"Huh. Maybe you should find out," Sophia said.

"Damn, why do you always end up telling me what I ought to know myself," Kelsey said.

"'Cause I'm your bestie. Maybe your dad knows more. When did he say he'd be back?"

Kelsey walked into the kitchen for another beer. Talking about this was a gut wrencher. She didn't use alcohol as an escape—her father's drinking problem had sworn her off anything more than two beers in one sitting, so this was her limit. Her avenue of escape was sex. Getting lost in the touch of a woman, the feel of her skin, the taste of her arousal, the mesmerizing sounds she made on her climb to orgasm—that was her road to sanity. "Yeah, and look where that trip led you to last night."

"What did you say?"

Kelsey didn't realize she had spoken out loud. "Nothing. Look, he left, and I don't know when he'll be back."

"He just…left you with everything that's going on?"

"Without a second glance." Goddamn, that hurt.

"Oh, hey, I'm so sorry."

"Me too. Well, actually, maybe I'm not. What kind of father does that? Bad enough he sold the ranch without telling me, but he left me to deal with the fallout."

"I'm so sorry," Sophia said again. "I don't know what else to say. I hate it that you're going through this. What can I do to help? You know I'll do anything you ask. Even what you don't ask."

"Nothing other than what you're doing now. Be here when I need to bitch or complain or feel sorry for myself."

"You know I'm here for you, babe."

"I know, and it means a lot to me. Listen, when I know more, I'll call, okay?" Even though Sophia lived in Phoenix, she was and always would be Kelsey's bestie. Kelsey could count on her for a shoulder, a hug, or a kick in the ass. Right now, she needed all three. Actually, what she really needed was someone to knock some sense into her and all the memories of Elizabeth Sutton *out*.

Elizabeth Sutton. *Who was she?*

Kelsey said good night to Sophia, hurried back to her casita, and dug out her iPad. She settled back on her bed to google Sutton Properties, now that she finally knew who the buyers were. If she'd been able to get even that much out of Red, she would have done it sooner. Now she had a lot more reason to know who she was dealing with.

As she read, she shook her head.

Welcome to the world where personal transformation is at your fingertips. Set among some of the most beautiful natural landscapes on the planet, our wellness centers offer our guests the luxury of the finest spas coupled with carefully curated sessions to help you achieve your long-term goals, whether physical, emotional, or spiritual. Our expert staff will guide you on the pathway of growth and discovery through individualized programs targeting your specific wellness needs. During your stay you can take advantage of our nutritional assessment plans, exercise physiology measurements, and one-on-one meetings with spiritual advisors to enhance your reflection and growth. At Sutton Wellness Resorts we are committed to providing you with the adventures and experiences that will set you on a lifelong journey to health and mind-body harmony.

Photos of the resorts looked nothing like Red Sky. The rooms were decorated in muted colors of blues and tans with overstuffed chairs and couches. Several lounge chairs surrounded a large fire pit that looked more decorative than functional. There were photos of massages at daybreak and Jacuzzis under the stars. The only picture that looked remotely like it would fit the ranch was a wandering path of rocks in concentric circles.

How did walking in circles lead anyone to any kind of awareness?

Kelsey snorted. "Holy crap. What does all that even mean?"

Whatever happened to hard work in fresh air to cleanse the soul or whatever? Okay, fine—she knew some people were into meditation and Reiki and a lot of those other mind-body connection activities, but that wasn't what the Red Sky Ranch was all about. How the hell did Sutton Properties expect to turn the ranch into one of these places? Elizabeth had her work cut out for her if she was going to reinvent the Red Sky as one of these frou-frou spas.

When she clicked the next link, an image on the cover of a magazine called *Real Estate Today* depicted Elizabeth leaning back against a sleek chrome and glass desk with an impressive skyline view behind her.

Kelsey stopped breathing. Elizabeth stared directly out from the cover *at her*, a smile on her face as if she had a secret, her arms crossed over her chest. She wore a bright blue sleeveless top with a pair of white linen trousers and the same expensive-looking watch she'd had on when she'd arrived at the ranch. The matching white jacket hung over the back of the desk chair behind her. Her arms were tanned and finely muscled. The top three buttons of her blouse were open, giving a peek at the gold chain around her neck. She radiated confidence and raw power and sexy all rolled into one.

And Kelsey wanted her, again.

Forcing herself to abandon the entrancing image, Kelsey scanned through other articles and press releases where Elizabeth was featured. The picture that came into focus of Elizabeth Sutton was damned impressive.

Thirty-seven, the only daughter of Jonas Sutton, one of the country's largest real estate holders, a graduate of an elite private university, and project manager of numerous Sutton Properties, including the launch of their flagship resorts in Europe, Singapore, and Tokyo. She was pictured in a variety of settings—in chinos and a hard hat on a construction site in Dubai, pointing to a set of blueprints in a boardroom in Tokyo, and attending countless society events wearing everything from a ball gown to a micro-minidress that barely covered her ass. And in each one, she had a different stunning woman on her arm.

Impressive. So impressive Kelsey couldn't help but wonder, with that prime real estate in her portfolio, why Elizabeth was in the middle of the Sonoran Desert in a town the size of Wickenburg.

And why had she been in a no-name, run-down lesbian bar picking up someone like Kelsey? She was nothing like those women in the photos. She didn't have a dress in her closet and couldn't remember the last time she'd gotten her nails done. Possibly because never.

Kelsey closed the iPad and turned out the lights. The answer to *why her* was probably as simple as she'd been in that bar looking for the same thing Elizabeth had been seeking—a brief few hours of pleasure with another woman. Kelsey had gotten what she'd been looking for. And now it was over.

Chapter Sixteen

Just as Elizabeth pulled behind a line of cars at Starbucks, Olivia turned to her and said, "All right, are you going to tell me or am I going to have to pry it out of you?"

Before Elizabeth could pretend she had no idea what Olivia was going on about, Olivia poked her in the arm and said, "And don't insult me by telling me there's nothing wrong. You haven't been yourself since you stepped out of this car last week."

Elizabeth had expected this conversation was going to happen, she just hadn't thought up a good story in response. She and Olivia had known each other for so long, Olivia probably knew her better than she knew herself.

She'd had a long, hard week of organizing stage one of the transition plans while trying not to think of Kelsey, despite running into her at every turn, and trying to tell herself she didn't want to talk to her, or touch her, or somehow ease the obvious pain that clouded her dark eyes. With her emotions already frayed, she didn't have the energy to fight Olivia.

"I met her the night I went out. The night we arrived." Elizabeth kept her eyes on the cars in front of her, but the silence in the SUV pressed in on her as if the air had suddenly taken on weight.

"I know what night that was. You ran into her at the bar you went to."

"Yes." *Ran into.* That was a polite way of saying it, all right.

"The tension between you two has been pretty obvious, but I attributed it to this whole situation," Olivia said slowly.

Elizabeth could almost hear Olivia's mind working as she started adding it all up and didn't have to wait long until Olivia made the connections.

"Wait! What? You *hooked up* with her? Are you out of your mind?"

Elizabeth shot her a look. "Give me some credit! I didn't know who she was. Until two weeks ago, I'd never even heard of the Red Sky Ranch."

"So you just—happened to go out to the same bar on the same night that one of the principals of the business Sutton had just acquired happened to be there?"

"Unfortunately and unbelievably, yes." Elizabeth sighed. She ought to regret it. Rational, career-before-all-else Elizabeth would have regretted it—no, somehow that Elizabeth would have avoided the entire...mess. *This* Elizabeth couldn't bring herself to be sorry.

"So, who picked up who?" Olivia asked.

"She asked me to dance, then asked if I wanted to get out of there." She didn't mention the part where Kelsey asked her if they were actually going to fuck right there in the parking lot, and she said yes.

"Your father is going to kill you."

"My father will never find out, will he?" Elizabeth looked at Olivia. "Why would he? He doesn't know about my other... engagements." She shrugged. "Other than Allison."

"Right," Olivia said. "And apparently Allison didn't mind talking about it to make her point. Is that going to be a problem with Kelsey? Did you talk to her about it?"

"I tried to. She wasn't too happy to discover who I was, but really—there's nothing to be gained by making a public fuss. Kelsey Brunel is nothing like Allison Wyland. She's angry about Sutton's involvement at the ranch, but what happened between us was just... an accident. We met, we didn't know each other—"

"You really didn't even know who..." Olivia sighed. "Okay,

maybe in this instance that's an advantage, but could you think about keeping it in your pants a little more often?"

"*It*? There is no it. Remember your anatomy?"

Olivia laughed. "Okay, but *try* to be a little cautious in the future when you're in the market for...whatever."

"Believe me, I am not interested in any more whatever any time soon."

"What, did she ruin you for other women?" Olivia teased.

Elizabeth handed Olivia her drink and put hers in the cup holder. She didn't want to think about that. "The only thing I'm interested in is getting this project off the ground and getting us out of here."

"So, you're not still lusting after her?"

Elizabeth sighed. "You know what she looks like. What lesbian wouldn't be attracted to her? She's gorgeous. But it will not happen again."

"You might want to keep telling yourself that."

"You know I don't mix business and pleasure." She'd been tempted many times, but never acted on it.

"Kelsey may not know that. She looks at you like she wants to nibble on you for a snack, eat you for dinner, and save the best part for dessert."

"What Kelsey may or may not want is not my problem."

Her problem was she might not say no to any of those things.

Chapter Seventeen

A commercial-sized white truck with a double cab, a utility rack over the bed, and the logo of Brinkman Construction on the side was parked in the middle of the circular drive when Elizabeth drove in. Leaving the drive open for guests, Elizabeth pulled around to the adjacent lot and walked around the building to deal with the contractor she assumed belonged to the vehicle.

"You want me to stay?" Olivia asked.

"No, why don't you get started with Phil on the specs for the golf course. This shouldn't take long."

Olivia passed Kelsey, who was just coming out of the main building, as Elizabeth walked over to greet a tall man in his late forties with a little too much beer belly, who stood with his arms across his chest, looking at his watch. His body language screamed macho, and Elizabeth got ready. She'd been here before, and it never got easier.

"Mr. Brinkman, I'm Elizabeth Sutton."

He shook her hand with one of those soft handshakes reserved for ladies, as if something might break if he grasped too tightly. Elizabeth wanted to rub her palm on her jeans.

Brinkman looked around as if expecting someone else to appear before narrowing his eyes in her direction.

"Miss Sutton. And Jonas Sutton is...?"

"My father."

"Is he coming?"

"No. I'm in charge of this project."

Brinkman's eyes gleamed a little too much. She'd seen that look before, too, on people—usually, but not always, men—who thought they'd discovered an advantage. She knew in an instant what Brinkman was going to do next, and he didn't fail her.

His gaze took a lazy, lecherous sweep over her body, starting at her face, down to her boots and back up again, pausing at places inappropriate for any type of business relationship. When his eyes met hers again, he smirked.

"Ms. Sutton," Brinkman said with a *there, there, little lady, let me tell you how it's going to be* tone.

"Mr. Brinkman?"

"Please, you can call me Dick," he said. "May I call you Elizabeth? Or do you go by Liz?"

Elizabeth saw Kelsey take a step down from the porch and head in their direction and shook her head slightly. Kelsey, thankfully, was *not* a jerk and drew up short. "I go by Ms. Sutton, Mr. Brinkman, which is what I would like you and every member of your crew to call me. I hope that's clear."

His face turned red, and he clenched his jaw until the muscles bunched, which Elizabeth took to mean yes.

"Good. Now that we've got all the formalities out of the way, are you ready to get to work?"

He glanced around as if seeking some backup, while probably calculating the dollar signs that would fly out the window if he walked. He pushed away from the truck and passed close enough to her to almost, but not quite brush, against her.

"My crew will be here in the morning."

Kelsey catapulted down the rest of the steps as if she'd been spring-loaded. She stared after Brinkman's truck as if she could gun it down with her eyes. "Tell me that asshole shouldered into you."

"He didn't." Elizabeth grasped Kelsey's arm without thinking. Her forearm was a steel band, and the rest of her body rigid.

Elizabeth squeezed gently. "It's fine. I've dealt with worse a dozen times over."

Kelsey's hot gaze met hers. "You shouldn't have to. I'm going to fire his ass before he gets back to town."

"Kelsey," Elizabeth said gently, "let it go. If I fired every person who thought they could blow one over on me because I looked too young or too soft or just too damned female, I'd never get a project completed *and* I'd look weak."

"You? Weak?" Kelsey shook her head. "If Brinkman had any idea what kind of projects you usually handle, he'd be kissing your ass and hoping you'd throw more business his way. Idiot."

"Oh?" Elizabeth tilted her head, caught between curiosity and a flush of pride. "And how would you know about what projects I've headed?"

Kelsey shrugged and cut her eyes away. "There's only about five hundred press releases from the last ten years or so about them."

Elizabeth laughed. "Tell me you googled me."

Kelsey shot her hands to her hips, the way she did when she was getting ready to make a point. A move Elizabeth found very, very sexy. "And if I did?"

"I imagine you were bored pretty quickly."

Heat flared in Kelsey's eyes, the same look she'd aimed at Elizabeth across the floor in the bar. The look that said she liked what she saw. "What if I said I thought you were even hotter than before?"

Elizabeth felt the flush but kept her gaze on Kelsey and quietly said, "I'd say that's a place I'd rather we didn't go."

Kelsey huffed out a breath and stepped away. "Just business. Right. And I apologize for interfering with Brinkman. I forgot for a minute that I can't fire anybody, can I?"

Disappointment and unexpected sadness took Elizabeth by surprise. For a moment she'd felt that connection again, the intensity between them that made her feel seen and wanted. Just for herself. But she'd been the one to pull away first, so she squared her shoulders and smiled. "No apologies needed. I'm late for a meeting, so I'd better get inside."

Kelsey touched a finger to her cowboy hat. "Of course."

Elizabeth reminded herself that keeping her distance from Kelsey was the right decision, but the fierce look in Kelsey's eyes when she'd stormed off the porch to confront Brinkman lingered in Elizabeth's mind for the rest of the day.

Chapter Eighteen

"What are you doing here?" Kelsey said when she opened the front door on her way out after breakfast and nearly ran into Sophia.

"Hi, you." Sophia gathered Kelsey into a tight hug. "I haven't seen you in forever, and the last time we talked, you sounded down."

"It's barely been two weeks, and you didn't need to drive two hours to check in on me." Kelsey backed out of Sophia's embrace. "You know, cell phones?"

"But this is where *you* are," Sophia said, as if Kelsey had just made the dumbest statement in the world. "And two hours is not a biggie."

"It's Monday. Don't you have to work?"

"I called in sick."

"*Sophia.*" Kelsey sighed. "I love you for it, you know that. But I'm *fine.*"

"You haven't been sounding fine. And you don't look fine." Sophia poked her in the gut. "You're too skinny. I'm worried about you, so I'd be worthless at work anyway."

Kelsey squeezed her hand. "Thanks. Talking with you always helps get me sorted out. And I'm glad to see you."

"You're welcome, and I'm glad, too." Sophia peered past Kelsey's shoulder toward the screen door. "Is she here? I didn't see her fancy ride anywhere. Is she off peeing on the saguaros somewhere?"

Kelsey chuckled at Sophia's newest reference to Elizabeth

marking her territory. She hadn't felt like laughing since Red had told her about the sale. In the next minute, her humor died a quick death. Sophia was *here*—in person—and she'd seen Elizabeth at the bar. Seen the two of them together. And Kelsey had never told her about Elizabeth being that woman.

The door opened and closed behind her, and she didn't have to look to know. She'd grown accustomed to the sound of Elizabeth's footsteps coming and going—the speed at which she walked, the way a minute after she heard the footfalls she smelled her distinctive honey-lemon scent, the way the air became electrified whenever Elizabeth was nearby.

And Elizabeth was right behind her now.

Kelsey glanced at Sophia and saw her eyes widen. So much for hoping Sophia wouldn't remember Elizabeth from that night at the bar.

"Kelsey?" Sophia whispered not all that quietly.

"Right," Kelsey muttered. "I, uh…"

"Hello," she heard Elizabeth say in her cool, I-eat-idiots-for-breakfast voice. "I'm Elizabeth Sutton."

Kelsey groaned inside and wanted to slide between the space in the boards under her dusty boots. Elizabeth held out a hand as Kelsey was incapable of making introductions. Like she was about to say *Elizabeth, this is my best friend, Sophia. Sophia, this is the new owner and oh, by the way, also the woman I told you I fucked in the parking lot.*

"Hi," Sophia said, sounding only a little confrontational. She did take Elizabeth's hand, so that was a good sign. "I'm one of Kelsey's friends. Her *best* friend actually."

Sophia stepped closer to Kelsey, and Kelsey tried to get her brain working.

"I see," Elizabeth said, and Kelsey immediately wondered what Elizabeth thought she saw. "Nice to meet you." She turned slightly to face Kelsey. "If you're free later, Kelsey, I'd like you to come to the meeting in Phil's trailer at four. We need to approve the final plans for the golf course, and I'd like your input."

"Sure," Kelsey said as Elizabeth walked off in the direction of the trailers parked on the far side of the barn. What could she say? *No thanks, boss, I'll be busy?*

"I'll *bet* she'd like your input," Sophia snarled, turning to watch Elizabeth stride away. A second later she rounded on Kelsey, fire in her eyes. "What. The. Actual. Fuck?"

"I can explain." Kelsey held both hands out in front of her like a shield.

"Try hard," Sophia said, exaggerating the two words.

"Please," Kelsey said. "I don't need this right now."

"And what exactly is *this*?" Sophia leaned closer. "Why didn't you tell me *this* before?"

"Because you would've ended up right where you are right now. In my face when I'm already in the middle of all kinds of fucked-up."

"Well, I'm sorry if your *best friend* caring about you is so hard for you."

"You know that's not what I mean. Can we sit down?" Kelsey's knees were weak, a common occurrence whenever Elizabeth was around.

The instant they were out of earshot of the open front door, Sophia said, "Just how big is the mess?"

"I'm not even sure yet. We're kind of at the cold war stage. But I'm stuck working with her—for her—whatever the hell—during the transition if I want to be sure all the staff keeps their jobs."

"Oh, that's real nice," Sophia said, glaring off in the direction Elizabeth had gone. "That's blackmail. You don't need to take that. You need a lawyer. I know just the—"

"No," Kelsey said, surprising herself. For the first time, she had to admit that Elizabeth wasn't the cause of all her problems, even if she was the head of Sutton's forces on the ground. "It's not Elizabeth's doing. She didn't negotiate the terms of the contract that Red *signed*. Her father or whoever offered the deal to Red did that."

Sophia studied her and sighed. "Did you know who she was?"

"Of course not!" Kelsey's anger matched her frustration. "Do you think I'd use what happened between her and me to somehow try to get out of the sale?"

"No, no, of course not. That's not what I meant, and you know it. Is that what *she* thinks?"

Kelsey flinched. Did she? Did Elizabeth actually think she'd be so low as to use sex with her as a weapon? Was that what she'd been trying to get at that night she followed her to the barn to talk? "I don't know. I hope not."

"Well, what has she said about…everything?"

"That we should be rational and adult and agree it was a one-time thing and that it wouldn't happen again." Kelsey sounded bitter even to herself. Damn it, she wasn't bitter. She was…pissed. Maybe she could be rational and adult and still want to get Elizabeth Madison Avenue Sutton into bed again.

"Well, I agree with her there," Sophia said, as if that settled everything.

"Why?"

Sophia pursed her lips and gave her a long look. "I can think of a thousand reasons why what you're thinking would be a very bad idea. Starting with the fact she has all the power here, *and* she's going to hightail it out of here back to the big city as fast as she can."

"You don't know what I'm thinking." Kelsey tried to make light of it, even though she could think of ten or twenty million reasons or however much Red had sold the ranch for. None of them mattered whenever she saw Elizabeth.

CHAPTER NINETEEN

On her way to the mini-trailer village that Sutton crews had erected for living and working quarters during the construction phases of the transition, Elizabeth fought the urge to look over her shoulder at Kelsey and Sophia. Kelsey had said they were just friends that night in the bar, but Sophia had been quick to point out they were best friends. Did that equal friends with benefits? That certainly seemed possible—probable, really. Kelsey hadn't had any other visitors to the ranch and didn't appear involved with any of the staff, sexually or otherwise. Every woman in her group had seen her leave the bar with Elizabeth, and considering their almost-sex on the dance floor, the reason they were leaving had to be obvious. Doubtful a girlfriend would have been okay with that. So Kelsey was apparently single, incredibly hot, and definitely not celibate. Sophia was attractive, if you liked the voluptuous in-your-face confrontational types, so friends with benefits seemed at the top of the list.

She found the idea annoyingly annoying. And what the hell?

Long-term coupledom was not in her vocabulary. She certainly wasn't jealous.

Kelsey and her best friend-whatever was a distraction she didn't want or need.

The planning meeting went until mid-afternoon, and once out of the air-conditioned but still uncomfortably crowded trailer, Elizabeth and Olivia escaped to a far corner of the patio behind the main building. Construction had begun on the remodel of the nearby bunkhouse into the main spa with new high-end suites for facials, massages, and immersion therapies. The sounds of power saws and machinery rumbled in the distance, a backdrop of noise Elizabeth found oddly soothing. Progress meant completion of a project and a return to her regular life. She quickly squashed a qualm of uncertainty. Of course she wanted out of this remote, barren place. Why wouldn't she?

"How are they doing?" Olivia asked, nodding toward the construction site. "Phil says Brinkman is a homophobic asshat."

"That pretty much rounds out the triumvirate," Elizabeth said with a sigh. "Phil is too refined. Misogynistic, racist, homophobic asshole is more like it. But his crews are here on time every day and put in a good day's work."

"Well, that's something, so far."

They'd both had far too much experience with contractors that were either late or didn't show up at all. Elizabeth and Brinkman had settled on keeping their contact to a minimum, which so far was working.

One of the staff stopped by their table, and they both ordered non-alcoholic summery drinks—a specialty of the bar which Elizabeth happily found top level. While the ranch offered alcohol, the wellness center would not.

She smiled at the memory of Kelsey's astonishment. "What do you mean, no alcohol?"

"It's a wellness center, remember? Health and alcohol do not play well together."

Again, the aggressive stance with hands on hips as Kelsey leaned forward, her very nice chin raised. "What about the studies showing a glass of wine a day may be protective from certain kinds of cancers?"

"I'm aware," Elizabeth said, and wasn't at all surprised that Kelsey was also. She could google, too, and she hadn't found much about Kelsey Sky Brunel, but she did see an old entry reporting her address at the state university where she'd been a student. What had really caught her attention was her middle name. *Sky.* How many times had she whispered or begged Sky to make her come?

"Who was the hottie with Kelsey?" Olivia asked.

"What? Oh. Sophia," Elizabeth said. "They were at the bar together where I met Sk—Kelsey."

"Together?" Olivia asked, her eyebrows raised.

"They were there together, but I don't think they're *together*." As if it mattered.

"She's cute."

"Don't touch," Elizabeth warned. "We've got enough complications already."

"Only in your dreams. By the way, the fire inspector is due in…" Olivia lifted her phone. "Twenty minutes."

"I didn't know he was coming today." Plans for the remodel of Red Sky had been submitted to every applicable agency as soon as the prospectus had been completed. She wasn't involved in that, so she'd have to rely on Olivia to get her through any documents he might have brought with him. "We've got the design review with Phil later."

"It wasn't scheduled," Olivia said, checking her phone again as it softly dinged. "That's why they call it subject to inspection at any time. And apparently, any time is now. They're here."

They finished their drinks and walked along the flagstone pathway toward the main entrance. "Where are we supposed to meet him?"

"*She* is apparently on the porch," Olivia said, "and *she* is H-O-T."

Elizabeth was happy to see the inspector was a woman, just because why not? And because they were usually old guys coasting their way to retirement. "Hot? Is that a play on words? The fire inspector is hot?"

"No, but she can throw me over her shoulder and rescue me anytime."

Elizabeth shot her a look. Olivia had never expressed any interest in women, but these little remarks were becoming more frequent. "Are you sure I haven't missed something?"

"Nope, just admiring one of God's finer specimens."

"If you say so," Elizabeth said. Olivia would tell her or not.

Being friends meant giving each other space. "Well, let's see what she wants."

By the time they reached the porch, Kelsey had come outside. Sophia's nondescript gray two-door sedan was gone, and hopefully so was its driver. Kelsey and the fire inspector turned their way, and Elizabeth paused.

Olivia was wrong. The inspector was cute in an androgynous sort of way with short, spiky brown hair, pale skin that had to be a nuisance in this climate, and a wiry build. She wore blue work pants, a long-sleeved, pale-blue button-up shirt, and a clunky no-nonsense watch on her surprisingly slender wrist. Kelsey, on the other hand, in her jeans, cowboy boots that were definitely not for show, and another of her western style shirts, was hot in all-caps.

Kelsey grinned, a slow, sexy smile, and Elizabeth mentally cursed. Way to be caught staring—no, make that ogling.

The fire inspector stepped off the porch, her hand extended. "Ms. Sutton, I'm Riley Mitchell, county fire inspector."

Riley was slightly taller than Elizabeth, her handshake firm, and her green eyes direct. Elizabeth judged her to be in her early thirties.

"Please call me Elizabeth, Inspector Mitchell. What can I do for you?"

"And I'm Riley. Aside from reviewing your plans and permits, all of which are in order, it's my job to see that fire safety regulations on the job site are enforced. Fire can be fast and deadly in the dry desert. All it takes is one stray spark or a misplaced cigarette butt, and we'll have a big problem."

"We both agree that's what we don't want. How can I help you?"

"I'd like to look around, if you don't mind."

"Absolutely. Where would you like to begin?"

"Let's start with the demo sites." Riley turned toward Kelsey. "Good to see you again. Don't be a stranger."

Elizabeth wondered if they had history. They sure didn't look like they had just met. But then again, Wickenburg didn't look like a hub of lesbian opportunity. Everybody had probably slept with everybody. What living, breathing lesbian wouldn't want to sleep with Kelsey or find out what was under the fire inspector's blue uniform?

"Riley, this is Olivia Martinez, my exec. She can take care of anything you need at any time."

Riley's eyes sparkled when she looked at Olivia. "Good to know. Nice to meet you, also."

"Yes, you, too," Olivia said, glancing at Elizabeth sideways and mouthing *take care of anything you need at any time?* "I'll call for a guest cart."

CHAPTER TWENTY

Elizabeth closed the gate to the outside pool and dropped her towel and cover-up on a lounge chair. The Olympic-sized pool at the Red Sky was top notch, and she'd been itching to get into it since the moment Kelsey had shown it to her. With the chaos of Sutton crews and managers arriving, setting up the base camp for living and work quarters, and reviewing all the plans for the various areas of demo and remodels, she hadn't had time to do much more than grab a bite to eat when Olivia reminded her, catch a few hours of restless sleep, and head back to the ranch for more work. She'd vacillated between being grateful when she didn't see Kelsey and wondering where she was. She wasn't sure if Kelsey was avoiding her or just as busy as she was. After the first few meetings with Sutton project managers, Kelsey had begun to offer some suggestions based on her experience with the climate, the terrain, and the ranch clientele that had provided valuable intel. Elizabeth had noticed her interacting more with the Sutton personnel. But not her.

And wasn't that just as she wanted it? What she needed was just what she'd come for—an hour in the water to clear her head. The instant she hit the water, she entered another world. Sounds were muted and gravity ceased to exist. Her mind calmed and her body and the water became one effortlessly. It had always been like this. When she'd been competing, her personal pleasure in the sport had taken second place to speed, precision, and lap times. She'd been driven then by the need to prove she was the best at one thing—to measure up to the Sutton standards. Sutton children were expected to be the very best at everything they did, from always finishing first and securing acceptance into the best schools to climbing to the top of their professions. What she couldn't manage academically, despite receiving more than average grades by working tirelessly and leaning on Olivia when she needed to, she could achieve in the water. Until she'd lost even that.

For years, she'd ignored the pain in her right shoulder. Pain was merely the price to be paid for winning. She'd been so close to proving to her family she was a Sutton until, on the last lap of the Olympic qualifying race, her shoulder had exploded and her arm had gone limp in the water. She'd known in that instant her Olympic dreams were over and she would once again fail in her parents' eyes. Before she'd even reached the hospital, she'd determined she would change course and focus on learning the family business. Failure was not acceptable.

❖

Kelsey woke before the sun was up for an early ride on Adira. She hadn't had nearly enough time to exercise her, what with meeting with the ranch staff to explain the details of the transition to Sutton and attending the damn Sutton planning meetings. How did they ever get anything done when all they did was talk about it? She had to admit, though, some of their ideas for expanding the ranch's offerings to attract a wider clientele were…interesting. And Elizabeth had made it a point that Kelsey's input was welcome during the interminable meetings. Hell, she even listened to some of Kelsey's suggestions.

After brushing down her horse and letting her out into the corral with the others, she skirted around the nearby construction area and headed to the house to see if Charmaine had any of her biscuits ready yet. As she crossed the patio, she saw a lone swimmer in the pool and detoured to let them know the pool didn't open to guests for another two hours.

When she recognized the lone swimmer gliding through the

water, she quietly slipped through the gate and sat in a chair to watch. Elizabeth's strokes were metronomic—smooth, regular, and seemingly effortless. Her kicks barely rippled the water.

Twenty-eight minutes later, her fast, efficient strokes slowed as she started her cooldown. The pool was a regulation fifty meters, and who knew how long Elizabeth'd been in the water before she showed up. Elizabeth could seriously swim. Spotting her towel, Kelsey retrieved it and stood at the end of the pool. When Elizabeth surfaced, she held it out to her and asked, "How long have you been swimming?"

"This morning, or in general? And how long have you been standing there?"

"In general," Kelsey said, recognizing the attempt at distraction. "About half an hour."

Elizabeth folded her arms on the edge of the deck, the rest of her body still in the water, and regarded Kelsey steadily. "It's just a hobby."

"Hobby my ass. You're better than good. Do you swim every day?"

"I try to. If I don't, I get cranky."

She smiled then and Kelsey's heart twisted. Damn, she was beautiful. Teasingly, she added, "Can't say I've seen you swimming much. Must account for the crankiness."

"Won't argue." Elizabeth laughed and effortlessly pulled herself up to the pool deck and took the towel. Kelsey's mouth went dry in direct contrast to the water seductively sliding down Elizabeth's body. Her blue tank brought out the color of her eyes, the legs cut so high they were almost to her waist. The fit was simple and efficient and still highlighted every curve and plane of her toned body. Kelsey silently cursed when Elizabeth pulled on her cover-up.

"How far did you go?" Kelsey's voice cracked. She hoped Elizabeth didn't notice it.

"I just swim for pleasure," Elizabeth said with a decided edge. "I'm not measuring."

That was an interesting answer. "Technically, you're not supposed to swim before the pool opens. Safety regs."

"Mm," Elizabeth said. "As I'm not a guest, the rules don't apply. And I'm perfectly capable of going for a simple swim."

Kelsey hadn't intended to be confrontational, but their conversations always headed there. She sighed. "I doubt there's anything you're not capable of."

Elizabeth hesitated, almost as if she'd changed her mind about what she intended to say. "Was there anything else?"

"Not a thing," Kelsey replied. "Have a good day."

❖

Elizabeth dropped into the lounger, still breathing fast, more from Kelsey's gaze on her than her swim.

Kelsey hadn't bothered to hide her interest. She'd taken her time gazing the length of Elizabeth's body. Kelsey had to have been aware of what she was doing and had to know Elizabeth would know it, too. How could she not? Kelsey knew her way around women and knew when she was sending you-look-fuckable signals. Elizabeth certainly recognized the look and, under other circumstances, would have been very interested.

She leaned back in the lounger, her suit drying rapidly in the hot, dry air, and closed her eyes. Thinking of the way Kelsey had watched her tightened her nipples and stoked a pressure in her depths she recognized all too well. God damn it, she did not want to spend the day horny and cranky. Trying to ignore the unwanted arousal, she took a series of long, calming breaths and let her mind drift. Meditation sometimes came in handy.

She decided to swim at midnight, alone under the stars to relax after a long, stressful day. At the end of her last lap, she surfaced and looked up at the shadowy figure standing at the end of the pool in jeans and boots.

"How long have you been standing there?" she asked Kelsey, her heart beating faster in anticipation.

"Fifteen laps." Kelsey glanced at her watch. "Eight minutes. It's late for a swim."

"I like to swim when the pool is empty. Helps to avoid bumping into people, and being alone is...restful."

"Do you want to be alone? In the pool?"

Was Kelsey asking to join her? God, she hoped so, or else she was about to make a fool of herself if she wasn't. "Not if the option is you being in here with me."

"What if I can't swim?"

"Something tells me you can do anything you put your mind to." Elizabeth waited for Kelsey to back off, to indicate she'd read the signals wrong. When Kelsey didn't move, Elizabeth added, "Did you have something particular in mind?"

She sounded like she was sending an invitation, and she didn't care. She was. She hadn't really flirted with anyone in recent memory—not the playful, foreplay kind of flirting that left her giddy and wet. Wet with anticipation.

Her heart lurched when Kelsey turned away and then just as quickly skipped a beat when she heard the gate lock. Silently, she watched Kelsey return, toe off her boots, and unself-consciously strip off her shirt. Her breasts were perfect ovals, the nipples small and hard. Elizabeth's clit pulsed, and she caught her lip between her teeth to stifle any sound. She didn't want to interrupt the best foreplay she'd ever experienced. Now all she could think about was Kelsey in the pool, touching her, inside her, making her come.

She held her breath as Kelsey unhooked the silver buckle, gleaming in the moonlight, and shimmied out of her jeans and briefs. Her legs, which Elizabeth knew from having gripped them with hers what felt like months before, were tight and muscular.

Elizabeth held her breath as Kelsey paused. Had she changed her mind? Come to her senses?

"Last chance," Kelsey murmured. "To be alone."

"I've already done that tonight. Show me what you can do."

Laughing, Kelsey dove in, her body a perfect curved blade, barely causing a ripple as she broke the surface and, a moment later, came up directly in front of Elizabeth.

Elizabeth gripped her shoulders and pulled her in for a kiss. She'd been living on the memory of that kiss for weeks and this was so, so much better. When Kelsey clasped her waist and pressed closer, their breasts melded, and she struggled to breathe.

"I knew you could do it." Elizabeth brushed her lips along Kelsey's jaw. Kelsey made a rough sound in her throat that made her clit ache.

"Swim?" Kelsey cupped Elizabeth's breast beneath the surface of the water, her thumb flicking across Elizabeth's nipple.

Elizabeth caught her breath. "Did you mean something else?"

"You're overdressed for what I have in mind."

"And what is that?"

"Take that suit off, and I'll show you."

Elizabeth braced her hands on Kelsey's shoulders. "Why don't you do it?"

Kelsey kissed her, a sure, hard kiss that streaked through her and struck lightning to her core. "Hold on."

They danced in the water as Elizabeth lifted first one arm and then the other while Kelsey drew her straps down. Kicking lightly to stay afloat, Elizabeth draped both arms around Kelsey's neck as Kelsey pushed the suit down and off. Kelsey wrapped one arm around her waist, keeping her close, and guided her into a smaller side pool with underwater seats designed for lounging.

"Here," Kelsey ordered, in a tone that unexpectedly caused Elizabeth's stomach to clench with a surge of need.

Elizabeth settled onto the seat and stretched her arms out along the edge of the pool, watching Kelsey, illuminated in moonlight, focus on her exposed breasts. Kelsey's hungry look grew wilder as Elizabeth cupped her breasts in invitation.

"Don't move," Kelsey said, her tone low and ominous.

Elizabeth laughed, still fondling her breasts. "Or what?"

"Or I'll stop." Kelsey's hot mouth closed over her breast, her teeth grazing her nipple.

Elizabeth threw back her head with a cry, need so sharp her sex clenched. "Oh my God. I am so ready to come."

Kelsey lifted her head. "Not even close."

"God, don't stop."

Kelsey drew her to the edge of the seat, slid her hands under

Elizabeth's ass, and pressed her thigh against Elizabeth's sex. "Let me feel how wet you are."

Elizabeth dug her fingers into Kelsey's shoulders and worked her clit against Kelsey's leg. "Oh, God, that feels good."

"Don't come yet," Kelsey warned, and went back to exploring Elizabeth's breasts, alternating satin kisses with taunting bites. Using her tongue and teeth, Kelsey took her time.

"I can't take much more," Elizabeth gasped. "You're so good at this. I want to come so much."

"Lift up," Kelsey murmured, and slid inside her. She fondled Elizabeth with just the tips of her fingers moving in and out, and Elizabeth shuddered.

"Yes, just like that." Elizabeth rocked her hips faster, the pressure building. "So close now. Oh my God."

Elizabeth grasped the back of Kelsey's neck and pulled her mouth against her nipple. "Suck it harder."

Elizabeth stared upward, the stars a swirling symphony as she reached for the peak. "God. Harder."

Kelsey's teeth closed around her, and Elizabeth exploded.

"There you are," Olivia said "Do you know it's almost seven thirty, and we have a planning—"

"Yes, I know." Elizabeth shoved upright on the lounger, stunned to be lying in bright sunlight and not the moonlight of her dream. She stared around, inwardly sighing in relief to see she was still alone by the pool. "I need to shower and get dressed."

"What about coffee?"

"What?" Elizabeth rose and wrapped her towel around her waist.

Olivia cocked her head and frowned. "You look a little... frazzled. Are you okay?"

"Yes, fine." At Olivia's hurt expression, she added quickly, "Sorry. I guess I must've dozed off there for a minute. I could really use a coffee, thanks."

"I'll bring it over to the trailer," Olivia said.

"Thanks," Elizabeth said, glad for the hundredth time they'd decided to move from the hotel to an on-site double-bedroom trailer for the duration. "I'll be quick."

"Okay, if you're sure," Olivia said, still regarding her with a worried frown.

Elizabeth squeezed her arm and lied. "I'm fine."

Chapter Twenty-one

"We're going to the rodeo Saturday," Olivia declared two weeks later.

"What rodeo?"

"The one at the rodeo arena." Olivia, hands on her hips in her *we're doing this whether you want to or not* pose, gave her a big smile.

"Well, that's an appropriate place to have a rodeo," Elizabeth replied, "but I really don't need this new experience. I get enough dust and dirt and horse poop every day."

"Come on, it'll be fun."

"I'm afraid I'm not seeing the fun part here."

"Consider it research, then," Olivia replied, exasperation in her tone, "seeing as you *do* like to work. Everyone will be there."

Elizabeth narrowed her eyes. "Define everyone."

"Um...Marie and Charmaine and some of the other staff. Kelsey. And I heard Kelsey mention Riley would be there."

"And which one of those individuals has convinced you *we* should go?" Riley dropped in every ten days or so for the routine safety reviews, and Olivia usually managed to be the one to take her around on the ATV. "I'm thinking Riley."

"Riley is interesting and laid back. Just...nice. And that's a refreshing change from the usual cutthroat Sutton people."

"Uh-huh. Nice." Elizabeth laughed, used to Olivia's secretive nature regarding her interest in other people—male, female, sexual, or romantic. "If you say so."

"Don't try to distract me." Olivia pointed a finger. "I can hear you changing your mind. Besides, it'll look good for the locals to see you there. Come on. It'll be fun."

Elizabeth wavered. Work on the new buildings was moving along, the crews had begun the landscape work for the golf course, and she had a full slate of interviews every day for staff in mind-body therapy, exercise physiology, the health spa, and outdoor activities. She started at sunup and fell into bed at sundown. If she had a chance to swim, she counted herself lucky. And every time she surfaced, she looked for Kelsey, but Kelsey had not returned except in the all-too-frequent dreams that left her restless and decidedly unsatisfied. The idea of an evening that didn't involve a video call to someone at Sutton and that just might give her a chance to spend time with Kelsey was too hard to resist. "All right, fine."

Four days later Elizabeth followed a mini-caravan of trucks and cars from the ranch to the outskirts of Wickenburg where a portly man exuberantly waved red flags to direct her into a large dirt lot with green and white flags indicating where to park. Elizabeth pulled in beside a Dodge Ram with a camper bed on the back and got out just as a Jeep with oversized wheels passed along the row behind her and kicked up a cloud of dust. She sneezed and waved a hand to dispel the dirt still swirling in the air in front of her.

"Bless you," Olivia said, walking up beside her.

"You didn't warn me I needed a respirator to breathe," Elizabeth said.

"Pretend you're at the beach." Olivia swung her purse strap across her chest.

"You brought a Tory Burch purse to a rodeo?"

"And why not," Olivia replied archly as she extracted her sunglasses from the side pocket and slid them on. "What did you expect me to carry? A saddlebag? Besides, I think the canvas version looks very…topical."

Elizabeth scanned the crowd. "I can't say it looks a lot like rodeo attire."

"Does it look like I'm a slave to rodeo fashion?"

"You're not even acquainted with rodeo fashion."

"That's why I asked Riley," Olivia replied, smugly.

"You asked Riley what to wear? When?" Elizabeth laughed. "And better question, why? Riley is more the plain pants and shirt type. Kelsey dresses fancier than her, and her nod to fashion is a silver belt buckle and pearl snap buttons."

Olivia cut her a look. "Pretty specific there."

Elizabeth flushed. Damn it all. Must that happen anytime she even thought of Kelsey? "Not the point."

"I asked her for the dress code when she was here last week," Olivia said. "It's bad enough that everyone will be checking us out, seeing as we're the strangers who came to town to take over one of the biggest businesses around. We don't need a fashion faux pas, too."

"Well, thank you for saving us from being on the front page of the local newspaper displaying our fashion faux pas. That would be humiliating."

"Anything I can do to help." Olivia smiled sweetly and craned her neck to look around the long line in front of them for the pair of ticket booths. "I think we're behind the rest of the Red Sky people."

"We'll catch up," Elizabeth murmured. Kelsey had already been driving out by the time she and Olivia left the ranch, and she hadn't gotten a chance to see what she was wearing. Or if she was with anyone.

They stood in a line that moved at a snail's pace. As they drew closer, she could hear the ticket taker, who apparently knew everyone, catching up on all the news about families, jobs, kids, and of course, the weather. Finally, they got to the booth, Elizabeth handed over two twenties to a man with what looked like a basketball stuffed under his blue rayon golf shirt, who stamped a big blue WR on the top of her left hand.

Elizabeth and Olivia followed the crowd like dutiful lemmings. Concessions stands under canvas awnings that offered burgers, dogs, fries, and beer lined the path that led to the grandstand. "Want a beer?" Elizabeth asked. "I doubt there will be anything else more interesting."

"No, maybe later. I'm going to find a little cowgirls' room before we sit. Keep an eye out for Riley and Kelsey."

"I'll be over there by the beer tent," Elizabeth said. She headed that way, skirting a family with a double-wide stroller carrying two toddlers, a cooler, and a year's worth of baby supplies. When the stroller veered her way she jumped aside, colliding with someone else trying to get by.

"Sorry," she said.

Kelsey steadied her with a hand on her elbow. "No problem."

Elizabeth had been right about the silver belt buckle, and though Kelsey hadn't worn her usual ranch attire, she hadn't strayed far from her normal look, which was pretty damn hot. She was the quintessential cowgirl in low-heeled boots, jeans that had been nicely broken-in in a way that said they weren't for show, and a pale-yellow shirt with snap-closed pockets on the chest. On the very, very nice chest.

"You look great," she said without thinking.

Kelsey's brows winged up and she laughed. "Thanks."

Elizabeth shook her head. "I mean, Olivia and I were just talking about rodeo fashion and—"

"Rodeo fashion?" As they walked, Kelsey's hand lingered just at her elbow. "What is rodeo fashion?"

"Something you obviously know all about." Elizabeth shook her head and moved her arm. "Never mind."

"Can I buy you a beer?" Kelsey asked.

"Thanks, but I can get it."

"It's a beverage, Elizabeth, not a bribe," Kelsey added.

Elizabeth sighed. She had to stop looking for some ulterior motive in everything Kelsey said. Old habits were hard to break. "Thank you, that would be nice."

"Good."

Kelsey's smile made her glad she'd said yes.

While Kelsey gave their order to the cowboy behind the counter, Elizabeth watched her talking with the others waiting for a beer. In seconds, she was back in the Last Stop, watching Kelsey across the room, knowing in some undefinable way that she was the one. The one for the night. The one she wanted—

"Elizabeth?"

Elizabeth jumped as Kelsey held out the clear plastic cup of beer.

"Sorry. Thanks." Her cheeks heated, and not from the sun.

"So, Olivia got you to come?" Kelsey said as they stepped away from the beer stand.

"I will admit that she dragged me here."

"Sounds like you aren't looking forward to it."

Elizabeth realized her comment might be construed as insulting. "No, not at all. I plan to stay open to possibilities and new experiences."

Kelsey smiled. "The Wickenburg rodeo committee appreciates that."

"Are you on the Wickenburg rodeo committee?" Elizabeth wasn't entirely sure Kelsey was serious.

"As a matter of fact, I am. Have been for years."

"It's all new to me," Elizabeth said. "I don't suppose you'd be a tour guide again."

Kelsey looked surprised, and Elizabeth didn't blame her. They'd both been adhering to their silent agreement to give each other a wide berth at the ranch, so what was she doing? "I mean—"

"Sure. I'd be happy to."

"Oh, wait," Elizabeth said, suddenly caught between disappointment and relief. "Here comes Olivia. I should stick with her."

"Hi," Olivia said, looking from Kelsey to Elizabeth. "Where is the rest of the group?"

"They headed up to the stands," Kelsey said. "I was just about to show Elizabeth around. You're welcome to come along."

"Oh, no," Olivia said quickly, glancing at Elizabeth with an aha look as she backpedaled. "I'll see you up there."

And then she was gone, and given no choice, Elizabeth set off with Kelsey.

"We'll do the vendors first," Kelsey said, once again gently steering her through the crowds to the booths displaying hats, belts, T-shirts, bags, wallets, and assorted western paraphernalia. "Got to get a memento."

"Ah…" Elizabeth quietly protested when she got a look at most of the offerings. She was so not wearing a T-shirt with a horse head—or any part of a horse—on the front. She stopped a moment later to look at what appeared to be hand-tooled leather belts. "The craftsmanship on these is nice."

"Let's see if they have one that will fit," Kelsey said, her warm breath so close to Elizabeth's ear, she shivered. "What's your size? That would look great on you."

"I'm not sure," Elizabeth said. "These aren't my usual style."

"Hold on." Kelsey took a dark brown belt with fine braiding along the edge off the hook and, stepping close, wrapped it around Elizabeth's waist.

Elizabeth froze. Her head knew that Kelsey's arms around her was completely innocent, but the rest of her shouted it was something altogether different. Something along the lines of *yes, get closer, touch me.*

"That might do it. Take off your belt," Kelsey said, stepping back.

"My belt?" Her body still vibrated with the anticipation of sex—she really needed to do something about exerting just the tiniest bit of rational thought whenever Kelsey was within visual range—but now was not that moment. "Why?"

Kelsey gave her a curious look. "Yes, your belt. The only way to guarantee an accurate fit is to actually try it on."

"Oh, of course," Elizabeth said. Of *course* none of this was about sex. They were in public, for God's sake. Yeah, that hadn't stopped them before. Her hands shook when she unbuckled her belt and slid it out through the loops. She took the new one and started inserting it through the first loop. It was much heavier than her thin fashion one and caught on one of the loops in the back.

"Here, let me help."

Kelsey leaned closer, and Elizabeth inhaled Kelsey's familiar scent. If she moved her head just a bit, their lips would be only a few inches apart. Her head grew light.

"There," Kelsey said. "That fits perfectly. What do you think?"

That I want you to drag me off to some corner somewhere and fuck me like you did the first time. Start with removing this belt.

The vendor, a skinny guy with deep creases etched in his tanned face, chimed in. "Looks awfully good on you, sweetheart."

Elizabeth's brain engaged, and she laughed. Odd, as ordinarily a stranger making a personal comment would have annoyed the hell out of her. But nothing was normal at this moment, including her. The simple yet unique belt gave her a completely different look. She glanced at Kelsey, who searched her face expectantly. "It's very nice."

Elizabeth caught a breath of fresh air when Kelsey stepped back. It helped clear her head—barely. "I like it, but—"

Kelsey turned toward the vendor. "She'll take it."

"You're not buying me this belt," Elizabeth said quickly. A five-dollar beer was one thing, a one hundred and thirty-five dollar belt something different.

Kelsey grinned. "You got that right. You are."

Elizabeth swiped her credit card and took the bag that held her original belt.

"Let's go to the chutes next," Kelsey said.

The tour ended with a stop at the first aid station, where Kelsey spoke to several of the techs. She'd been stopped any number of times along their path by people wanting to say hello, many of whom gave Elizabeth a less than friendly once-over. She was happy to finally reach the crowded grandstands where hundreds of spectators crowded the long aluminum benches waiting to cheer on their favorite cowboy and cowgirl. She recognized more than a few faces from the ranch as she followed Kelsey through the maze of people. Trying to navigate the seated people, the drinks and food on the ground beneath their feet, and five million screaming children was like walking through a minefield. She almost stepped on several things that might have been alive.

"Elizabeth."

She looked up to find Kelsey's hand extended. "Here."

The offer felt like more than a simple assist. Much more. What her heart heard was *If you take my hand and trust me, I will show you things you have never seen before.*

Elizabeth paused. Was this really the next step with Kelsey—a place she'd never gone to with anyone before? Was Kelsey even feeling what she was? Their eyes met, and Elizabeth read patience and expectation in Kelsey's gaze. And what she dared to think might be hope.

Elizabeth clasped her hand. "Thank you."

Kelsey gripped her hand with a sure and steady touch. "Almost there."

Elizabeth didn't care how long it took to find a seat. Not when fire raged through her from the heat of their touch. Finally, she settled on the backless bench between Kelsey and Olivia. Riley sat beside Olivia with some of the other Red Sky people beyond her.

"This is such fun," Olivia said. "You didn't miss much."

As the stands filled up even more and spectators shuffled back and forth to get a beer or a snack, Kelsey was forced to scoot closer to her. Their thighs often touched, and she tried to ignore the hot pulse of pleasure that the contact shot through her. When Kelsey leaned close to point out some detail of what was happening in the arena below, all Elizabeth could think about was how little it would take for her to just turn her head and kiss her.

Just great—kissing Kelsey Brunel in the middle of most of the population of Wickenburg would seal her reputation as a…a gold digger? Opportunistic bitch? Money-hungry corporate troll? She had a feeling quite a few of those terms had floated around about her after her arrival, and she'd been trying to change those opinions. The success of the center depended in a substantial way on the involvement and support of the townspeople. Clients did not want to spend thousands to vacation in a hostile environment. God knew, the climate, the terrain, and the wildlife were hostile enough.

So no kissing in public.

No kissing anywhere.

Somehow, Elizabeth kept her attention on the events in the

arena. Horses bucked, cows were caught, cowgirls raced around barrels, and bulls more often than not tossed their rider into the air. All in all, she had more fun than she thought she would. As they made their way out of the stands, Kelsey walked beside her, following Riley, Olivia, and the others.

When people split off from the group, Riley turned and said, "Want to grab a bite?"

"I'm in," Kelsey said instantly.

"Sounds like fun," Olivia answered.

Elizabeth glared at her.

"What?" Olivia said, feigning innocence. As if she didn't know Elizabeth had been avoiding close proximity to Kelsey for weeks. "It does, and I'm hungry. Come on, Ellie."

Traitor, Elizabeth thought. She could either look unfriendly in front of Riley, an important official in the county who she'd have to work with closely for the long term, or she could take one for the team, something she'd been doing for years.

Smiling while moving slightly away from Kelsey to avoid the appearance that they were together, she said, "Love to."

She even managed not to snarl.

CHAPTER TWENTY-TWO

"Everyone apparently had the same idea," Riley commented as they waited for their name to be called by the hostess.

"Yep," Kelsey said, the extent of her conversation for the last twenty minutes. Several people had stopped her on the way into the restaurant to congratulate her on another successful event. She'd answered them politely and subtly tried to squelch the topic. Now what she really wanted was to be somewhere else. She did *not* want to sit across from Elizabeth all through dinner and pretend not to be looking at her eyes or her mouth or any other part of her, but she didn't want to be beside her either. Any more of their legs touching, however inadvertent, and she was going to spontaneously combust.

She didn't want to have dinner with Elizabeth, and it would be another hour before it was over. She'd been a nervous wreck the entire evening. Why had she started a conversation with her in the first place? And playing tour guide again? She could have just said no, couldn't she? Except she hadn't wanted to say no.

She'd told herself that by showing Elizabeth what Wickenburg and its people were really like, Elizabeth might yet decide that Sutton Properties and their high-end spa did not belong in her small town. She'd told herself that she'd hoped Elizabeth would feel out of place in the dirt and dust and horse poop, and that maybe wishes did come true, and Elizabeth would see the venture was a bad idea and pack up her crew and leave the Red Sky alone.

She told herself a line of BS because what she'd really wanted was to be with Elizabeth without the tension and lingering anger they couldn't seem to shed. She could admit it now. What choice did she have? She'd do it all over again at the first chance. Elizabeth was impossible not to desire.

The air between them had shifted when she'd put that belt around Elizabeth's waist. When she'd leaned in, close enough to kiss her, and had desperately wanted to. When she'd inadvertently touched her while threading it through the belt loops and the memory of all the other ways she'd touched her set every nerve on fire. She'd broken out in a cold sweat while her vow to hate everything about Elizabeth and Sutton Properties went racing off into the distance, like a thoroughbred bolting out of the starting gate.

And now here she was, forced to act casual when her head filled with thoughts she could do nothing about. She finally settled on sitting across from Elizabeth. Safer. Mostly. Besides, she liked looking at her and hearing the sound of her voice almost as much as touching her.

"So what's on tomorrow's schedule?" Olivia asked as she helped herself to nachos.

"There's more?" Elizabeth blurted.

Kelsey laughed. "Last night and tonight were the qualifying rounds. Tomorrow is the finals. Gates open at three."

"You sound like a card-carrying member of the Wickenburg Rodeo Association," Elizabeth said.

The teasing note in her voice made Kelsey's heart stutter. "Well, I…"

"She's the president," Riley interjected.

Elizabeth looked at her and raised her eyebrows.

"Somebody had to do it," Kelsey said off-handedly.

"Don't let her fool you, Elizabeth," Riley said. "Kelsey was unanimously elected."

Kelsey tried to brush it off. "Like I said—"

"I imagine that takes a lot of coordinating, and a fair amount of time," Elizabeth said, watching her. "That's impressive. I can't imagine you have much spare time."

"The ranch takes up pretty much all my time," Kelsey muttered. Damn, she wished they'd find something other than her to talk about.

"Yeah," Riley laughed, "that and dancing."

Elizabeth glanced at Riley with a quizzical expression. "Dancing?"

"She loves to dance," Riley went on. "Not much around here, but in Phoenix there's always someone at the bars to dance with. Right, Kelsey?"

"So, you like to dance?" Elizabeth asked in an oh-so-casual voice as she carefully spooned guacamole onto her plate.

Kelsey might have thought Elizabeth was trying to make her uncomfortable, except for the glint in her eye. Flirting. She was playing with her, and damn, but she liked it. "Yes, I do. It's one of my favorite things."

"Are you any good?"

"I haven't had any complaints, but I've been pretty busy the last couple of months. I might be a bit rusty, but it all comes back to me pretty quick."

"How did you learn? Lessons?"

Kelsey laughed. "Practice. A woman asks, or you ask her, and each time you get a little bit better."

Elizabeth's eyes darkened. "Yes. Practical, too, if you've got the time."

"Well," Kelsey continued, "you can always practice by yourself. No one wants to dance with someone who doesn't know what they're doing."

"Mm. True. Not as interesting, though."

"Are we still talking about dancing? As in on a dance floor with music?" Olivia asked, looking between her and Elizabeth.

"What else would we be talking about?" Kelsey asked, her question directed to Elizabeth.

"Sounded kind of hot to me," Olivia replied, waving her hand in front of her face as if to cool off.

"That's why they call it dirty dancing," Kelsey replied, and Elizabeth blushed.

"We should all go sometime," Riley said, reaching for the salsa verde.

Elizabeth eased back in her chair, her gaze still on Kelsey. "I don't think we've got time for that kind of entertainment."

Kelsey sucked in a breath. Entertainment. That's what their encounter had been, so why did it bother her to hear Elizabeth call it that?

CHAPTER TWENTY-THREE

Laughter spilled out into the quiet night when Elizabeth opened the door of the Wickenburg Civic Center. She hesitated and half turned around. "Really, this is a terrible idea."

"Come on, they won't bite," Olivia said, giving her a little shove. "We need to make nice with the locals."

"Why exactly is that?" Elizabeth sounded petulant and knew it.

Olivia was right, but she really hated these kinds of things. She loved the planning and getting projects off the ground. The hustle of meeting deadlines, coordinating contractors, and making decisions was exciting and energizing. Schmoozing with people was her father's area of expertise, but it was part of the job, especially in a situation like this one. Her father had reiterated that for the umpteenth time earlier that week.

"The townspeople are not too happy with the construction traffic," he'd said.

"People like who?"

"People like the ones behind the three calls I've received from the mayor," he'd snapped. "You need to get in front of this. We have too much invested in this for it to go bad. We don't need a bunch of protestors at our gates like we had in Milan."

Her father never missed the chance to remind her of past failures, even when they weren't her doing. But then she did believe that as the project head, all responsibilities ultimately fell to her.

"I know. I'll take care of it," she'd replied.

"The sooner the better. You're already close to falling behind schedule."

Elizabeth's trouble-ahead antennae shot up. "I'm sorry? What makes you think that?"

His pause told her all she needed to know. She had a mole somewhere at Red Sky who was reporting back to her father—or through Wyland to him. They weren't behind schedule—yet, but there'd been some slowdown when materials hadn't arrived and the geological surveys for the new golf course had mysteriously been misfiled at the county clerk's office and hadn't surfaced for almost a week.

"I'll take care of it," she'd repeated.

"Just keep the locals pacified," he'd said and hung up.

So there she was, all prepared to pacify. She had her doubts that something called a Hoedown, spelled H-O-E not H-O, as Olivia had so helpfully explained, would do the job of soothing the ruffled feathers in town, but she put on her game face and followed Olivia.

"I love the way they decorated this place!" Olivia exclaimed when they stepped inside. "This is cute."

Hay bales bordered a large stage occupying one end of the cavernous space. Banks of halogen lights illuminated the four band members belting out a western tune. From what Elizabeth could tell, their instruments constituted guitars, violins, a keyboard, cymbals, a ukulele, and bass guitar—not all played at the same time, clearly. Additional bales lined the walls, creating seating areas, and several more were scattered around the room in semicircles. A farm wagon in one corner had been transformed into a large bar. Under strings of lights crisscrossing the ceiling, wooden planks lay over the geometric carpet, creating a makeshift dance floor.

"I'll get us drinks. Then we can mingle," Olivia said and headed toward the bar across the room.

Elizabeth eased out of the fray and moved to the side of the room where she checked her watch. One hour—max. She hated mingling. Small talk was not only boring but a waste of time, something she never had enough of.

Several of the Red Sky staff and a few local residents she'd met over the past few weeks were already on the dance floor. Her gaze landed on Kelsey, who of course she knew would be there, and right on cue, Kelsey turned and their eyes met. When Kelsey cocked her head and lifted her beer in greeting, the butterflies dancing in Elizabeth's stomach migrated downward. Damn it. No amount of telling herself *no way, no how* seemed to get through to the parts of her body so clearly not under her control. In all fairness, any lesbian with a pulse would give Kelsey a second look. Kelsey always looked amazing, but tonight she'd shed her rough and tumble ranch look for cowboy finery—black jeans with black cowboy boots along with a shimmering black western-style shirt featuring white piping around the pockets and cuffs and white studs in the buttonholes. She'd finished off the look with a matte black cowboy hat. Oh yes—she was fine in all respects.

"I know you're not a big fan of beer, but this crowd is, so, when in Rome…" Olivia trailed off and passed her a clear plastic cup with nary a hint of a head. Keg beer—yum.

"Yippee." Elizabeth took a sip. The beer was cold, though, and really not too bad.

"Well, Kelsey dressed to impress," Olivia said in a suggestive tone.

"Really?" Elizabeth turned away. "Hadn't noticed."

Olivia snorted. "Wow. The BS meter just imploded."

Elizabeth sighed. "I thought we were supposed to be mingling."

"We are. You should mingle your way over to Kelsey. Let the good folks in Wickenburg see there are no hard feelings." Olivia shrugged. "Really. Kelsey is a big deal round here, and quite a few people are put out that Sutton—aka *you*—are stealing her ranch."

"Really? And you know this how?"

Olivia looked momentarily nonplussed. "Riley might have mentioned it when she was out for the last inspection."

Elizabeth sighed. "God, small towns. Fine. I'll talk to her. For a minute. Where will you be?"

"Mingling. I saw Riley come in. She can introduce me around."

Elizabeth quirked a brow. "Handy."

Olivia blushed. "Expedient. I'll find you soon."

"Make it earlier than that," Elizabeth muttered as Olivia headed off. If she didn't know any better, she'd say Olivia had a girl crush on the handsome inspector. That was interesting. Olivia hadn't mentioned it, but everyone had their secrets.

And now it was time to do her duty. That was why she'd come, after all.

❖

Elizabeth was the last person Kelsey had expected to see. Elizabeth was not a small-town-dance type of woman. Kelsey'd seen the articles picturing her—and the women with her—at high-end New York and Vegas clubs. The type of places where you had to know somebody or *be* someone just to get in. Definitely not clubs with hay on the floor, plastic decorations hanging from the ceiling, and a four-piece band belting out country favorites.

Elizabeth had dressed for the event, though. Gone were her fashion jeans and silk shirts. The Wrangler patch on the rear pocket of her jeans showed from across the room. Her tailored cotton shirt wasn't overly fancy, but with the top three buttons undone and a layered silver necklace nestled in the hollow of her throat, she turned heads. Kelsey smiled to herself. Elizabeth wore the belt from the rodeo. Seeing it on her gave her a little surge of possessive satisfaction—undeserved maybe, but pleasant nonetheless. With Elizabeth in the room, Kelsey couldn't look anywhere else.

"You better stop looking at her like that." Sophia handed her a fresh beer. "And don't say you're not. You haven't taken your eyes off her since she came through the door."

"So? She's an attractive woman." Kelsey took the beer. "I don't plan on getting into any trouble."

"I'm your wingman, here to see you don't," Sophia said, her eyes narrowing as Elizabeth headed their way.

Kelsey watched her approach, and everyone else in the room disappeared when Elizabeth said hello. Kelsey smiled. "Glad you made it. So what do you think of our local entertainment?"

"It's nice." Elizabeth glanced at Sophia. "Hello, Sophia."

"Nice?" Sophia said, not bothering to return the greeting. "Is that a word you use when you're bored out of your mind?"

"Actually, no," Elizabeth replied with cool pleasantry. "If I was bored, I'd leave. I meant it's nice. Not overcrowded, the music is good and not too loud, the drinks are reasonably priced, and it looks like everyone is just here to have a good time."

"As opposed to what?" Sophia asked, a slight edge in her voice. Kelsey shot her a look. What was she doing?

Elizabeth shrugged. "Trying to score something, make a connection, or work some deal."

Sophia snorted. "Sounds like you spend your time with a bunch of assholes."

"Yes, it does, doesn't it." Elizabeth sipped her beer, watching Sophia with a faintly amused expression.

Uh-oh. Kelsey had a feeling Sophia didn't know she was poking someone with teeth.

"Is that what you do, when you're not building resorts? The whole asshole thing?"

"Sophia," Kelsey snapped. "Come on."

"If you're asking if I'm good at my job," Elizabeth said, "then yes, on occasion, that's exactly what I'll do."

Elizabeth's tone held an edge, and Kelsey started to sweat. She needed to get these two into opposite corners—of the universe preferably.

"Does that include seducing people?" Sophia said.

Elizabeth laughed. Actually laughed, and the sound sent a chill down Kelsey's spine. This was not going to end well. She grasped Sophia's arm. "Come on. Let's go get some air."

Sophia jerked her arm away, her glare fixed on Elizabeth. "Well. Does it?"

"I've noticed that tactic is only necessary for people who don't have the brains or ability to get the job done on their own." Elizabeth tilted her head and smiled. "I imagine you understand what I mean."

"I'll tell you what I know," Sophia said, leaning into Elizabeth's space. "You blow into some little town like this and take people's jobs, ruin people's lives, *fuck* with people's feelings, and then you leave without another thought."

"Okay, that's enough." Kelsey slipped an arm around Sophia's waist and steered her toward the door. "What the hell are you doing? You were rude, insulting, and a complete ass."

"Just trying to protect you."

"I can protect myself."

"Not against that one." Sophia turned her head as if looking to see if Elizabeth had followed. "She is way out of your league."

"Well, thank you very much. So glad to hear what you really think of me." Kelsey managed to get Sophia outside while she worked the Uber app with one hand.

"That's not what I meant." Sophia sounded confused.

"You obviously don't think much of my judgment. Or what kind of person I deserve to be with." Maybe Sophia had had too much to drink or maybe she really couldn't see the bigger picture. Elizabeth wasn't to blame for her losing the ranch, and there'd been two of them in that parking lot outside the Last Stop. One of them had been her. Maybe she had a reason for it to take her this long to see that, what with Red pretty much cutting her legs out from under her, but Sophia had no business going after Elizabeth for no reason.

"You're making a big mistake with that one," Sophia said, stomping off in the direction of the waiting Uber.

Kelsey, thankful the wait was never more than a minute when any kind of event was going down, gave the driver the address to the ranch. Once she'd made sure the driver knew how to find her casita, she hurried back inside. She needed to find Elizabeth and try to apologize. A line dance was in full swing, the dance floor crammed with people jockeying for real estate. With so many people shuffling their boots on the wooden floor, it was easy to spot Elizabeth talking to the mayor in the corner. Kelsey wouldn't have interrupted, but the mayor saw her and waved her over with a big fake smile.

"Kelsey," the mayor said cheerfully. "Miss Sutton and I were just talking about you."

Kelsey tried not to imagine just what Elizabeth had been

saying. She glanced at Elizabeth, who smiled as if she was enjoying her discomfort, damn it. She opted to feign innocence. "Things have been…busy…out at the Red Sky. What with all the changes."

"So I understand." He beamed at Elizabeth. "I hear you've been helpful and wonderful with the remodel. It has to be tough to see what you've worked for your entire life sold out from under you."

Elizabeth's congenial expression changed instantly. "I would suggest, Mayor, that you not express opinions about something you obviously know nothing about. Something that must happen quite frequently, I imagine."

Kelsey laughed. "You don't need to defend me, Elizabeth, but thanks. The mayor's opinion doesn't carry a lot of weight with me."

The mayor had never been a friend to her or Red. He was usually too busy with his nose up the butt of the people with money who would help him get reelected to know much about what was really going on in Wickenburg. Or to care. How he kept getting reelected was a mystery to her—but then, money could buy pretty much anything.

"Your father would be ashamed of you for talking like that," Swigler said, although his gaze was already roving over those nearby—probably looking for the next person whose influence he'd try to pander.

"Since I am ashamed of him, I guess that makes us even." Kelsey turned her back on him and said to Elizabeth, "Can I speak to you a minute?"

"Of course."

"We can talk out on the back patio." Kelsey led Elizabeth outside, where the air was cooler and the noise level much lower, although the band could still be heard. She walked to the far corner, away from the few people who'd had the same idea they had. "I want to apologize for Sophia. She was completely out of line."

"She knows about us, doesn't she?" Elizabeth asked quietly.

Kelsey's heart jumped in her throat, and she nodded. "I didn't tell her. She saw us leave the bar together and did the math when she saw you that morning at the ranch."

"I see. For a one-time thing, which I presume you told her that was all it was, she seems to hate me."

"She doesn't know you."

"Apparently that doesn't matter. She loves you and she hates me because I'm the one that's taking Red Sky away from you."

"Sophia is my friend," Kelsey said, "and I love her the way you can love family without agreeing with them—or even liking them sometimes. But she doesn't know everything about me or what I feel, and she's wrong about you. Besides, I don't hate you, and that's all that matters."

As soon as she spoke the words, Kelsey realized they were true.

"When did that change?" Elizabeth asked softly.

Somewhere between the minute you got out of that ridiculous car and the first time you actually smiled at me, Kelsey thought, struck once again by what she'd been avoiding for weeks.

She took a breath and said, "I've had some time to see what Sophia can't—or doesn't want to accept. The people I should be angry with are my father first, and yours second—although I suppose for him the deal was just business as usual. You aren't behind all of this."

Elizabeth held her eyes for a long time, and Kelsey hoped she saw truth.

"Thank you for that," Elizabeth said finally.

Relieved, Kelsey said, "And I like some of what you're doing out at the ranch—especially the golf course."

Elizabeth smiled. "Phil has mentioned you've had some key input on that, especially considering we have no idea what happens to the landscape when it rains."

"I noticed." Kelsey laughed. "The redesign will prevent the eighteenth hole from flooding with the run-off."

Elizabeth cocked her head. "Tell me, how much influence does Mayor Swigler have with county officials?"

Kelsey snorted. "Those he didn't outright appoint as a reward for helping him get elected, he likely bribes to go his way on important issues. Why?"

"Just wondering," Elizabeth mused. "He seemed very interested in our progress out at the ranch."

"Probably trying to figure out how he can make money from tourists who aren't here for long and don't own property."

"Possibly." Elizabeth smiled. "Thanks for the input. I think I should find Olivia. I believe it's time for us to leave."

"Not yet." Kelsey caught her hand, and Elizabeth looked down at their suddenly clasped fingers in surprise. Kelsey quickly let go. She couldn't let the night end this way—not when every instinct told her she'd regret it. "You can't leave without a dance. It's a rule."

Elizabeth laughed. "A rule?"

"Absolutely. Come on." Kelsey's blood thundered in her ears. What she really wanted was to kiss her, which happened just about every time she saw her, but they'd agreed that was not happening. She was a woman of her word, but a dance ought to be safe. At least she could touch her, something she ached to do.

"I don't know how to two-step," Elizabeth said.

"It's easy. We can do it right out here—just follow my lead."

"You know, the last time we danced, we…" Elizabeth lifted a hand.

"I know. I was there." Kelsey sensed her wavering. "It's just a little small-town dance. You can handle it."

Kelsey's insides churned as she watched Elizabeth struggle to decide. She'd been turned down plenty of times, and none of those no's ever bothered her. Right this moment, she knew Elizabeth's next words might take her somewhere she'd never been. She held her breath, wondering what was going through Elizabeth's mind as the silence grew. When she saw the nearly imperceptible shift in her expression, she steeled herself for disappointment.

"All right," Elizabeth said, "I'll give it a try."

CHAPTER TWENTY-FOUR

"Okay," Kelsey said, relief so great she was breathless. "Don't think, just move."

Elizabeth laughed a little shakily and took the hand Kelsey extended. "I'm not going to say how dangerous that sounds."

"No thinking," Kelsey murmured and drew her closer, careful not to scare her away before they'd even started. This dance was not like any other dance she'd ever had—this was not like the first time with Elizabeth when sex was all she had on her mind. This dance was her chance to savor everything about her. Her scent, the softness of her skin, the magic of a tendril of her hair whispering against Kelsey's cheek.

With Elizabeth's hand in hers, warmth spread up her arm and settled low in her belly. As Kelsey led her through the simple steps, Elizabeth tipped her head down to watch their feet, and one of them stumbled. It could've been her. She was too lost in Elizabeth to know.

"Sorry." Elizabeth smiled at her, her face flushed, her eyes like diamonds in the moonlight. She was breathtaking and so close, Kelsey struggled again not to kiss her.

"You're doing great," she somehow managed to choke out.

"You're a good teacher," Elizabeth said. "This is really kind of fun."

"Yep," Kelsey said. *Fun* was not quite the word she had in

mind. Tormenting, tempting, and tantalizing were more what she was feeling.

When a couple who'd had too much to drink staggered across the patio, Kelsey automatically pulled Elizabeth against her. Elizabeth's hand slid from her shoulder to the back of her neck, and Kelsey tightened her arm around Elizabeth's waist. Elizabeth fit against her body everywhere, and adrenaline spiked her arousal. She risked turning her head and resting her cheek against Elizabeth's. The contact, feather-soft, filled her with longing and desire like she'd never known. Her fingers tingled where they intertwined with Elizabeth's. Her stomach turned somersaults, and her heart beat against her chest as if trying to escape.

Elizabeth met her gaze, and the quickening of her breath, the slight tremor of her body, assured Kelsey she was not alone in her desire. Like that first night—that mind blowing, life altering night—Elizabeth felt what Kelsey felt. Knowing that, *feeling* that, left her equal parts exhilarated and terrified. That first dance had been all about sex, and need, and the driving urge to banish loneliness and isolation with raw, physical intimacy. This dance was every bit as powerful and touched her somewhere she hadn't known she wanted—needed—to be touched. But at what cost?

Part of her signaled a warning to back off before she risked too much and opened the floodgates to too much need, too much hope. But the pull of Elizabeth's eyes was like a magnet. Kelsey didn't even try to fight it. Why? This was where she wanted to be. Lost in Elizabeth's arms, but somehow home in her eyes.

"Elizabeth," she whispered, her mouth against the tender skin just below Elizabeth's ear, "do you know how much I—"

Elizabeth tensed and dropped her arms from around Kelsey's neck. Kelsey registered the silence around them. The band had stopped playing, and she'd never noticed.

"I…thank you for the lesson." Elizabeth stepped back, her gaze averted. "I need to find Olivia. It's time for us to—"

"Elizabeth," Kelsey said quickly, hoping to convince her to stay. She wanted this dance to end how their first dance had—with her making Elizabeth come, with Elizabeth driving her wild. But not fast and hard in a nondescript parking lot. This time she wanted Elizabeth in her bed, naked, all night.

"I can't, Kelsey. And you know why."

Kelsey didn't follow her. She'd let Elizabeth see her need, and Elizabeth had turned away. Lesson learned.

❖

Elizabeth found Olivia talking with a few of the crew and didn't bother to make excuses.

"Sorry, something's come up," she said to the group and motioned to Olivia. "Let's go."

She didn't wait for a response. Olivia was used to her quick exits from business gatherings, which was what this should have been, after all. She skirted around the crowd and headed toward the main entrance. She could not get out of there fast enough. She needed to put serious distance between herself and Kelsey. She didn't trust herself to look back, to see if Kelsey had followed her, to see if she looked hurt or angry or still wanting. If Elizabeth saw her, she might turn back, and she might say yes when Kelsey offered another night together, and from what she'd seen in Kelsey's eyes—she *would* offer. And she'd end the night in Kelsey's casita, in Kelsey's bed, in her arms. She'd want to lock the door and never come out, but she couldn't do that, could she? And then what about the morning?

A night with Kelsey would not be the anonymous trysts she'd limited herself to for years. Everyone at the Red Sky Ranch and on the Sutton Properties crew would know before noon that they were sleeping together. Whoever was reporting back to her father, and she knew there damn well was someone, would be filling him in five minutes later. Her reputation, her credibility in a world where women were never granted the same respect or authority as men, would be in tatters. And Kelsey—some would say she was trading sex for some advantage in the new organization. Those were all reasons enough not to give in to what every cell in her body urged her to do. She didn't even need to consider the reason that mattered most—the one she'd been avoiding thinking about for weeks. Possibly since the night they'd met. One night, two, a dozen with Kelsey would never be enough. Not when she was more than halfway in love with her already.

"Okay." Olivia hurried to keep pace as Elizabeth rushed outside. "Are you all right?"

"Yeah, I'm fine." Other than needing someone to rattle her brain back on track.

"Are you sure? Did someone say something to you?"

"No, I'm fine," Elizabeth said again. "We've talked to everybody we needed to, so mission accomplished. Business is concluded."

She tried to sound nonchalant but doubted that she had succeeded. Olivia was still frowning. She just couldn't talk about it. She needed to back away, remember why she was there, remember who she was.

Mercifully, Olivia was happy with casual conversation on the way back to their temporary quarters in the Sutton compound at Red Sky. As she stopped the SUV in front of their trailer, Olivia squeezed her arm.

"Are you sure you're okay? Because, you know, I know you pretty well, and I can tell when *fine* is just BS."

"Yes, you can, and you're right, but I'd rather not talk about it." Or even think about it, she thought, but that was never going to happen.

"Did Kelsey do something to upset you while you were dancing?"

"Hell," Elizabeth groaned, dropping her head into her hands. "Did everybody see it?"

"I doubt it," Olivia answered. "I just happened to end up by the patio door when I wanted to get out of the crush for a while."

"Thank God. I so do not need to give the town anything more to talk about."

"So what happened?"

"I almost made a serious mistake." She drew a deep breath. "But that's all settled now."

CHAPTER TWENTY-FIVE

Kelsey found Sophia asleep on the couch in her living room when she walked in. She'd escaped from the damn social at the civic center as quickly as she could after Elizabeth pulled another disappearing act, leaving her confused and horny and aching. Why had she expected anything different than the first time? Elizabeth obviously was not interested in a repeat performance—she'd said that pretty clearly more than once. Kelsey stood staring at her best friend, anger and remorse and self-recrimination a bitter brew churning inside.

Sophia, her hair tangled and her shirt askew, rolled onto her side and slowly sat up. "Oh. Hi."

"What the holy hell was that all about?"

"Huh? What?"

"Tonight—the attitude with Elizabeth. Where did all that crap you were spewing come from? You embarrassed me, and if you cared, which obviously you don't, yourself, too."

Sophia grabbed her head with both hands. "Could you lower the level a notch, or ten? I have a headache."

The half-empty wine bottle she'd left in her fridge now sat empty beside the sofa.

"No, I won't. If I thought in a million years you'd pull some-thing like that, I never would have invited you." Kelsey shoved her hands in her pockets and crossed the small living room to the window. With her back to Sophia, she said as quietly as she could through the haze of fury, "Why?"

"I thought you might need some help seeing your fuck-buddy for who she really is." Sophia sounded almost sober now, except for the careful way she said each word. "She's a cold-hearted, manipulative bitch who has ruined your life, and you can't see past your clit long enough to know it."

"My what? I am not believing this." Kelsey turned, the anger in her middle turning to stone. "Whatever Elizabeth is to me is no one's business, not even yours." She walked to the door. "Sleep it off. You can get one of the hands to drive you back to your car in the morning."

The sky was clear, the night air cool and crisp as Kelsey walked down to the barn. Tonight wouldn't be the first time she'd slept out there. As a kid, sleeping in the loft had been an adventure. Tonight she just wanted an escape. She was so very tired.

The weeks since Elizabeth had arrived had been a constant barrage of tension, uncertainty, and confusion. She'd lost the ranch, her father had deserted her, and Elizabeth had turned her inside out with one look. Pretending she didn't care what Elizabeth was doing or thinking or hiding that just being near Elizabeth made her lose focus was exhausting. Some days her hands shook so badly she could hardly hold her cup of coffee without spilling it all over herself.

She murmured to the horses as she passed them in their stalls and climbed up to the loft. The familiar sweet smell of hay surrounded her as she tossed one of the horse blankets stacked against one wall down on the floor. She toed off her boots and stretched out, doubting sleep would come. Not when the past few hours were so fresh in her mind.

Dancing with Elizabeth. What was that? One minute they were talking, the next arm in arm, their bodies close and their legs intertwined. She'd never thought she'd hold her again, never feel her body pressed against her, never inhale her scent or sense her breath quicken as they touched. She hadn't thought at all. She'd simply drowned in her.

And now what?

Now she had to forget all that all over again.

She closed her eyes and took a deep breath. Elizabeth's scent lingered on her skin, or she imagined it did. The excitement of being close to her again definitely remained. The pressure in her clit hadn't relented despite the drive home and the scene with Sophia. Other than the almost-orgasms she had in the midst of vivid dreams about Elizabeth, she hadn't come since the night they were together. Dancing with her again brought the need roaring back.

Eyes shut, she opened the button on her jeans and slid one hand down the front while pushing her shirt up with the other. Her hand became Elizabeth's on her breast, tweaking her nipple, her fingers were Elizabeth's, stroking across her clit and teasing at her entrance until her hips lifted. So fast now, just a little harder, a little deeper, and the surge of pressure burst into her core and down her thighs.

The orgasm exploded behind her eyes, robbing her of all sensation except pleasure. Her hips jerked as the last spasms ended, and she rolled onto her side, curled around the fading image of Elizabeth.

CHAPTER TWENTY-SIX

Elizabeth woke exhausted and was still sluggish after two cups of coffee. Her brain finally caught up as Brinkman fed her his most recent excuse for the work slowdown.

"Your entire crew has come down with some mysterious GI ailment," she repeated, impatience and frustration clearing the cobwebs from her head.

Brinkman shrugged with one of his just short of mocking smiles. "Happens. Bunch of guys, eating out at the same places."

"If your crew is not back on site tomorrow," she said, "I'll need to bring in a temp crew."

"Won't make you real popular with the men."

Elizabeth kept a thin rein on her temper. "Tomorrow, Mr. Brinkman."

"He's lying," Olivia said, watching Brinkman drive away in a plume of exhaust and dust.

"I know. I can't understand why," Elizabeth said, squeezing the bridge of her nose. The headache did not relent.

"Maybe just to prove who's boss in his own little mind," Olivia said. "Did you get any sleep last night?"

"Enough." When Olivia gave her an I-don't-believe-you expression, she added, "I've got a lot on my mind with this project. We keep running into little problems that are starting to add up. I need to keep us on schedule so we can get the hell out of here."

"Wow. Okay. You're really having a bad morning."

"Sorry. Ignore me."

For some reason, this project seemed unlike all the others, and the deeper she got into it, the more the feeling grew. She'd thought at first the encounter with Kelsey was the cause, but in the past few months they'd been able to at least work together without as much tension. As long as she didn't let herself think about all the ways she found her attractive. Whatever was going on, she'd gone from the normal tired that went along with any big project to weary—the bone-deep sensation that her life had become nothing more than a succession of projects in the never-ending quest to prove... something. What, she wasn't even sure she knew any longer. She'd always loved the work, but now she was questioning if she still did or if she had just grown used to the routine.

"You know what you need?" Olivia said. "A hooky day."

"Hooky?" Elizabeth stared. "Are we in grade school now?"

"Just say yes."

Elizabeth shook her head. "I never agree to something unless I know the terms."

Kelsey said from behind her, "Sounds like good advice."

Elizabeth spun around. Kelsey didn't appear to have slept well either, and for some reason, that bothered her. Dark circles shadowed Kelsey's eyes, and lines of fatigue framed her mouth. The mouth that Elizabeth had almost allowed to kiss her. That she had wanted to kiss her. "Good morning."

"We have three checkouts today," Kelsey said in an all-business voice. "Rudy and I are going to move a few of the horses to the paddock on the far side of the barn. That'll get them out of the dust. All the machinery makes them a little jumpy."

Olivia glanced at her phone and stepped away. "I need to take this. See you, Kelsey."

"Bye," Kelsey said, her attention still on Elizabeth. "I'm sorry about the scene with Sophia."

"You already apologized last night—and you didn't have to then. You certainly weren't out of line," Elizabeth said, relieved her nervousness didn't show. The horses weren't the only jumpy ones. Facing the woman she'd almost kissed and had most certainly wanted to was not what she needed right now. Not that any other time would be any easier.

"Wasn't I?"

"Of course not." Elizabeth rubbed her eyes and stepped into the shade. "God, this place is hot." Kelsey grinned, damn her, and she looked so good when she did, Elizabeth had to smile. "Can we not pretend we both didn't know exactly what was happening last night?"

"I can't pretend that wasn't the second sexiest dance I ever had, if that's what you mean," Kelsey said, lowering her voice and stepping closer. "I can't even stop thinking about it."

"I'm sorry if I let things get out of hand."

Kelsey sighed and her expression cooled. "Don't apologize. I know the score."

"Then we understand each other."

"That we do." Kelsey squinted toward the road as another vehicle approached. "Looks like you've got another fire inspection coming up."

"What? This is the third time this month." Elizabeth took in the official county fire inspector's white vehicle with red logo as it slid to a stop and Riley stepped out. Ordinarily, she'd be more annoyed, but the interruption was welcome. "I need to go see what she wants this time."

"And I've got horses to see to." Kelsey paused. "By the way, Sophia won't be a problem again. I asked her not to visit the ranch until you're gone."

Until you're gone. The words almost took her breath away, leaving her shaken and confused. Of course that was what she wanted, wasn't it?

CHAPTER TWENTY-SEVEN

"All right," Elizabeth said as they followed the signs to Lake Pleasant, "this might have been a good idea after all."

"I told you a hooky day was in order," Olivia said smugly, glancing at her watch for the third time in ten minutes. "After the last few weeks, we've earned it."

Elizabeth's almost good mood took a dip. She'd seen plenty of delays at other work sites, but this one seemed to be plagued with them. From dealing with equipment breakdowns to mislaid work orders to crew absenteeism that Brinkman couldn't seem to control, she'd done nothing but put out metaphorical fires every day. Added to that, her inability to quench her attraction to Kelsey had her stretched to the breaking point. They'd taken to interacting only when they needed to discuss a change in a blueprint or order replacement parts for the machinery that mysteriously kept breaking down or reschedule yet another guest who complained about too much noise. Actively trying not to think about her was as exhausting as the persistently sleepless nights. On top of that, she missed her. How ironic was that? She missed walking through the job site with her and talking out the plans for future guest events or simply stopping to watch the sunset before Kelsey went off to check the horses. Ordinary things people who just liked being together did.

Annoyed that she couldn't stop thinking of her even when she'd taken a day off to do just that, she saw Olivia check the time again and said grouchily, "Are we late for something?"

"What? No. Of course not," Olivia said.

Elizabeth pulled into the small lot by the Lake Pleasant marina and boathouse that bore a sign declaring the same. "All right. We're here. What do you suggest?"

Olivia pushed open her door and jumped out. "I think we should rent a boat."

Elizabeth locked up and joined her. "A boat?"

"They have boats to rent."

"What kind of boats?"

"All kinds. Plus water skis, pontoon boats, Jet Skis, kayaks, and paddle boards. They even have a cruise boat you can charter for events."

"I don't want to have to work at anything. I just want to relax, unwind, and worship the sun. Let's do the pontoon." She'd been on one several times while visiting friends in Louisiana. They were large enough to comfortably move in without danger of tipping it or yourself into the water, you could simply just cruise around, and most importantly, it had a bathroom.

The marina store carried the requisite sunscreen, snacks, ice, and beer. Several shelves in the rear held fishing gear, bobbers, bait, and more than a few things Elizabeth didn't recognize. The rental counter was against the wall to her right.

Olivia took care of the paperwork and Elizabeth used her American Express for the deposit. A few strokes of the pen, a cooler full of fruit, ice, and a twelve-pack of beer—no other alcoholic beverages available—and they were ready to go. Olivia carried a plastic bag containing chips and cookies while Elizabeth pulled the cooler across the aluminum dock.

Their eighteen-foot rental had a front wraparound bench for seating and a rear side-by-side lounger. Lake Pleasant Rentals was painted on the side in turquoise. The seats were gray with red stripes and the gray carpet looked new, as did the Bimini top that provided shade over half the boat.

"This is pretty big," Elizabeth said.

"More room to stretch out," Olivia said and showed her

paperwork to a baby dyke, who had to be no more than seventeen, standing by the side of the pontoon.

Her half-bored expression turned to definite interest as she spied Olivia. After a quick rundown of the safety procedures and a warning about the heavy traffic in some parts of the lake, Bing—as the teenager introduced herself—released their tie ropes and they were away.

Elizabeth kicked the throttle forward. "Wasn't that cute? *Bing* could not keep her eyes off you."

Olivia kicked off her flip-flops and slipped out of her shorts. Her bikini was red and minuscule. "What can I say? I'm irresistible to all persuasions."

Elizabeth snorted. One of them at least was already in a party mood. "You just about gave her a heart attack when you took off your shirt before we left the dock. Too bad for her, her boat will never be parked in your slip."

Olivia laughed and pulled her towel and sunscreen out of her bag. "Considering she's a baby dyke—for sure. Why are we going so slow?"

"Because it's a no wake zone. See those buoys over there?" Elizabeth pointed. "A no wake zone means you can't go fast enough to kick up waves behind you. Too rough on the shoreline in narrow straits and dangerous for boats behind you, especially when returning to dock."

"Well, aren't you Captain Smart." Olivia smeared on sunscreen. "Beer?"

"Not while I'm piloting."

"Against the law?"

"Probably. I know it is in most states. I didn't look up Arizona. It's no different than driving a car. Only you don't need a license, which is totally wrong. Boats are so much harder to handle."

Elizabeth picked up a little speed once in open water and checked the laminated map duct-taped to the dash. The lake was larger than she'd first realized. She wondered how many rescues the marina had to do each year because boaters didn't pay attention to where they were and had no idea how to find their way back. Small coves dotted the shoreline of the main lake, some with inlets cutting into the surrounding mountains. She was used to lakes in the middle of the woods or near a bayou. But this was nothing like that. Scraggly, rocky mountains bordered the shore in shades of brown and tan with cactus dotting the landscape. The sky was crystal clear, the winds calm. All in all, a picture-perfect day to be on the water.

Their speed, a comfortable ten miles an hour, according to the speedometer, didn't give Elizabeth much of a chance to observe the scenery. Boats were going in every direction, and she had to pay attention to the traffic on the lake. Jet Skis were the worst. Depending on their size, their speed could go anywhere between forty and seventy miles an hour and they could turn on a dime. In her experience, the drivers were the most inconsiderate, and the Ski itself, the most dangerous vehicle on the lake. Surprisingly, the three off to her left moved at a reasonably sedate pace.

Slowing to a crawl, Elizabeth maneuvered through a narrow canyon. Red rocks with horizontal stripes of varying colors were almost vertical in their ascent to the sky. The water was clear to the rocky bottom. Several ducks swam alongside them.

"How about we anchor here for a while?"

"Good for me." Olivia stood and peered back behind them. "I have nowhere to go and nowhere to be."

"You get the anchor." Elizabeth guided Olivia through what she needed to do to secure the boat to the bottom. Then she repeated the steps with the anchor at the rear, and Elizabeth killed the engine.

It was quiet in the canyon, two other boats anchored near, but not too close to invade their privacy. Elizabeth shucked her shorts and shirt. She favored a little more cloth than Olivia, more to avoid the sunburn than anything else.

"Look," Olivia cried, pointing to the shore. "Are those donkeys?"

Elizabeth looked, and sure enough, a pack of six donkeys perched on a small hill. The largest lifted its head and brayed, or was it honked? Whinnied? She didn't know, and it didn't matter. For some reason, the greeting felt as if it was just for them.

"*That* is awesome," Olivia said, taking a picture. "Best day so far."

A padded deck covered the compartment in the rear where the motor was located, and Elizabeth picked that as her spot for the rest of the day. She spread her towel out, slathered her front with sunscreen, and lay down, her sunglasses keeping most of the sun out of her eyes. She had to admit, so far it had been a very good day. If she could only stop thinking about Kelsey, and secretly wishing she was there to share the beauty, she might even be content.

CHAPTER TWENTY-EIGHT

"Do you see them yet?" Kelsey shouted, shading her face with a hand on her forehead as she maneuvered the Ski around an outboard cabin cruiser that had anchored smack-dab in the center of the narrow inlet to the cove.

"Off to the right!" Riley yelled back.

"You sure?"

"Yes! Olivia said a pontoon with a big striped awning."

As Kelsey steered them closer, she picked out the blonde in the bikini lounging on the sundeck. Although her face was mostly covered with sunglasses, she was instantly recognizable. Kelsey would know her anywhere just from the curve of her jaw and the long lean line of her arm. Elizabeth sat up and looked right at her. Her expression of confusion turned to surprise and then, hopefully, to anticipation.

Kelsey looked from Elizabeth to Olivia, waiting for an invitation. She'd told Riley they were taking a chance just showing up this way, but Riley swore to her Olivia had invited the two of them to join them if they could when she'd texted to ask the best place to spend a day away from work. She sure hoped they'd be asked aboard, as the last thing she wanted to do was be less than a million miles from Elizabeth in a bikini. Or work clothes or anything at all.

Olivia waved and called down, "Hey, you made it. Can you park that thing and come up?"

"Yes," Kelsey called back, idling the big three-seater Kawasaki

Jet Ski by the side of the pontoon boat ladder. "Throw down a couple of your tie lines."

Elizabeth climbed down from her perch on the sundeck to give Olivia a hand, and Kelsey got a stunning view of all the parts of her she'd fantasized about that were even better in the flesh—long lean legs that went on for miles, curving hips barely covered by the high-cut lavender bikini bottom, softly rounded breasts, and a pale stomach a shade lighter than her tanned legs. She didn't have to try hard to imagine kissing every inch.

Riley poked her in the back. "Yo, Kelsey. The rope."

Kelsey blinked and raised her gaze to Elizabeth, who leaned down with the rope dangling from one hand and an amused look on her face.

She couldn't read the rest of Elizabeth's expression as, unlike her, Elizabeth kept her sunglasses in place.

"Can you reach?" Elizabeth called.

Kelsey jerked into motion. "Oh, yeah. Right. Got it."

Kelsey grabbed the rope, tied off the Ski, and reached for the ladder. Elizabeth waited at the top. With each rung she climbed, her view tracked perfectly up the length of Elizabeth's body. She had to work hard not to ogle. Or worse, drool.

"Welcome aboard," Olivia said. She handed both Kelsey and Riley, who'd hopped aboard right after Kelsey, a beer.

"Thanks," Kelsey said, absently glancing at Olivia, who looked great in her bikini, and immediately back to Elizabeth. She doubted she'd notice a boatful of naked women at that moment.

"This is a surprise," Elizabeth said, looking Olivia's way. Sunglasses still hid her eyes.

Olivia smiled a totally fake-innocent smile. "Oh, I guess I didn't mention Riley was the one who suggested this place when I asked her about a good day trip. And it's always more fun with a group, right?"

"Of course," Elizabeth said dryly.

"Come on, Riley," Olivia said, "let me give you a tour."

Kelsey waited until they'd moved forward out of earshot and asked, "So, uh, would you rather we left?"

Please say no, please say no.

Elizabeth shook her head and motioned to the sundeck. "No. Do you mind the sun?"

"Love it," Kelsey said and followed her up the stairs. Anywhere Elizabeth wanted to go was fine with her.

"So, the Jet Ski," Elizabeth said when they settled in the loungers. "Is it yours?"

Kelsey unbuckled her life vest and dumped it on the floor. In her surf shorts and sports bra, Kelsey felt way overdressed. For a second, she thought Elizabeth was checking her out. "No, a friend of mine. She keeps it here, and lets people use it."

"Nice."

"I didn't know you were going to be out here—I mean—I did, after Riley invited me and we were on our way."

"I'm glad you're here," Elizabeth said quietly.

"You are?"

"Why wouldn't I be? We've been working together for three months now—I think we can agree we're friends."

Friends. Not where her mind or any of the rest of her had been headed. Kelsey was glad she'd put her sunglasses back on so what she really wanted between them didn't show.

"Hey, Kelsey," Riley called. "Okay if I take Olivia out on the Ski?"

Kelsey kept her gaze on Elizabeth. "Sure. You can give her my vest to wear."

"Great." Riley climbed up, grabbed the vest, and said, "we might be a while."

"That's fine," Kelsey said, watching Elizabeth take off her sunglasses and set them in the built-in table between the loungers. A minute or so later, the roar of the Ski signaled they were alone.

Elizabeth reached up and took off Kelsey's sunglasses. "That's better. Now I can see your eyes."

"Now you'll know that I can't keep my eyes off you."

Elizabeth groaned. "That is such a bad line."

"Not working?" Kelsey asked, swinging around sideways on

the chair so she could lean closer to Elizabeth. Kissing close if she moved just a little more.

"I didn't say that," Elizabeth murmured. "Your persistence is… admirable."

Kelsey grinned. "Are you flirting with me?"

"Sorry."

"No, you're not."

"You're right. I'm not." Elizabeth's gaze slowly moved over Kelsey's body. "You know I find you attractive." She shook her head. "More than that, obviously, since I couldn't wait for you to get your hands on me."

"Elizabeth, come on, you're killing me here."

"I want to say what I should have said that night at the Last Stop."

Kelsey nodded, barely breathing. Her head pounded, her clit pounded, her entire body trembled. "Go ahead."

"I think you're incredibly hot. I'd like to find out just how hot you can make me. I'd like to do the same to you." Elizabeth touched her face, and Kelsey jumped. "Here's what I didn't say. Just sex. No strings. No involvement. No regrets."

Kelsey silently shouted *Too late for that. I am so involved, I'll never stop wanting you.* She took Elizabeth's hand. "Agreed. Can I ask you one question?"

Elizabeth nodded.

"Why now?"

"Because I am so damn tired of trying not to want you. Is that reason enough?"

Kelsey knew it wasn't, not anymore, but she'd never let her better judgment make her decisions for her. Why stop now? "Let's move down out of the sun. Bring your towel."

CHAPTER TWENTY-NINE

Elizabeth refused to think as she followed Kelsey to the lower deck.

When she'd realized Kelsey was on the Ski, in the last place she'd expected to see her, on a day when she'd finally left behind all the baggage of the job and her father and her never-ending quest to live up to standards she'd never understood, all she could feel was desire. More than that—joy. Kelsey was the one person she wanted to see. The one person she wanted to share the day with. The one woman she wanted to touch her.

And she'd seen the same longing in Kelsey's eyes.

She needed an hour, just one hour, when all she knew was the sensation of Kelsey's body next to hers. Of Kelsey's hands on her, of Kelsey's mouth bringing her off. She needed to lose herself in the magic of stroking Kelsey until she came, long and hard and only for her. She *needed* to be with her again.

"Are we really going to do this here?" Elizabeth asked, breathless.

"Yes. We just agreed, remember?" Smiling, Kelsey cupped Elizabeth's face, desire lighting her eyes, and pulled her close.

Slowly Kelsey leaned closer and kissed her. Her lips were incredibly soft, exploring Elizabeth's like she was completely new territory. She dropped gentle kisses over her eyelids, on her cheeks, and along her jawline. Elizabeth gripped Kelsey's arms as the rest of her floated away. Could that really be happening? When Kelsey returned to her lips, her kiss was deeper, more demanding, with a wild edge that hadn't been there before. Elizabeth thrilled to the evidence of Kelsey's need. The urgency that echoed her own. "I like the way you kiss."

"Do you?" Kelsey murmured, caressing Elizabeth's breast through the thin bikini top. "I'll have to kiss you more, then—everywhere."

Elizabeth arched and caught her breath as Kelsey massaged her nipple. "Not too soon. I'm too ready."

Kelsey groaned and rested her forehead against Elizabeth's. "Do you know how much I want you? How many nights I've dreamed of this?"

"I know." Elizabeth framed her face and kissed her, letting her own need explode as she teased the inner surface of her lips, then delved deeper and bit ever so gently. The kiss, meant to excite Kelsey, stoked *her* arousal until she had to pull away. Shakily, she said, "I've wanted you the same way. Every night since the first night."

"Then don't make me wait."

Elizabeth couldn't have said no even if she'd wanted to. Her body clamored for Kelsey's touch—for her hands and her mouth to drive her to the edge and beyond. "Then don't."

Kelsey pulled a cushion off the side bench and tossed it on the deck. "Here. Spread your towel out."

Elizabeth took one quick look around. The only other boats were well out of sight and Olivia and Riley nowhere around. Watching Kelsey watch her, she slowly released the tie on her bikini top and let it fall.

"Perfect," Kelsey whispered. "You're perfect."

"Wait," Elizabeth said, when Kelsey reached for her. "Watch."

Kelsey groaned. "If you keep this up, I'll come right here."

Elizabeth laughed. "All right."

"Just hurry," Kelsey said, sounding anything but tortured.

Elizabeth untied each side of her bottom and flicked the swatch of fabric to the deck. "Now your turn."

Kelsey had her board shorts and sports top off in a millisecond. "In a hurry?" Elizabeth asked, her voice catching. Kelsey's breasts were gorgeous, and Elizabeth knew they would fit perfectly in her hands. Wanting to prolong the moment for just a bit longer, Elizabeth ran her fingers across Kelsey's collarbone, across soft, sensitive skin until she filled her hands with Kelsey's breasts. The last time she had barely tasted Kelsey's skin, not nearly enough to feel how her nipple came to life under her tongue and teeth. Not able to wait any longer, she lowered her head.

"Yeah," Kelsey exclaimed, threading her fingers into Elizabeth's hair. Her hips rocked as if seeking a way to relieve an ache. The same ache consuming Elizabeth now.

"God, you have a great body," Elizabeth said, pulling away. "I can't wait to feel you on top of me."

That was all the invitation Kelsey needed. In an instant, she'd wrapped her arm around Elizabeth's waist, guided her down to the cushions, and stretched out on top of her. She shifted her weight onto an elbow, freeing one hand to explore. Her touch was electric, setting Elizabeth's nerve endings ablaze. Elizabeth wrapped her legs around Kelsey's hips, trying to press her center against her.

Suddenly Kelsey sat up, shifting to kneel between Elizabeth's legs. "Now who's in a hurry?"

Elizabeth made a sound she'd never made before in her life— somewhere between a growl and a plea. "Will you please for the love of God touch me?"

"You're so beautiful," Kelsey said, stroking her breast and her stomach. She leaned forward, her hips cradled between Elizabeth's legs, and pressed her mouth to Elizabeth's breast. Kissing her way to Elizabeth's nipple, she slid her hand lower to the delta between Elizabeth's thighs. Almost, but not quite, to her clit.

"God, yes, that feels good," Elizabeth managed. She wanted Kelsey like she'd wanted no one before, and she wanted her now. "I need to feel your mouth on me. I need you to make me come."

Elizabeth lifted her hips, and Kelsey instantly pushed lower on the cushion until she was lying between her legs.

Elizabeth looked down and met Kelsey's eyes looking back. "Your mouth. On me. Damn it."

Kelsey grinned and covered her with her mouth.

Elizabeth arched and pressed her forearm to her lips to stifle the scream. Kelsey knew just where she needed her. She licked and stroked and teased. Elizabeth moaned. "Fuck me now. Now, and you'll make me come."

Kelsey pushed to her knees, leaning over her on one arm. "Watch me."

Elizabeth wrapped her fingers around Kelsey's nape and looked into her eyes. What she saw nearly pushed her over. Desire. Need. Wonder. "Hurry or I'll come."

Slowly, Kelsey teased her opening before sliding inside. Elizabeth raised her hips to draw her deeper.

"That's it," Kelsey murmured. "Just like that. Take me."

"More," Elizabeth gasped.

Kelsey stroked faster and deeper, and Elizabeth's clit tightened. "I'm coming. Don't stop."

"Never happen," Kelsey murmured and pressed her clit.

The orgasm hit fast and Elizabeth cried out, pumping her hips in time to the wrenching spasms. When her muscles finally relaxed, she groaned. "Well, all right then. Nicely done."

Kelsey burst out laughing and kissed her as if she'd die if she didn't. Elizabeth grabbed her ass and pressed her leg between Kelsey's. "Ready to come?"

"Fuck, yes," Kelsey said through gritted teeth and buried her face against Elizabeth's neck. She rode Elizabeth's thigh in long, hot, hard strokes until she threw back her head with a sharp cry and went rigid.

Elizabeth watched Kelsey climax, glorying at the sight that had never been more powerful or more beautiful. Her chest tightened, and she bit her lip. Oh, God, this could not be happening. She could *not* be falling in love.

❖

"Are you all right?" Kelsey asked, not sure what part of *all right* she meant. Satisfied? Happy? No regrets?

"Fine."

"You know? I hate that answer," Kelsey muttered. "It could mean anything—including *I can't want to get away from here.*"

Elizabeth cupped her cheek. "Hey. Look at me."

Kelsey sighed. "Sorry. Not quite myself yet. I think I left my brain somewhere around Pluto."

"Pluto?"

"Only planet I can think of right now."

"By *fine*," Elizabeth said, sounding serious again, "I mean that was awesome sex—as I expected based on our past experience…" She waited while Kelsey stopped laughing. "And I think you are about the sexiest—no, make that *the* sexiest—woman I've ever seen. That kind of fine. How about you?"

Kelsey nodded and kissed her. "I'd be more fine if we could do that again."

Elizabeth hesitated at the familiar sensation of needing to extricate herself from any further connection before she risked getting in too deep, creating distractions and complications. Needing not to disappoint. Kelsey watched her with a small frown, as if sensing the sudden distance, and Elizabeth searched for something to change the subject. "Today is the first time I've seen Riley without long sleeves. That burn scar on her left arm looks like it was a serious injury. I guess firefighters have to be prepared for that to happen, but it's got to be hard."

"She's gone through a lot." Kelsey gave Elizabeth a narrow-eyed look. "Are you trying to distract me? Because it's not working. When I'm anywhere near you, I'm thinking about what I wish we were doing. And when you're naked—"

A loud blaring sound saved Elizabeth from trying to hide her sudden uncertainty. "What is that?"

Kelsey cursed colorfully. "*That* would be the horn from my Jet Ski."

"Get *dressed*." Elizabeth grabbed the bits of her bikini.

Amused, Kelsey pulled on her shorts and sports bra. "They're going to wonder."

"Let them," Elizabeth said, tying her bikini bottoms. "Supposition is not fact."

"Okay," Kelsey said, drawing out the word. "I won't make any announcements."

"Thank you." Elizabeth didn't see the point of repeating what she'd already said—what Kelsey had agreed to. No involvement. They weren't a couple, and what they had done or might possibly do again was no one's business.

"Ahoy the ship," Olivia shouted.

Kelsey gave Elizabeth one long look before walking toward the ladder. "I'll help them tie on."

CHAPTER THIRTY

"Everything okay?" Riley asked as she helped Kelsey winch the Jet Ski into the custom berth on the side of the dock.

"Sure," Kelsey said briskly, giving the tie-down strap an extra yank. "Why wouldn't it be?"

Other than she had no clear recollection of the ride back to shore. Good thing Riley had wanted to drive on the return trip. She'd been too busy reliving the moments with Elizabeth and recovering from the abrupt change when Riley and Olivia climbed back aboard. Elizabeth was friendly enough, in a distant way, but she'd gone back to the sundeck after saying she wanted to take advantage of the sun when she wasn't actually being baked to death by it.

Kelsey'd hung with Riley and Olivia for another beer and boat snacks she didn't feel like eating, all the while trying not to look in Elizabeth's direction or let her mind wander back to what they'd just shared. Or start with the endless questions—which she was no closer to answering now than she had been the day Red dropped the nuke on her life.

What would she do when the transition at the Red Sky was done and Elizabeth left? Would she still have a job of some kind there? Would she even want one? Would she ever look at another woman and want her the way she wanted Elizabeth? Would she ever want to *know* another woman the way she wanted to know her?

She sighed.

Riley cocked her head. "See, that's what I mean. You're somewhere else."

Kelsey forced a smile. She had to do a better job of keeping her feelings to herself, especially since they weren't likely to go away. "Just tired. It's been a madhouse out at the ranch lately."

"Not surprised," Riley said as she grabbed their gear bags. "I mean, I am, actually. I can never remember having so many orders come through for permit checks and code evaluations as we've had for the Sutton project." She must have seen Kelsey wince, and said quickly, "Sorry. That's how it's registered with the county clerks."

Kelsey frowned, remembering Elizabeth complaining about the frequent fire inspections. "Are there problems at the site?"

"Not that I can see," Riley said. "But you know, these inspections are never quick—plus the paperwork for everyone piles up. Has to cause a bit of work slowdown."

"Yeah," Kelsey mused, "there's a lot of that going around."

"So," Riley said, climbing into Kelsey's truck. "do you want to hit Cowboy's for dinner? I think Olivia and Elizabeth might be headed that way."

Cowboy Cookin', a restaurant in a run-down building painted a putrid gold, was a local favorite. A statue of a saddled horse, its reins tied to a hitching post, stood in front of the wide, wood plank porch. Kelsey hit the place at least twice a week for dinner. Her pulse skittered at the thought of seeing Elizabeth again, but that passed in the next heartbeat. She needed a bit of time before she could work herself back to being casual around her. She shook her head. "Thanks, I'll pass tonight."

❖

"I think whoever picked the paint might have gone a bit too far with the local color thing," Olivia said as they walked into Cowboy Cookin'. Paintings, horseshoes, and other western knickknacks covered the walls and shelves behind the long bar. "At least the color scheme is a little less eye damaging in here."

"Hmm," Elizabeth answered. When no one approached, she decided it must be seat-yourself and headed toward one of the smaller tables in the far corner. Most heavy wood tables had six or seven spindle bow back chairs around them, and she had no intention of family-style seating, let alone conversation. She didn't feel the least bit sociable. She wasn't hungry either, but Olivia had flat-out refused to get in the SUV unless Elizabeth promised they'd stop for dinner.

After scanning the laminated menu offering the usual diner-type fare, she ordered a burger and fries. Seemed the safest option. She even got a draft beer, which, when it came, was ice cold and very good. She took a long pull and let out a long breath. God, what a day.

"I thought you were having fun," Olivia said, munching from the bowl of shelled peanuts on the table.

Elizabeth tilted her head. "What? Oh, it was fun. Great idea."

"Uh-huh. That's why you look miserable."

"I am not miserable! Too much sun, probably."

"Uh-huh. Because it's not sunny or hot at the ranch. Where you never look like you want to be someone else, somewhere else."

"I'm just tired," she tried feebly.

"It's Kelsey, isn't it?" Olivia asked casually.

Yes. No. Of course it is, Elizabeth wanted to shout, but said instead, "No. There's no problem there."

"You two sure seemed to be avoiding each other out on the boat—at least after we came back from skiing." She paused. "In fact, you were a bit rude the rest of the afternoon. So what gives?"

"Nothing, really."

"This is more than nothing—it's not like you to get involved with someone."

"Who says I'm involved? We had a thing. It was great sex. You should try it." Elizabeth really wanted to divert Olivia from this conversation, and the fastest way she knew to do that was to put the spotlight on Olivia instead of her. She'd already been down the road of What the Hell Am I Doing, and had no answers for herself, let alone Olivia.

"That's another topic for another time," Olivia said, all too used to Elizabeth's defense mechanisms. "You're different since you've started *not* being involved with her." She frowned. "It's not like you're not on top of the job, because nothing will ever get in the way of that, but your ice shield is cracking."

"My ice shield?"

Olivia actually looked discomfited, a rare situation for her. "You usually project an aura of untouchability—as if you're the boss, which obviously you are—and that's all you ever let people see."

"You mean I come across as cold and indifferent?" Elizabeth said, feeling the chill inside as her defenses automatically clicked into place. She acted that way so other people couldn't get close enough to hurt her. That had aways worked—until Kelsey, who somehow seemed to slip around her protective barriers to excite and terrify her in equal measures.

"Don't be angry," Olivia said. "I'm only mentioning it because the longer we're here, the more I see you showing the other sides of you—you didn't even rip Contreras a new one yesterday when he failed to notice the new mix of concrete they'd sent was wrong."

"He didn't order it," Elizabeth said feebly, "so I didn't think he needed to be reamed out in public."

"I'm just saying," Olivia said, "something has changed, and I think Kelsey has something to do with it. And that's why you couldn't get far enough away from her this afternoon. She shakes you up, doesn't she?"

Elizabeth fought not to look away from Olivia's prying eyes. She wasn't having much success getting Olivia to drop the bone she wanted to chew on, and she didn't like lying to her best friend. But just now she was feeling raw and vulnerable. Kelsey shook her up all right. Kelsey not only turned her on with a flicker of a smile and made her come faster and harder than any woman she'd ever been with, she reached into some place deep inside her that she kept locked away for safety's sake. The place that wanted to curl up in the arms of a lover who would cherish her and support her and value her for who she was, and not just reward her for a job well done.

She didn't want to think about that right now, when she could still feel Kelsey's hands on her, and she didn't want Olivia psychoanalyzing…certainly not in the middle of Cowboy Cookin' on a Thursday night. She didn't even want to think about it when she was lying in the dark in her solitary bed. "If there's anything between Kelsey and me, it's about sex. Just sex."

"There's nothing else there?" Olivia idly fished another peanut out of the dish on their table.

"No." Elizabeth didn't ask for examples of what the *else* might be.

"You sure?"

"Positive." Okay—stretching the truth some, but Olivia was pushing into territory where even best friends should tread carefully.

"I'm just trying to look out for you. I have never seen this side of you, and neither have you."

"I appreciate that, I really do, but I've got it handled." And she *did*, until the reins of control slipped out of her hands, and she let Kelsey close again. She'd posted the No Involvement sign, and Kelsey had agreed. If she didn't follow her own rules, she'd be hurt. She'd left relationships that had mattered before, and every time, a little bit of herself was left behind. This would be no different, but if she wasn't careful, she'd leave more than a little piece behind.

"All right," Olivia said, "so I have this to say. You and Kelsey had a thing—you hooked up. People do, you know. You surely have plenty of times before this. If you don't want a repeat—fine. If you do, fine again. But make a decision and make it clear to her. From where I'm standing, the two of you are making each other miserable. This is not like you—so whatever is going on, fix it."

Elizabeth stared. What could she say? She could hardly tell Olivia that everything was settled, that she'd be happy having sex with Kelsey, as long as that's all it was. Not when her feelings for Kelsey already went far beyond just sex. "You'll just have to trust me on this. I've got it under control."

Olivia rolled her eyes. "Just try not to get hurt."

Elizabeth suspected it was already too late for that.

CHAPTER THIRTY-ONE

"Sorry I'm late." Kelsey sat down next to Elizabeth at an empty table on the patio. The kitchen was closed, as all the guests were out on scheduled events or private outings, but Maria had left sandwiches for them to have an early lunch. Which wasn't early at eleven when she'd been up since four.

"You're not late," Elizabeth said. "Two minutes is within the grace period."

Kelsey smiled. "Good to know. I need all the grace I can get." She gestured to the plates covered with snow-white napkins. "You waited."

"Of course." Elizabeth pulled a dish over and lifted the napkin. A turkey club—with actual meat carved from a turkey—a side salad, and slices of apple. "How is that something so basic looks so delicious?"

"It's the air and the exercise," Kelsey said. "Makes you hungry."

"Then you have no excuse. You need to eat more. You're looking thinner," Elizabeth said as they both started on the sandwiches.

Kelsey blushed. "Ah—okay, sure?"

Elizabeth glanced at her and laughed. "Sorry. But it's true."

"I'll work on it. So, you said there's something you wanted to discuss?"

Elizabeth squeezed the bridge of her nose. She hoped she wasn't making a big mistake—one of many she'd been making since she'd arrived in Wickenburg. She might as well get right to the point. "I think someone or a…group of someones…is trying to sabotage this project."

"And you think it's me?" Kelsey shot up straight in her chair, a blaze of anger flashing across her face. A look Elizabeth hadn't seen in the last few weeks. Not since the afternoon on the boat. Since then, they'd been easier with each other, for want of a better word. The heat was still there, more than ever—at least for her. She'd awake as if from a daydream and find she'd been watching Kelsey work the black colt in the corral and think of how good she looked, how strong and sure and just…right…doing what she loved. Or she'd see her ride back on Adira after checking out the trails the guests would be riding later, dusty and windblown and gorgeous, and want nothing more than to drag her off to…anywhere they could be alone and naked. Oh, the desire was there all right, but they'd also begun to work better together. Conferring about a problem on the site—of which there were more than there should be—or reviewing a new design plan sent down from corporate unexpectedly or just somehow ending up together on the porch after the evening meal to watch the sunset. What they hadn't done was have sex again, and that was slowly driving her mad.

"Of course I don't think it's you." Elizabeth shook her head. "If I did, would I be sitting here telling you this? And besides, subterfuge is not your style."

"Oh, really?" Kelsey sounded slightly less outraged. "And my style is?"

"Direct, brash, a bit shoot-from-the-hip."

"You make me sound like an ass."

Elizabeth pressed her lips together, but Kelsey narrowed her eyes, so the smile probably showed. She quickly added, "I find your style quite effective in some situations."

"Don't flirt if you don't mean to follow through," Kelsey said softly.

"I plan to deliver," Elizabeth said, knowing she'd made the decision she'd been struggling with since they'd last been together, "at a better time."

Kelsey nodded, apparently satisfied to wait. That was different, and...nice. That little bit of trust.

"So, tell me what's going on," Kelsey said.

"You've probably noticed we're behind schedule," she began.

"Not really." Kelsey grimaced. "There seem to be so damn many changes going on everywhere at once, it's like a tornado touched down."

"Well, we are, a little bit more every week. I didn't worry at first," Elizabeth said. "Every project has its glitches, especially in the early stages. But little by little, our glitches have been adding up—work delays due to equipment shortages, breakdowns, missed deliveries, misfiled paperwork, miscommunications with interviewees. Small things by themselves, but when put all together?" She shook her head. "They add up to something bigger."

"What are you saying? That these things are deliberate? Who would do that?" Kelsey asked. "You think it's someone from the Red Sky staff? Is that what you're telling me?"

Elizabeth held her gaze. "That's what I'm *asking* you. That would seem to be the likely source—since Sutton is viewed by quite a few people in town and here as the enemy who invaded your world and is systematically destroying it. Perhaps someone is trying to stop us from succeeding."

Kelsey sighed. "I used to be one of those people, and I can't pretend I'm happy to have Sutton move in here and start telling me what I should do with my own damn ranch, *but* I don't think everything you're doing here is a bad idea. And I don't sneak around stabbing people in the back."

"I know that," Elizabeth said patiently. "Which is why I've come to you with this. What about one of the longtime hands? They might not trust we'll keep them on, or they might just want to stop us out of loyalty to you."

Kelsey shook her head. "I don't see it. I'm the only one with an interest in seeing you fail—or I suppose I *would* be, if I thought that would get me the ranch back—but I know that's not happening." She leaned forward, her eyes bright and intense. "I'm not an idiot, so I know that's not possible. I just needed time to work that out. And," she said, cutting off Elizabeth's protest, "I don't want *you* to fail."

"You don't?" Elizabeth asked. Were they at last on the same side, somehow?

"You and I don't see the ranch the same way, but"—Kelsey blew out a breath—"I can see the big picture, what you're building here, and it's not all bad." She shrugged and grinned. "If I'd had more money and more time to actually think about what I wanted to do with the ranch, I might have come up with a few of the changes you're making."

Elizabeth smiled. Had they been anywhere else she would have kissed her. Because she was gorgeous and sexy and honest. "Thank you. That means a lot."

Kelsey covered Elizabeth's hand where it lay on the table. "I've been so busy telling you how much I wanted to get you into bed again, I haven't told you you're one impressive businesswoman."

"I still think you're trying to get me into bed."

"True." Kelsey left her hand where it was. "So do you think it's someone on the Sutton crew?"

"Not the crew," Elizabeth said, wishing she wasn't heading toward the most likely answer. "The rank and file have no reason to want the project put on hold for budget reasons—if we fall behind schedule, if we start costing the corporation more than expected, the board may put this project in the deep freeze and pursue something more lucrative."

"And what happens to the ranch?" Kelsey asked grimly.

"We liquidate, sell it off, and take the loss as a write-off."

Kelsey pushed her chair back and jumped to her feet. "The hell you will."

"Not my decision," Elizabeth said, "but there's still time to salvage things if I can stop the slow bleed."

"If not someone on the crews, then one of the Sutton team managers?"

"Someone here on the ground would have access to everything we're doing," Elizabeth admitted, "but I can't figure out why anyone would want to sabotage the project. None of us get paid if we fail. And besides, I handpicked these people. I've worked with them all before."

"You've just eliminated all the possibilities, then," Kelsey said, running a hand through her hair as she paced.

"Not necessarily." Elizabeth caught her arm. "Sit down."

With a grunt, Kelsey dropped into her chair. "You're awfully calm."

"Trust me, inside I'm boiling." Elizabeth sighed. "I think we have a mole—someone who is reporting back to my father, or someone close to him. He knows things that have happened before he should, and he knows things about our progress that aren't in any reports I've sent him."

"Sure sounds like one of the Sutton team."

"Or it's several someones here," Elizabeth said, "working together with someone at corporate."

"Say you're right," Kelsey said. "The question is still, why? What's to be gained by sinking this project?"

"You mean besides ruining me?" Elizabeth grimaced. "Once we figure that out, we'll have all the answers."

❖

"Excuse me," Maria said tentatively from the far side of the patio, "but there's someone in the parlor asking for you, Kelsey."

Kelsey frowned. "Who is it?"

Maria shook her head. "She wouldn't say. She is not from around here—she came in a rental car."

"Not a guest," Kelsey asked. "Early arrival, maybe?"

"No. She said she wished to speak to you."

Kelsey sighed and glanced at Elizabeth. "I'd better go see what this is all about."

Elizabeth set her napkin aside. "I have some calls to make, also." She tilted her head, her smile one Kelsey hoped she'd get to see a lot more of, as it promised something special. "I'll see you for dinner?"

"I'll be there."

Kelsey left feeling lighter and more optimistic than she had since this all began, even with the new complications Elizabeth had just brought up. Elizabeth no longer kept her at arm's length—and for the first time in longer than she could remember, she had hope. Hope for something more in her life than work and one-night stands.

A slender woman in a sleeveless, pale-green linen shirt that complemented her honey-gold hair and decidedly suntanned arms stood with her back to the room studying the framed photos—mostly of Red or Kelsey on a succession of horses over the years.

"Can I help y..." Kelsey's words died in her throat when the woman she hadn't seen since she was seven years old turned around.

"Hello, Kelsey, dear. How are you?" her mother said.

Kelsey really wished this was a bad dream, rather than a living nightmare. The last time she'd seen her, Lois Brunel had been thirty-three years old. Thirty years later, she was still trim, with no visible streaks of gray in her perfectly coiffed updo, and a flawless face free of any laugh lines. If Kelsey didn't know better, she'd guess her age as not a day over forty.

Shock turned to anger, but she managed to keep her voice steady. "What are you doing here?"

"Aren't you even going to say hello?"

"No. I don't think manners are required here. What are you doing here?"

"No need to be so ugly, Kelsey," Lois said in a disapproving tone as if Kelsey was ten years old.

"No need to..." Kelsey bit her lip. She would not let this woman know how much she'd hurt her. She would not give her that power over her. "You walked out on us, on me, if you remember correctly. Not a call, not a card, not one goddamn word. You lost the right to tell me anything when you walked out that door."

"Yes, well, there were...circumstances."

"Circumstances?" Kelsey heard her voice break and cleared her throat. "How about the *circumstances* of a husband and kid?"

"I can understand why you're upset."

Kelsey straightened. Unbelievable. But then...what about any of this was believable? "Understand? How does a *child* understand why her mother left and never came back?"

"I had to go. This place"—Lois waved her perfectly manicured hand—"was not for me."

"Then why are you here now?"

"I heard your father sold the ranch."

"And?"

"And I want my share of the proceeds."

Kelsey couldn't help but laugh. Wow. What world did this woman live in? "Your share?"

"Yes, my share. I was with your father on this godforsaken ranch for eight years. I deserve something for that."

"You deserve to be thrown out of here on your Pilates ass is what you deserve." Kelsey finally raised her voice. "The door is right where it was the last time you left. Get out."

"Don't speak to me—"

Elizabeth walked up beside Kelsey. "Is there a problem?"

"And you are?" Lois asked, sounding as if she still owned the Red Sky.

"Elizabeth Sutton. Is there something I can help you with?"

"I'm Kelsey's mother, and this is a private matter."

Surprise flickered across Elizabeth's face for an instant before her cool professional look returned. Kelsey had never mentioned anything about her mother. Now here she was sitting in the living room like she owned the place. Obviously, she thought she did.

"I wasn't aware you were coming, Ms. Brunel." Elizabeth glanced at Kelsey as if gauging the temperature in the room before asking, "Will you be staying with us?"

"What business is it of yours, Miss Stratton?"

Kelsey grinned as Elizabeth transformed from politely professional to *I'm* not *in the mood for your crap*. It was something she'd seen more than once on the job site.

"It's Sutton, and I own the Red Sky."

"Congratulations," Lois said with no enthusiasm. "Or maybe I should offer my sympathies. I don't know why someone would spend good money on a plot of dirt."

"I imagine there are a great many things you don't understand," Elizabeth said coolly. "Now, is there something I can do for you?"

Lois ignored the question and turned to Kelsey. "I'd like to know where your father is."

"Like you told *him* where you were all those years." Kelsey's voice was brittle.

"He always knew where I was."

He always knew? If he'd known where her mother was, why hadn't he told her? Shocked, Kelsey replied, "You want him, you find him."

"I have a right—"

"No. No, you don't. You have no rights at all here." Kelsey shook her head. "You lost those when you walked out."

"Seeing what you've turned into, I can see I made the right choice." Lois lifted her chin. "Because of you, I was trapped here on this ranch in the middle of hell. Your father and I were perfectly happy living in Palm Beach until you came along—an accident, by the way, and suddenly he wants a different lifestyle for his *family*." She picked up her designer bag and carefully smoothed back her hair with one hand—despite not a strand being out of place. "I waited for him to come to his senses, but he never did."

"What *I* turned into?" Kelsey staggered at the vitriol from someone who, in her imagination at least, had once loved her. What a fool she'd been believing *that* all these years. Never in her entire life had she heard anything as cruel.

"Yes," Lois went on, "a rude, dirt-covered, trashy—"

"That's enough," Elizabeth said. "I'd like you to leave, Ms. Brunel. As you can see, Mr. Brunel is no longer here. You'll need to inquire elsewhere."

"You may think I have no rights to this property, but you're wrong," Lois said haughtily. "We're still married, and I know my rights." She took her time walking to the door and looked over her shoulder with a malicious smile. "My attorney will be in touch."

Kelsey's hands shook so badly she had to shove them in her pockets. "Just when I thought no one could be more of a bastard than my father, she walks in."

Elizabeth touched her arm. "Kelsey, I'm so sorry."

"Yeah, me, too. Sorry that I didn't know all these years what a cold, heartless bitch she was."

"Let's sit down."

Kelsey sat because she had to. She had no fight left in her, and Elizabeth's company was unexpectedly comforting—even though Elizabeth had just seen Kelsey at her worst with her family garbage strewn all around. The room started to spin, and Kelsey laid her head back. In the last ten minutes, her entire life had come crashing down—again. Everything she'd known, or thought she'd known, had changed with a few icy, hurtful words.

"Well," she finally said, "now you know my whole sad family history."

"You didn't know she was coming," Elizabeth said gently.

"I haven't seen her in thirty years. I didn't even know if she was alive. And I certainly didn't know they were still married."

"She'll get nowhere with that threat. Her name was not on the deed. She has no rights to the ranch."

Kelsey jumped up, the hurt and frustration boiling over. "Do you think I care about that? If Lois wants her pound of flesh, then she can get it from my father. If she can find him. Obviously, he took a page from her book and disappeared without a fucking trace."

"I can't imagine how you feel right now," Elizabeth said. "You deserved better from both of them."

"Do I?" Kelsey's emotions ricocheted from fury to confusion to deep, untouchable pain. "Maybe she's right. Maybe I ruined her life. She sure looks to have done fine without us."

Elizabeth stood, her eyes filled with sorrow. "Kelsey—"

Kelsey couldn't breathe, couldn't think. She needed to get away—from the memories that had turned to ash, from the loss and the betrayal. She bolted out the door in search of the only comfort she could count on.

CHAPTER THIRTY-TWO

Elizabeth sat up, rubbing her eyes, still groggy from her night on the porch chair, a wooden lounge-type affair with a well-worn cushion the color of the surrounding desert. She glanced at her watch—5:30 a.m., and over the mountains, another beautiful sunrise. The sweeping palette of reds, purples, and oranges painted a picture she would always remember.

Kelsey had been gone all night. When Elizabeth had followed her outside and seen her ride out a few moments later on Adira, she'd walked around the job site for a while, knowing no sleep was in her future. The conversation between Kelsey and her mother that she'd walked in on had been stunning in its cruelty. Lois Brunel was a malignant, vicious woman with thoughts only for her own well-being. Lois was an older version of Kelsey physically, with the same color eyes and the same build, but the similarities stopped there. Kelsey had her edges and didn't trust easily—well-deserved self-protection mechanisms, from what Elizabeth had seen of her parents—but she was also honest, loyal, forgiving, and tolerant. Her word meant something, and so did her actions.

Despite the incredible pain Lois's accusations must have caused—saying that Kelsey was an unwanted burden from which Lois had to escape—Kelsey had held her temper and kept her dignity in the face of devastating revelations. Elizabeth marveled at how much strength Kelsey had shown not to crumble under the onslaught.

The wounds had gone deep, though. Despite Kelsey's strength, the tremors in her hands and the anger and confusion in her eyes had shown just how much she'd been wounded. Elizabeth understood the need to hide pain, not to show weakness when at her most vulnerable—just as Kelsey had been in that room with her mother. She also knew how badly she'd needed to be able to show her need, to cry out for help. Until Olivia, no one had ever answered.

Elizabeth wanted to be there when, if, Kelsey reached out for help, so she waited. She wanted to be the one woman—maybe the first woman other than Sophia—who did not abandon Kelsey when she needed someone to share her pain.

She rose and stood at the top of the steps as Kelsey walked toward her from the barn.

"What are you doing here so early?" Kelsey looked around as if she could spot the trouble. "Was there a problem with the horses?"

"Nothing like that. I was worried when you didn't come back at sundown." Elizabeth wrapped her arms around herself, feeling the chill in the morning air now that she was awake.

"It's not safe to ride in the dark. The gopher holes are everywhere." Kelsey shrugged and stepped up beside her. "Adira could've stepped in one and broken her leg. I'm used to sleeping out. It's not the first time I've used a saddle for a pillow."

Kelsey didn't look like she had slept much, if at all. Her face was pale and gaunt, and her eyes shadowed with the ghosts of her past.

"Well, I just wanted to make sure you were okay," Elizabeth said, slipping past her. "I'll go so you can get some sleep."

Kelsey grasped her upper arm. "What if I said I'm not tired."

"Then I'd…" Elizabeth trailed off. "I'd ask you if there's anything you needed. Anything I could do."

Kelsey's gaze never left her face. "If I said I needed you, would you run away again?"

Elizabeth squared her shoulders. "I don't think I've been running away."

"Then why haven't we had sex again since that day on the boat? Did you get it out of your system? Over and done now?"

"What is this about?" Elizabeth said. "You're angry and hurt. I get that. Your mother—"

"*Lois*—not my mother."

"Lois said hateful things, and I'm sorry—but this is not about us." Elizabeth pulled away, and Kelsey immediately released her arm. "I'm not going to do this here, and certainly not now."

"You're right," Kelsey said as she pulled open her front door and walked inside, "there *is* no us."

❖

Kelsey stopped just inside and closed her eyes. What the hell was she doing? She'd just turned on Elizabeth for no reason, and practically equated her to Lois to her face. Elizabeth would probably never talk to her again. And for what reason? Because Elizabeth didn't want to fall into bed with her every other minute like she wanted to? Because Elizabeth had a damn job to do here that kept a hundred people employed, a lot of them *her* people, and cost more than she could imagine? Because Elizabeth wanted no strings, and she did?

Kelsey stopped cold. Did she? Did she want more than a string of one nights? But ties that actually lasted? She didn't have an answer, but she knew where to start.

She turned around, yanked open the door, and nearly ran Elizabeth down in her hurry to get outside and find her. She blurted, "You're still here."

"Yes, I am," Elizabeth said, her chin tilted in that way that said she was steamed but keeping it under control. "Apparently, your attempts to get rid of me failed."

"I don't—" Kelsey grabbed her shoulders, yanked her close, and kissed her. "I don't want to get rid of you. I want you to come inside."

"Then yes," Elizabeth shoved her back through the doorway with both hands on her chest, "I will. Thank you."

"Come on." Kelsey took her hand and didn't let go until they were inside her casita with the door closed and locked behind them.

Elizabeth said, "Before we go any further, I want you to know how sorry I am about Lois. She has missed the chance to know an exceptional woman by walking out on the child you were. You survived and you won, and I'm impressed and proud of you."

"Ah..." Kelsey swallowed hard. "Thank you. I needed to hear that. I forget sometimes—most of the time—that she made a choice that had nothing to do with me. I wasn't the cause of her leaving, no matter what she tells herself."

"No, you weren't. Now tell me why you're angry with me."

"I'm not..." Kelsey grimaced. "I'm mad at myself."

"Oh?"

Kelsey said, "So here's the thing. I wanted you from the moment you walked into the Last Stop. You were gorgeous, sexy, and confident, standing there like you owned the place. And I could not keep my eyes off you. Every time I've touched you since, I've wanted you again."

"I'm following," Elizabeth said with a slight smile. "Is there a *but* coming?"

Kelsey nodded. "But right now, I want more. More than sex—which is amazing—every now and then before we get on with our lives as if the sex hadn't happened. I want to spend all night exploring every inch of you, then I want to do it again as often as possible. *But* I also want to fall asleep in your arms and wake up with you and share the morning sunrise with a cup of coffee. I want to sit down with you at night over dinner and hear about your day and your problems or what victory you scored over one of the grade-A jerks you deal with every day."

"I'm leaving in a few weeks." Elizabeth's voice was quiet, as if she whispered the words, they wouldn't be real.

"I know."

"We could get hurt."

"I know."

Elizabeth leaned forward, their foreheads touching. "I don't want to hurt you."

"You won't."

"I'm afraid leaving will really hurt." Elizabeth shook her head.

"Shh," Kelsey murmured, as she gently kissed Elizabeth's neck. "We're here right now. This moment right now is what matters—not tomorrow, not next week, but right now. This is what we have, and we can make it what we want."

Elizabeth hesitated. "I want these moments and the ones that come after them, too. I've never done anything like this before." She laughed, her voice shaky. "Of course, I've never known anyone like you before." She threaded her arms around Kelsey's neck and kissed her. "Let's try something new."

Kelsey grinned. "We've got a king-size bed in the other room. We can start there."

Chapter Thirty-three

Olivia walked with Elizabeth from the trailer toward the main building. "You weren't paying attention in there."

"Hmm?" Elizabeth glanced at Olivia, startled. "Yes, I was."

"No," Olivia shook her head, "you weren't. And you've been distracted for the last week. Ever since you've started sleeping somewhere besides our trailer."

Elizabeth knew she was blushing like a teenager caught coming in late after a party. "Was I supposed to ask permission?"

Olivia laughed. "No—you were supposed to tell me all about it."

Elizabeth stopped in the middle of the wide dirt road that circled through the Sutton camp. "I have been spending time at Kelsey's."

"I knew that. And?"

Elizabeth shook head. "And that's all you get."

"I figured that," Olivia said. "And I also figured that's not the reason you've been so distracted. Some maybe—but even great sex isn't enough to make you lose focus in a meeting with the project managers."

"I was just focusing on something else," Elizabeth said, checking to see that no one else was nearby. "Do any of them seem to you to be dropping the ball intentionally?"

Olivia frowned. "*Trying* to slow us down? No—am I missing something?"

"I don't think so, because I agree."

"Then why did you ask?"

"I wanted an unbiased opinion—to see if I was imagining things. I think we have a problem." Elizabeth repeated what she'd told Kelsey.

Olivia grimaced. "And you really don't think it's someone from the ranch?"

"I don't think anyone there, other than Kelsey, would even know how to begin to disrupt a project like this." Elizabeth set her shoulders. "And I don't think it's her."

"Neither do I." Olivia's eyes grew distant, the way they did when she was working out a problem. "Let me do what I do best—some research."

"Do it quickly. My father is going to be very unhappy with the next report I send. We're not so far behind that we can't make it up without too much extra cost, but we're edging deeper into the red zone."

"I might know someone who can help," Olivia said. "I'll be in the trailer if you need me."

"Call me if you learn anything. I'll be on the site."

Elizabeth resisted detouring to the barn where she knew Kelsey was working with the horses. They both had work to do, and admitting that she missed her seemed…foolish. She'd seen her just a few hours before, after all. She'd left her casita before most of the ranch was awake—after seeing the sunrise while drinking coffee on Kelsey's porch. If she could have frozen time, she would have described her life as perfect at that moment. She'd spent the night with a complex woman she found more fascinating every day—a woman who challenged her and excited her and saw her for who she was. Or who, at least, was content with what Elizabeth had allowed her to see, and that was more than she'd hoped for in a relationship.

If only she could sort out who wanted this project to implode, she'd be very nearly content.

❖

Kelsey stopped in the mudroom adjoining the kitchen to wash the dirt off her forearms before lunch. The last of the guests were just finishing lunch. They'd all hustled inside out of the heat after the trail ride ended while she and Rudy rubbed down and fed the horses. Work she didn't mind doing, especially since she didn't know how much longer she'd be able to. Elizabeth said she was behind schedule, but to Kelsey's eye, the changes to the ranch were monumental. The grading and landscaping for the eighteen-hole golf course was nearly done, one of the two bunkhouses had been converted into a state-of-the-art spa, and four new guest casitas were well underway. Somehow Elizabeth had managed to accomplish all of that while keeping the feeling of the ranch intact—for which Kelsey was grateful.

She'd just sat down to eat the lunch Maria had put aside when Brinkman stormed through the front door, spied her at the table, and barged over.

"*Where* is Ms. Sutton?" Brinkman practically hissed the word *Ms*.

Kelsey wasn't directly involved in the remodel, thankfully, because the contractor was an ass. She hadn't liked him from the minute he'd shown up and tried to push Elizabeth around. He was loud, managed his crews with threats, and was basically a bully. She'd asked Elizabeth why the hell she'd hired such a jerk, only to learn that he'd been hired before Elizabeth had even arrived in Wickenburg, part of what Elizabeth called the pre-plan stages.

"Sorry," she said, "I'm not her keeper. You might try over at the Sutton camp."

"You certainly don't need a leash around her neck to keep track of her, the way she sniffs around you all day." He leered. "Unless you like that sort of thing."

Too stunned for words, Kelsey started to rise, intending to toss him out on his ass. "You're way out of line—"

"Is there something you needed from me, Mr. Brinkman?" Elizabeth said, walking through the archway from the kitchen.

Kelsey couldn't tell from her expression what she'd heard, but Elizabeth rarely showed her cards until she was ready to play.

"I need you to okay this change order." He waved the papers in his hand. "Just sign on the last page. That's all I need."

Elizabeth regarded him steadily. "Olivia handles all of that."

"She said it was okay. We talked about it, and she told me to write it up and get you to sign it. The guys are here to start the work." He placed several sheets of paper on the table, the pages stapled and turned to the last page. He held out a pen.

Elizabeth picked up the papers and flipped through them too quickly to have read them all. Brinkman fidgeted. Finally she dropped them on the table. "This is not the way we do things, and you're aware of that. Now what's this all about? I'd like to hear the highlights from you, and why you think they're necessary."

"I just need your Jane Hancock, that's all," he repeated, obviously eager for Elizabeth to sign. "You want the highlights for a small change?"

"If it's a small change, then what's the hurry?" Elizabeth held the papers out to him. "Otherwise, drop these off with Olivia, as I already told you."

Kelsey frowned. God damn, this man was condescending. Something else was going on.

Brinkman gave Elizabeth a short synopsis that didn't sound too coherent, his tone clipped and anxious, before holding out the pen again. "I told you, Ms. Davis already approved it. I just need your signature."

"I just wanted to be sure you were aware of the terms on the order."

"Already said that, didn't I?"

"Yes. You did." Elizabeth set her phone down on the table.

Kelsey glanced at it. Holy crap. She'd been recording. Brinkman, his expression murderous, didn't seem to notice.

"Look, you pis—" Brinkman caught himself. "All I need is your signature, and we can save everyone a lot of time. You're already behind, so I think you—"

"Mr. Brinkman," Elizabeth said quietly, "you're fired."

"What?"

"You're fired."

"You can't do that!"

"I can, and I just did." Elizabeth was so cool, ice could have formed on her words.

Brinkman's face was getting redder by the second. "We have a contract."

"And I have an attorney." She pointed to her phone. "I also have you verbally agreeing that you are aware of the terms outlined in this document, which I think you already know is a problem. Your crew stays. It's up to you if you embarrass yourself by being escorted off ranch property."

"You can't do this, you stupid bitch."

Elizabeth picked up her phone and pressed a number. "Ms. Huerta, would you and one of the other officers please come to the main house and escort Mr. Brinkman to the main road...No, thank you. We're fine."

"You have no idea who you're fucking with," he shouted on his way out of the room.

"Actually, I have a pretty good idea," Elizabeth said.

Kelsey stared at Elizabeth. With two words, Elizabeth had essentially shut down all the work underway. That was monumental. "None of my business, but why did you just fire your general contractor?"

"A number of reasons." Elizabeth tapped her phone before sitting down at the table with a sigh. "Firstly, I heard what he said to you. No one who works for me harasses one of mine." She smiled. "Especially not you."

Kelsey's heart jumped at the word *mine*. Man, she was in trouble—and trouble had never felt so good. "Thank you. Anyone who works for you is lucky, then. And secondly?"

"Brinkman is not just a bad boss—he's a liar and apparently a thief." Elizabeth let out a long sigh.

"I get the first part, and believe the rest of it, but how did you know?"

Elizabeth gave her a long look and rubbed the bridge of her nose. Uh-oh. Decision time.

Kelsey sat down beside her. "You might not believe this just yet, but you can trust me."

"I already do." Elizabeth pushed the papers Brinkman had left toward Kelsey. "Read this and tell me what you think."

❖

Surprised, Kelsey read though the paperwork and looked up at Elizabeth. "This is a change request, all right, but it's not in your favor. It gives him an additional three hundred thousand dollars for, and I quote, miscellaneous expenses." Kelsey snorted. "What an idiot. There's no way you would have signed this."

"Brinkman assumed if he approached me when Olivia was not with me, I would sign it without reading it."

"Why would he think something so stupid—I mean, yeah, the guy's a snake, but he's a smart snake."

"Because he knows I can't read it," Elizabeth said flatly, her gaze never leaving Kelsey's. "What he doesn't seem to know is that numbers are not a problem. I'm very, very good at math, and the invoices don't match."

Kelsey was still back at *I can't read it.* "What do you mean?"

Elizabeth had an instant to decide. Did she trust Kelsey enough to confide in her more than she already had? She'd dodged people discovering her reading disorder all her life. Kelsey would be just one more. Only Kelsey was not just anyone, and she had to stop hiding from her. She had already gone so far down that road, she'd be lying to herself if she thought she could turn back now.

"I have a form of dyslexia that makes it difficult—practically impossible—for me to interpret sentences. I can do it, but it takes a very long time, and then I often still need an assist." Elizabeth smiled sadly. "It's a secret I've kept from almost everyone my whole life."

Kelsey didn't answer immediately, although a dozen things came into her mind. How good Elizabeth was at her job. How hard it must have been for her as a kid—and how scary. Plus college and a business career? She'd just assumed, before she'd gotten to know her, that because Elizabeth was wealthy, she'd had it easy. She'd been wrong about that. "I'm grateful you told me—that you trusted me. And you should know your secret is safe with me. Maybe you don't totally believe that right now, but I hope you will someday."

"Thank you," Elizabeth said quietly, her eyes shining with what Kelsey hoped were not tears. "I wouldn't have told you if I didn't already trust you."

Kelsey slid her chair closer and slipped her arm round Elizabeth's shoulders. "I don't know what it's been like for you, but I'm guessing it sucked."

"You could say that."

Thankfully Elizabeth laughed a little and didn't pull away.

"And since you're amazingly good at what you do," Kelsey added, "you must have superpowers."

"Not even a little." Elizabeth sighed and leaned in to Kelsey. "With the help of Olivia, and the fact that I am something of a numerical savant, I manage. Don't ask me to read a simple email. It'll take me an hour."

"Olivia—of course she would know. She's a tiger where you're concerned."

Elizabeth smiled. "A bestie, like your Sophia, but maybe a little more subtle." Kelsey chuckled. "Other than Olivia, my parents were the only ones—" She stopped.

"What?"

"Brinkman had no way of knowing I couldn't read—except he did." Elizabeth kissed her and stood up. "I have to find Olivia, and then I need to get out in front of this with my father."

Kelsey called, "When will you be back?"

Elizabeth turned at the door and smiled, a truly devastating smile that had parts of Kelsey throbbing that really didn't need to be in the middle of the afternoon. "I did mention I intended to follow through. Tonight, your place?"

"That works," Kelsey said, silently praying another disaster on the work site didn't get in the way.

CHAPTER THIRTY-FOUR

Elizabeth left Kelsey's before the sun came up, but Olivia was already at her desk when she walked into the trailer.

"Have a good night?" Olivia said smugly.

"Yes, thank you." She hadn't slept and already had a blazing headache, but she couldn't help but smile. Memories of the night before sent a flurry of butterflies dancing in her stomach. If she thought Kelsey had rocked her world the other times they'd made love—God, there was that word again. Had sex—had sex, the night before had shattered any thoughts of anyone else ever touching her in the same way. Kelsey had been attentive and gentle when Elizabeth needed it, hard when she demanded it, and oh so thorough. Elizabeth had lost touch of the number of orgasms, not sure when one ended and another began. She'd somehow mustered enough strength to demand Kelsey stop so she could have the only other thing she needed—the joy of pleasing Kelsey. They'd finally collapsed into a light slumber, but she hadn't really slept. She'd been too entranced by the beat of Kelsey's heart against hers as they lay wrapped up in each other, a light breeze—thankfully cool in the hours before dawn—wafting through the open window and the sounds of the ranch drifting in. She had never in her life been happier.

Elizabeth leaned against the door and rubbed her forehead. And now she had to face the next crisis. She hadn't gotten out of a late Zoom meeting with the attorneys until after seven the night before—yet another complaint had been filed by the town about traffic disruption—this time claiming Sutton's presence was endangering schoolchildren. The route Brinkman was supposed to be using for hauling in the drainage culverts was nowhere near a populated area, but somehow the tractor trailers had been diverted through a residential area. Despite that, no children or anyone else had ever been endangered, but facts seemed to have nothing to do with reality. The complaints still needed to be handled. So she'd decided, for once, to put what she wanted before the project. And what she'd wanted was to spend the night with Kelsey.

"There's something we need to discuss."

"More trouble?"

"Yes, and no. I fired Brinkman."

"When we're behind schedule and overbudget?" Olivia spun her chair around from the small desk tucked in the corner of their trailer's main room where she'd set up her computer and widescreen monitors. "I thought it was awfully quiet out there. No one's working. Did you have a good reason?"

"More than one," Elizabeth said. "He's a misogynistic, disrespectful prick. Oh, and a thief."

Elizabeth relayed the entire conversation she had overheard between Brinkman and Kelsey before handing Olivia the change order. "And then there's this. He told me you'd approved it."

"What? As if I'd ever go around you—or give *him* anything for you to sign." Olivia's placid expression turned to a frown, then a deeper one as she flipped the pages. "Well, this is bullshit."

"Yes, well, he wasn't as well briefed as he should have been," Elizabeth said. "And the only reason he tried to pull this off is he thought I would sign it rather than admit I couldn't read it. Someone had to have told him that—someone who knows about me but clearly underestimated me."

"That limits the field quite a bit," Olivia said. "And makes this all very messy."

"This has been a mess since the beginning. I'm just starting to see how big a one." Elizabeth sighed and pulled out her phone. "I'm afraid it's going to get worse."

❖

"Hello, Dad."

"What the fuck did you do, Elizabeth?"

Elizabeth winced. He only used her full name when he was well and truly pissed.

"What exactly did you hear?" Elizabeth had learned long ago not to assume two people were talking about the same thing. She'd rather learn from him what he knew—or thought he did. She might be able to tell from that exactly who was feeding the information back to corporate.

"You fired Brinkman when the job is barely three-quarters finished."

"Yes, I did."

"Do you mind telling me," he said in a tone that sent icicles through the ether and nearly froze her ear, "What. The. Fuck. For?"

Elizabeth repeated once again the events of the morning, leaving out her suspicions as to why exactly Brinkman had presented the paperwork the way he had. "He was attempting to bilk us out of several hundred thousand dollars. What would you have done?"

The silence told her he hadn't known.

"The moron," he said in a low brutal tone, and she could tell he was beyond furious. Finally, he said, "Just how do you plan to finish this project?"

"I'll hire another contractor. I have good local contacts here. I'll handle it."

"You'd better get someone in there who will take orders and get the work done. These contractors will take you for everything they can. I've never met an honest one or one who's worth a damn. All they want is to do as little work as possible for the most money."

Elizabeth took the phone away from her ear and let her father continue to rant. She had heard it all before, so why did she need to hear it again? When blessed silence finally fell, she said, "I've been doing this a long time. I know what I'm doing."

"Well, these reports don't make it look that way. You're hemorrhaging money, and this little project isn't worth it."

Little project? Elizabeth clamped her jaws together. This might not have been the largest project she'd ever headed, but the ranch was perfectly situated for the kind of expansion into spin-off events that...

"Are you hearing me?" her father said.

"Oh, yes," Elizabeth said, "quite clearly. I've actually heard this a hundred times, and I've told you a hundred and one times, I know what I'm doing. We will be ready for the grand opening."

"Then you had better have a solution by eight tomorrow morning, my time. Otherwise, I'll have to make some changes."

The call disconnected. Elizabeth pictured him tossing his phone onto the desk and it bouncing off. He went through three or four a year.

"What's the plan?" Olivia asked when Elizabeth related the conversation.

"We're going to find Riley Mitchell."

❖

They tracked Riley down at the fire station in Wickenburg. The two bay doors on the long, single-story building stood open and the requisite shiny red firetruck and an equally spotless ambulance were parked, facing out, in each bay. Wickenburg Fire Department was emblazoned on the side of each, in old-fashioned lettering inside a shield logo. A portable basketball hoop hung on the side of the building, and Elizabeth pulled in just beyond it and parked.

"I think we're in Mayberry now," Olivia said as they walked around to the front of the building.

"What?" Elizabeth asked.

"Sorry—old sitcom reference."

"How old?"

"The sixties." At Elizabeth's stare, Olivia hastily added, "My parents watched all these old reruns when I was a kid. I thought every kid knew about them."

"That's a no," Elizabeth said as a ruddy-faced, strapping blond sauntered toward them.

"Help you ladies?" he asked. His nametag said Sven Sorenson. Not locally grown, apparently.

"Yes," Olivia said quickly. "We're looking for Riley Mitchell."

"In the kitchen. You can walk on back—it's the door on the left just inside the truck bay."

Riley stood at the sink rinsing a coffeepot when they walked in.

In addition to the compact kitchen area, the big rectangular room held a pool table and a circle of several chairs plus a couch in front of a ginormous TV. Elizabeth counted six sets of eyes looking their way, and they were all focused on Olivia.

Riley's surprised look turned to pleasure as she glanced from Elizabeth to Olivia. "Hey, I didn't expect to see you." She pulled out her phone and swiped a few times. "Did I miss a meeting or something?"

"No, nothing like that." Elizabeth looked around at their audience. "Is there someplace we can talk?"

"Sure, let's go out back on the patio."

Elizabeth and Olivia followed Riley across the room. Someone muttered in a not at all quiet tone, "Yo, Mitchell. Two? So not fair."

Chuckling followed.

"Ignore them," Riley said, and gestured to a picnic table under the green-striped extended awning. "I'm afraid it's not fancy."

"It's shade. Thanks," Elizabeth said, sitting on one of the bench seats. Olivia sat beside her, and Riley circled around to sit across from them.

"What's up?" Riley asked, looking from Olivia to Elizabeth.

"I've got a problem, and I need your help," Elizabeth said. She usually hated asking for help from anyone. A sign of weakness, her father had always said. But then her father, she'd finally learned, was not always right, and she didn't mind asking now.

"Sure, whatever I can do," Riley said.

"You know our job site and the kind of work we're doing out at the ranch," Elizabeth said. "I was hoping you could recommend a contractor to take over for Brinkman ASAP."

"What happened to Brinkman?" Riley asked carefully.

"I fired him."

"Ookaay. None of my business why, but is everything all right?"

"Yes. Or it will be as soon as I can get the work going again," Elizabeth said.

"Harris Construction." Riley scrolled through her phone. "I know Clive Harris is just finishing up a job. He's a good guy and does solid work. Here's his contact info."

Olivia automatically took out her phone. "Send it to me. Thanks."

Riley stood as they rose to go. "If there's anything else you need, let me know."

"Oh," Elizabeth said off-handedly, "I did have one other question. The inspection orders you've been getting for our job. Who issues those?"

"They come from the county fire commissioner's office," Riley said. "That would be Brant Sherwood."

"Right," Elizabeth said. "Same as our permits."

"Yep."

"Thanks again," Elizabeth said. "We'll contact Harris."

As they walked back to the SUV, Olivia said, "You want I should get acquainted, figuratively speaking, with Mr. Sherwood?"

Elizabeth smiled. "As always, you're one step ahead. Yes, I would like that very much."

CHAPTER THIRTY-FIVE

Kelsey woke at the first ring of her phone. The bedroom was barely light. Had to be a little before five thirty in the morning. Definitely not Sophia. Elizabeth stirred beside her as she reached to grab the phone. The alarm would be going off any second. On the rare nights when Elizabeth spent the night in her bed, she always left the casita well before the guests or the Sutton crew started to stir. The sex was better than any she'd ever imagined, but what she hadn't imagined was how good it felt to talk over the day or recount some amusing story about a guest or listen to Elizabeth's new plans for the project. What she hadn't expected was how much she looked forward to Elizabeth arriving in the evening, and the disappointment when she didn't.

"Damn it." She didn't recognize the number. She hated answering unknown numbers. They were typically robocalls asking if she wanted to extend the warranty on a truck she didn't even own any longer, but the timing seemed wrong and she couldn't chance that a guest had wandered off and was lost somewhere. "Hello?"

"Tell your mother to stop looking for me."

Kelsey's heart flip-flopped at the sound of her father's voice. It had been over a month since her mother's surprise visit, and though she couldn't succeed entirely, she'd tried to put her parents out of her mind. She couldn't make the hurt of what they'd done go away, but she wouldn't let them keep on hurting her.

"Where are you?" His voice sounded thinner than she

remembered. A loudspeaker in the background announced something she couldn't quite make out. Train station, maybe?

"Never mind that. Just tell her from me I'm gone, and she ain't getting anything from me."

"Are you okay? I've been worried—"

"No reason to. I'm fine."

He sounded defensive, the way he always had when he'd been drinking. She wasn't managing this conversation very well, but the shock of hearing his voice after all these months had thrown her. Elizabeth pushed the covers aside and started to get up. Kelsey grasped her hand and shook her head. Elizabeth settled back and lightly rested one hand on Kelsey's arm. The touch was like an anchor, and her racing heart steadied.

"When are you planning to come back?"

"What for? Nothing there for me anymore."

"Nothing here? *I'm* here." Kelsey's shock made her voice crack. "You ought to know that—you made that part of the deal."

"You could have walked," he said.

Kelsey squeezed her eyes shut. How had she never known him all this time? "I don't walk out on a deal, even one I didn't make."

"Just do as I said and tell your mother—"

"No," Kelsey said, "no more." Hurt and betrayal turned to anger. The two people who were supposed to care about her had left her, and their reasons, purely selfish ones, no longer mattered. She finally understood she wasn't to blame. Not when she was seven years old and not now. "If she finds you, you deal with it. I'm done with both of you."

She ended the call, and when Elizabeth reached for her hand, she pulled away. Her rage was so huge, she couldn't think. "I'm sorry. I just can't—I need to get away from here."

❖

Elizabeth debated exactly thirty seconds before jumping out of bed, throwing on her clothes on the way to grab an apple off the table, and hurrying outside. She knew where Kelsey would be.

She'd heard enough to know she was hurting, although she couldn't fathom how much. And she knew she couldn't let her bear it all alone. She reached the barn just a few minutes later. As she walked down the row of horses, Rebel, the black colt, nosed his head out over the stall gate and whinnied at her.

At the sound, Kelsey looked over her shoulder and frowned.

"Hello, Mr. Handsome," Elizabeth said gently as she held out the apple on her palm. With a toss of his head, which said he knew exactly how special he was, he delicately grasped the apple between velvet soft lips and munched on it, watching her as she walked the rest of the way to Kelsey.

"What are you doing here?" Kelsey asked.

"I knew you'd be here." Elizabeth nodded at the saddle Kelsey had propped on top of the horse stall gate. "Going for a ride?"

"I'm not good company right now," Kelsey said, turning away to finish placing Adira's tack. She tossed the blanket over her back and then hefted the saddle into place.

"You don't have to talk," Elizabeth said. "I'd like to go with you. It's a gorgeous dawn out there. I don't think I've ever seen a sky as beautiful as the one over this ranch."

Kelsey spun back to her. "Do you even know how to ride?"

"As I believe I mentioned the first time you asked," Elizabeth said, smiling at Kelsey's frown, "I do."

She held her breath, knew she was taking a chance. Kelsey would either admit she needed her, or needed someone, anyone, at that moment, or she'd keep the walls up between them. Elizabeth couldn't really blame her. As many times as they'd made love, they both knew the relationship was temporary. She'd accepted the risk she was taking, knowing how much she would lose when she had to leave. Kelsey might make a different decision and shut the door now.

"You can have Adira," Kelsey said. "I'll get one of the other horses ready."

"Actually, I'd like to take Rebel."

"Rebel?" Kelsey didn't bother to hide her amusement. "I don't think so. He's a lot of horse to handle."

"I'm used to handling difficult mounts." Elizabeth backed up, and Rebel immediately put his head out of his stall again. She stroked his neck. "Besides, I've been watching you work with him the last few months. He's not that difficult."

Kelsey narrowed her eyes. "Just how much experience do you have riding?"

Elizabeth sighed. "Mostly dressage, but a fair amount of jumping."

"Show jumping," Kelsey said in a decidedly dismissive tone.

Elizabeth nodded.

"Of course. The pastimes of the rich equestrians."

Elizabeth gave her that one, as she knew Kelsey was hurting and feeling prickly. "Actually, I only rode seriously until I was fourteen and I discovered I was a much better swimmer than an equestrian. But I can handle this one, and besides, he likes me."

"All right then," Kelsey said, surprising her. "His saddle is the middle one on the wall there."

"I'll just be a minute, then." Elizabeth paused. "We might want some water, and a bedroll would be good."

Kelsey's brows rose, but she strapped the items to her saddle. She watched Elizabeth saddle up Rebel and said, "All right, you do know what you're doing."

"I wouldn't lie to you," Elizabeth said, "and I certainly wouldn't take him out if I didn't think I could handle him."

"All right, but let me lead the way. He hasn't had that much trail experience, and if we come across a rattler, I don't want him spooked."

Elizabeth grimaced. "Please, be my guest. I'm more than happy for the two of you to deal with any creatures we come across."

Elizabeth was pleased to see that Rebel didn't feel the need to be out ahead, and she kept him just half a neck back as they rode away from the ranch and out into the foothills. The sky was awash with flame, the dawn a riot of blood reds, oranges, yellows, and over the mountains, deep purples. Twenty minutes later Kelsey slowed Adira and swiveled in her saddle.

"Why don't we sit for a while. The sun will be full up in another forty-five minutes and we'll want to head back."

"Here's fine," Elizabeth said.

They tethered the horses loosely to a mesquite bush, and Kelsey spread the bedroll in the shade of an outcrop of boulders.

"The view is gorgeous," Elizabeth said, her back to Kelsey as she looked out over the mountains. When she turned, Kelsey was watching her. Waiting. She liked that. "I think you should stretch out."

She enjoyed Kelsey's look of surprise. She hadn't expected any of this, and that was exactly what Elizabeth wanted. She wanted to keep Kelsey there in the present until some of the pain of the past dissipated. And more than that, she wanted her. She always wanted her whenever she looked at her.

Kelsey sat on the bedroll, stretched her legs out in front of her, and leaned back on both arms. "There's no way I'm taking my boots off out here."

Elizabeth laughed and knelt beside her on the bedroll. "I'm not taking anything off. We'll just have to work around things."

Before Kelsey could say anything, Elizabeth kissed her. Kelsey tasted of the heat of the morning and apple, one she'd probably shared with Adira. Elizabeth kept kissing her while she opened the buttons on her shirt and slipped her hand inside to cup one of her breasts. Kelsey drew a sharp breath, the sound she made when she was pleasured. Elizabeth had intended to go slowly, to give Kelsey time to move away from sadness, but Kelsey moaned into her mouth, her need raw and urgent. Elizabeth's heart pounded, and she was instantly and urgently aroused. She'd never found so much pleasure in pleasing another woman as she did with Kelsey.

"Lie back," she murmured, and started in on that damn belt buckle. Usually Kelsey let her work at it, but this time Kelsey brushed her hands aside and flipped it open herself.

"In a hurry?" Elizabeth whispered against the corner of Kelsey's mouth before nibbling at her lower lip.

Kelsey growled, an exasperated, impatient sound. "I woke up next to you this morning, didn't I? That means I was already wanting to come. So yeah, I'm ready."

Elizabeth's mind grew hazy for a second. Kelsey's excitement always drove hers, and if she wasn't careful, she'd lose her focus and Kelsey would know. Kelsey would take over, and Elizabeth wouldn't be able to say no. But not this time.

She opened the button on Kelsey's jeans, something she'd gotten very good at, and unzipped her fly. When she spread the denim open, she groaned. Nothing underneath.

"God, I love it when you don't wear underwear."

"Would you just fucking touch me," Kelsey said, raising her hips to give Elizabeth room to slide her hand inside her jeans.

When she did, she found her hot and hard and ready.

"I love your clit," she whispered as she kissed Kelsey again.

"Do it then," Kelsey gasped.

"Mm," Elizabeth murmured, tracing a finger along her length, circling below, and then up and around each side. "Watch the sky, baby. Watch the sun come up over this magnificent land. I don't want to hurry."

"You better. Come on. You know I'm ready."

Elizabeth did know. She could feel the swollen length of her pulse beneath her fingertips. She knew exactly where and how to touch Kelsey to make her come. She always planned to make her wait, but she never could. She loved to hear her groan as she brought her to orgasm, to feel her body grow rigid and her sex pulse beneath her palm. She stroked her the way she knew Kelsey needed and Kelsey came, hard and fast and with a sharp cry that pierced Elizabeth's heart.

"God, you're gorgeous," she breathed.

After a moment Kelsey opened her eyes and pulled her down beside her on the bedroll.

"How did you know I needed that?" she said, her voice rough and her eyes drowsy.

Elizabeth cradled her cheek against Kelsey's shoulder. "There weren't any words that would help, not now, but I knew you shouldn't be alone, and I wanted to be the one who was with you."

Kelsey looked into her eyes. "You're the only one who could be here now."

"Kelsey," Elizabeth whispered, "I—"

Kelsey pressed a finger against her lips. "No, don't. If you say it, you'll break me when you leave."

Elizabeth closed her eyes and pressed her face to the curve of Kelsey's neck. "Nothing will change it."

"I know." Kelsey kissed her forehead. "If I tried to do what I want to do out here, we'd run the risk of cactus and—"

Elizabeth hastily sat up. "Oh no, not a chance. I'll save it for you."

Kelsey laughed. "Promise?"

Elizabeth rolled her eyes. "Swear."

Kelsey pulled her jeans up, buttoned her fly, and buckled her belt. She sat next to Elizabeth, and for a moment, silence cloaked them as dawn broke.

"What a gorgeous sky," Elizabeth said, "our two amazing animals"—she glanced at Kelsey—"and an amazing woman. I couldn't ask for more."

Kelsey framed her face and kissed her. "Thank you for being here."

Elizabeth wanted to say *always*, but she couldn't, even though her heart would always be there.

CHAPTER THIRTY-SIX

Tuesday evening after Labor Day weekend, Kelsey sat on the front porch of the main house with a beer to watch another Arizona sunset. She'd sat in this same spot thousands of times since she'd been a kid, but she never got tired of the view. The ache of knowing she'd likely be leaving soon never left her but took up residence with the pain of the other things she'd lost, including her parents.

Elizabeth came out behind her and said softly, "Do you mind company?"

"Not if it's yours." Kelsey saw that Elizabeth was in what she thought of as her video clothes, the ones she wore when she had meetings virtually. She preferred Elizabeth in her casual on-the-job-site tailored pants, tony boots, and plain silk shirts. She looked sexy as hell and like she belonged on the ranch at the same time. "Long day?"

Elizabeth sighed and sat down in a rocker beside her. "Complicated one."

"I saw Clive Harris earlier," Kelsey said. "He told me his crew is making progress to get you back on schedule."

Elizabeth gave her a curious look. "Do you know him well?"

Kelsey nodded. "Clive and my...Red go way back. Growing up, Clive was always around." She blew out a breath. "Sometimes, maybe more times than I realized back then, he was more of a father to me than Red. He even stood in for me at things a father should have been there for—like father-daughter breakfasts at middle school and taking me to the father-daughter dance. When he'd bring Red home too drunk to drive, he'd make sure I got to bed and had food in the fridge for morning."

"He sounds like a good man. He seems that way to me now, too—working with him." Elizabeth reached across the space between their chairs and gripped Kelsey's hand. "I'm sorry for all the times your father let you down."

"I got used to the way things were," Kelsey said softly, "until they just became normal. When I came back from college, I thought things had changed. That *he'd* changed." She rubbed a hand over her face. "For a while it seemed like we were going to make this place into something special. Then the money dried up." She glanced at Elizabeth, whose face glowed in the last rays of the sun as it splintered over the mountaintops. "But he'd gambled or drunk it away."

"And none of that was your doing, and nothing you could have helped," Elizabeth said softly.

"No. It's taken me quite a while to see that." Kelsey took a deep breath. "And to see that you being the one to take over here wasn't your doing either. And even if it had been, there's no fault there. Red sold the place."

Elizabeth shook her head. "I can only say that had I been in charge from the beginning, I would have done things differently. But it wasn't my call."

"I know." Kelsey smiled wryly. "Our fathers backed us into some dandy corners. Who exactly did you piss off to get assigned this project?"

"Why do you think that?"

"You've built resorts in all kinds of exotic places. Why here? Hell, even what you have planned here isn't the usual Sutton kind of place—at least from what I've seen online of your other places."

"No, it isn't, is it?" Elizabeth said, her tone distant. Elizabeth had a very good poker face, but right now she'd clearly thought of something important and wasn't trying to hide it. That was new— her letting Kelsey see what she was thinking or feeling. "That's the missing piece—this place is off-brand."

"Okay—so then why is Sutton even interested? And why are *you* here?"

"Presumably because I slept with the wrong woman."

Kelsey choked on her beer. "Wow, I didn't see that coming. So, who was the lucky lady, and why was it a problem?"

"The sister of our chief financial officer, and he seemed to think I was corrupting her."

"Well," Kelsey said, "I know it wasn't because she was underage."

"Oh, not by six or seven years," Elizabeth said. "But she'd kept her interests in women from her family and presented a slightly different version as to why her brother saw us kissing than was actually true."

"*Saw* you?" Kelsey laughed harshly. "Was he having you followed?"

"No." Elizabeth winced. "Unfortunately, I'd broken one of my own rules and played too close to my own backyard. She'd spent the night and I was dropping her off at her car. Michael saw us kissing."

"Huh." Kelsey squashed the surge of jealousy that blasted out of nowhere. Like, this was in the past. They both had a past. Still... "Did you love her?"

"What?" Elizabeth laughed, her expression incongruous. "*Love* her? Of course not—she was a hook-up that went on too long."

A hook-up, like her. Kelsey stiffened. "Yeah. Big mistake."

Elizabeth tilted her head and gave Kelsey a look. "You stopped being a hook-up a long time ago."

"Sorry," Kelsey said softly. "I got a little territorial there for a minute."

"You don't need to apologize," Elizabeth said. "It's unnecessary, however."

Kelsey wasn't sure quite what that meant, but she definitely liked the way Elizabeth looked at her. Like she saw her and understood her.

"At any rate, Michael apparently wanted me far away from his sister, not that I wouldn't have done that myself—but he has my father's ear, and here I am."

Kelsey shook her head. "That's pretty crappy. Why don't you go work somewhere else? With your skills and experience, you could probably name your terms."

"I could never work anywhere else," Elizabeth said softly.

"Why not?"

"My dyslexia would be a major roadblock."

"So you go around."

Elizabeth laughed without humor. "What?"

Kelsey pulled her chair closer, leaned over, and kissed her. "You're a smart, capable, successful businesswoman. You're also motivated, driven, and honest." She kissed her again. "On top of that, you're a fair boss and an all-around good person."

"Stop," Elizabeth murmured, then grasped Kelsey's shirt when she tried to pull away. "*Not* the kisses."

"Are you listening?" Kelsey said. "I think you have a challenge. Just like every single person on this earth has challenges. You said yourself you can read, just slower. You sure as hell don't have any problem with blueprints, design, and the finances."

"But…"

Kelsey held up her hand. "No buts. Our parents, the people who were responsible for loving us unconditionally, for supporting us and for guiding us, failed miserably. But we've managed—we've survived, and we made our own successes. We know how to do that, and we can keep doing that."

Elizabeth cupped Kelsey's face. "How come it took me so long to realize what an amazing woman you are?"

Kelsey grinned. "I hide it well."

"Mm, well, now your secret is out."

"I trust you'll keep it." Kelsey's heart swelled. She could live on the look in Elizabeth's eyes for the rest of her life. Desire, yes, but more than that. Something she'd never known she wanted, and now feared she'd never be able to live without. The feeling was so huge, so amazing, she couldn't deny it. "I love the woman you are."

❖

Kelsey's words shot through her like heat lightning—setting the night ablaze with hope and promise. Could Kelsey mean what Elizabeth hoped she meant? Could she be loved by this incredible woman who had become the center of her days? Who never failed to challenge and entice her? The woman she'd come to trust and rely on. The woman who touched her as if she was fragile as glass and strong as bedrock. Did she dare?

Could she love when nothing was certain, when what she'd known all her life was that no one ever accepted her for herself? She searched Kelsey's face and found her answers in the tender regard that embraced her with tenderness and desire.

"This woman," Elizabeth murmured, "loves you, too."

Kelsey pulled her upright into her arms and kissed her long and hard. "This thing we have between us. You know we've got a rocky road ahead."

"I don't care, do you?"

"Not a bit. As long as I have you." Kelsey trembled. "But when this job—"

"I need you to trust me," Elizabeth said. "Can you do that for a little while?"

"Baby," Kelsey said, "I can do that forever."

Elizabeth pulled away and with her eyes on Kelsey, took out her phone. "Hi. Make the calls…I'm sure. It's time.

"Now," Elizabeth said when she hung up, "this woman who loves you wants you to take her to bed."

❖

The numbers on the bedside clock said 3:15 a.m. Elizabeth had been watching the numbers change for the past hour. A million thoughts careened into each other as she lay in the dark with Kelsey's arms wrapped around her. Could she really change the course of the future—one her father designed for her, even now? Did she care if her relationship with him would be forever changed, possibly ended? Despite him saying she was *a Sutton*, he'd always treated her as if she was just another employee, and not a very important one at that. Was she strong enough to stand up to him?

And what about Kelsey? She had fallen in love with Kelsey, and love was nothing like what she'd expected. When she looked at Kelsey, when she touched her, the joy was indescribable—as was the fear that she could lose her. Lose her before they'd even had a chance.

Before she could wake Kelsey with the tears that threatened to fall, she slipped out of bed, gathered her top and panties, and slipped out of the casita.

She made her way quickly down the flagstone path to the patio and through the gate to the pool. A moment later, she dangled her legs in the water and watched the ripples stream away into the dark. The water—any water, even the pool, calmed her. She needed a clear head to deal with her father, and she didn't have much time.

Why don't you go work somewhere else?

Kelsey's words came back to her, along with her certainty that Elizabeth could handle herself in the business world. But could she? Without Olivia to help her? Would her father just let her go?

We've managed—we've survived, and we made our own successes. We know how to do that.

But would Kelsey really trust her enough to try? She was due to leave in a few weeks. She shivered, although the air was warm. She could choose the safety of her old life, or she could risk everything she'd worked for on the chance that Kelsey would want…something…with her forever. Hide or take control of her future? Run or fight?

Become her father, or make her life what she wanted it to be?

"Hey," Kelsey said. "I woke up and your side of the bed was cold."

Elizabeth warmed at the words. She had a side of the bed. She'd never had a *side* of the bed. "I didn't want to disturb you."

"Want company?"

"Only if it's you." Elizabeth laughed and stroked Kelsey's bare leg. She'd come outside in just a pair of cut-off sweats and a T-shirt that had been similarly modified—no sleeves and cropped to show a swath of skin that stirred body parts that by rights should be satisfied for days after the night they'd just had.

The water rippled again when Kelsey sat beside her and dropped her legs into the pool.

"You're not swimming," Kelsey said.

Elizabeth leaned her shoulder against Kelsey's. "No. Just thinking. It's beautiful out here at night."

"Something wrong?"

"Now that you're here, no." Elizabeth sighed. "I've never been anyplace as peaceful, or as beautiful, as right here, right now."

"I've loved this place all my life, even before I was old enough to know what I was feeling. Now it's as much a part of me as my blood and my bones." Kelsey slipped her arm around Elizabeth's waist. "I've never wanted anything else—or didn't think I did— until I met you."

"And I've threatened everything you love, haven't I?"

"Not everything," Kelsey said in a tone Elizabeth had never heard before. "I learned something watching you transform parts of the ranch these last few months. The ranch is a place, and places change. Sometimes the change isn't all bad."

Elizabeth smiled. "Thank—"

Kelsey turned Elizabeth toward her. "Not done yet." She kissed her. "I could be happy in a different place, if I had you."

"I could be happy doing a lot of things," Elizabeth said, "if I had you."

"Let's start with doing something that will make us both happy. Come back to bed."

Elizabeth wrapped her arms around Kelsey's neck and kissed her. The problems would still be there in the morning, and maybe, just maybe, she'd have a solution soon. Now if she could only find a way to settle old scores that wouldn't break Kelsey's heart.

CHAPTER THIRTY-SEVEN

"I'm sorry. I keep waking you, don't I." Elizabeth pushed the covers back. "I'll head over to the trailer. It's only four. You can get another hour's—"

Kelsey grabbed her arm. "No way. I'm awake. You're awake. I'm horny. I'm sure we can think of something to do for the next hour."

Laughing, Elizabeth kicked the sheet aside and straddled Kelsey's hips, the familiar rush of desire swamping every other sensation. Like that first night in Phoenix, she needed a mind-blowing orgasm to give her restless mind some peace and clear her head for the most important negotiations she might ever have. But unlike that time, she didn't need to drive into the night to a forgettable bar in an unfamiliar town to hunt out a nameless stranger for sex that would leave her body sated but her heart unfulfilled. She leaned forward, increasing the pressure on her clit, and kissed Kelsey. Slowly. Toying with her. Teasing her. Teasing herself as the pressure built and spread deep inside.

"I love you," she whispered, bracing her hands on either side of Kelsey's shoulders. Watching Kelsey watching her. Shocked at how much she craved this. The overwhelming need to give Kelsey anything she wanted. "I love your ranch. I love your horses. I love your stubborn pride, and your tenderness. I love everything about you."

Kelsey cupped her breasts, her eyes in the dark in the emerging dawn light. "If you love me, wait for me no matter what happens. Don't leave me."

Elizabeth's eyes fluttered closed, stars dancing in the periphery of her mind as the tension spread. "Never…God, I'm going to come so hard. God."

"I love when you come this way," Kelsey whispered, cradling Elizabeth's hips and sitting up. She skimmed her lips over Elizabeth's breasts and nipples.

"Just for you." Elizabeth moaned. "Harder. I'm coming."

Elizabeth's breath caught as the orgasm ripped through her. Her vision blurred, her head spun, and the world disappeared. Except for Kelsey. Kelsey was everywhere and everything. When the relentless waves of release finally quieted, she collapsed onto Kelsey's chest, her heart hammering beneath her breast.

Kelsey lost herself in the sounds of Elizabeth's pleasure. She was close to orgasm herself, her skin awash with sweat, by the time Elizabeth sagged into her arms. She was strung so tight every muscle ached. "I need to come. I need you."

"Mm," Elizabeth murmured lazily. So much more than sex, this intimacy she'd never known with anyone else. She slid her hand down Kelsey's taut abdomen. "Here?"

"Yes. Just a little…oh, fuck." She jolted as the climax wrenched the words from her throat. Groaning, she pressed her face to Elizabeth's neck. "You kill me, you're so beautiful."

"I don't think that's what just got you off."

Kelsey laughed weakly. "Yeah, well, you're pretty amazing when you come, too."

"Ditto." Elizabeth kissed her and curled into her arms, her mind finally quiet and her soul at peace. This was what she never knew she'd wanted—this connection to the one woman who could fill her heart with joy and her life with excitement and promise. Whatever she had to do, she would not let this slip away.

❖

A terrible screeching noise plummeted Elizabeth out of a wonderful sex dream—oh, that hadn't been a dream—into an eardrum-bursting nightmare.

"What the hell!" Kelsey jumped out of bed and was into her jeans and shirt before Elizabeth was fully awake.

Boom! A thunderous blast drowned out even the screeching sound.

"What is *that*?" she cried.

"Shotgun," Kelsey said grimly. "And that's the barn alarm. Someone is after the horses."

Elizabeth jumped out of bed. Not bothering to sort through the clothes scattered about where they'd left them the night before, she pulled on the first thing she could find. A pair of Kelsey's jeans—too big, screw it, she'd wear them—and a shirt off a pile on the dresser. She raced after Kelsey, buttoning the front as she ran.

She'd almost caught up to Kelsey when Kelsey yanked the door open and nearly ran full out into Ruben, their lead trail hand, with Clive Harris a few steps behind. Rubin's shirt tail was flapping, his Stetson askew, and his face a study in fury.

"Ruben, what the hell—who's shooting?"

"Josie. Some men just drove in with two horse trailers. Said they'd come for the horses. Josie's in front of the barn doors holding them off, and she ain't too happy," Rubin said breathlessly.

Clive Harris jumped up onto the porch, not even bothering with the steps. He waved a printout at Elizabeth. "What is this? It was under the door in our office trailer."

He waited, apparently expecting Elizabeth to take it and read it. Elizabeth reached for it, but Kelsey got to it first. She scanned the single page and stared at Elizabeth.

"Someone has ordered Clive to raze the barns." She sounded as stunned as she looked.

"Who signed it?" Elizabeth snapped.

Kelsey looked again, her hand shaking. "A Michael Wyland."

"Yes, well," Elizabeth said, stepping forward to address Clive, "Michael Wyland has no authority here. I determine what work is to be done. Ignore it." She turned to Rubin. "Take me to these gentlemen who've come for the horses. And for heaven's sake, someone tell Josie to put the gun away."

"I'll take care of it," Kelsey said, "I'm going to the barn. No one touches our horses. Not today—not ever."

Elizabeth gripped her arm. "I don't know what this is about, but I'll find out. I had no idea—"

"I know that." Kelsey held her gaze. "I know you."

Olivia arrived just in time to hear that last exchange. "I'm afraid we might have bigger problems on the way."

Elizabeth watched the black limo emerge from a cloud of dust and turn toward the main house.

"Now what," Kelsey said grimly.

"That," Elizabeth said, "if I'm not mistaken, would be my father."

CHAPTER THIRTY-EIGHT

"Hello, Dad, what are you doing here?" Elizabeth hid her shock behind the cool façade she always adopted when dealing with her father. His disdain for emotions had taught her well how to hide her own. "The site inspection isn't for another two weeks."

"I wanted to assess the situation here," her father said, ignoring everyone but Olivia and Elizabeth, as if they didn't exist. For him, they didn't. They weren't Sutton people. Kelsey, after a quick look at Elizabeth, walked off with Ruben and Clive in the direction of the barn.

Elizabeth kept her focus on her father. *Assess the situation? As in he doesn't trust my reports?* Clearly he didn't, but she doubted that was the only reason he had arrived just as new work orders came through. Orders she had no knowledge of and that he would know she would never agree to. "The major construction is complete, the landscaping for the guest areas underway, and the finishing work on the interiors is scheduled to begin next week. The construction of the new indoor pool has been delayed as well as the final grading on the golf course, but we expect that—"

"I'll see things for myself." He turned to Olivia. "Bring me the project schedule and some means of transportation."

Olivia glanced quickly at Elizabeth, who nodded. "Sure thing."

"Why didn't you let me know you were coming?"

"I wanted to see for myself where you were with the construction."

"I've been giving you briefings every week. You never said you had any concerns."

"I didn't."

"Did you issue the new orders to raze the barn and remove the horses?"

"There have been a few changes in the plans," he said, not meeting her eyes for the first time.

"And you didn't include me—considering this is my project?"

"It's a Sutton project," he said sharply. "And you work for Sutton. That means you'll do what needs doing here, because *that's* your job."

Elizabeth heard what he didn't bother saying. That he didn't trust her to know what was really going on. Didn't trust that she would do the job she'd done for seventeen years. She'd always known how little he'd valued her, but she'd refused to stop trying. Until she'd learned what love—the love she'd hoped to get from him and never had—really felt like. His words hurt, but no longer wounded as deeply as they once had. She was stronger now, and that strength was her shield. "Since you're here, let me show you around."

"No, I'll look around myself." He walked toward the cart as Olivia pulled around the drive toward them and got out with the project folder in her hand. He took the folder, got into the cart, and drove away.

"What is he doing here?" Olivia asked. "He's never come during construction."

"I don't think this has anything to do with the project—not this project anyhow." Elizabeth rubbed her forehead, trying to stem the rising headache. "It's time for you to finalize the paperwork. We're out of time."

"You're sure?"

"Never more."

"Give me two hours." Olivia's gaze hardened. "Let's do this."

❖

His tour took a little over two hours. Elizabeth had left word she'd be in the office. If he was surprised to see Kelsey there, along with Olivia, he didn't show it. He simply tossed the project folder on the desk and said, "This place is not ready."

Her father never disappointed her, not where business was concerned. He never sugarcoated his words or even tried to make them less hurtful. He'd taught her well—how well, he was about to find out.

"Of course it's not. We don't open for another two weeks," Elizabeth said.

"It won't *be* ready."

"Are you responsible for trying to steal my horses?" Kelsey said flatly.

Jonas Sutton raised his brows. "And you are?"

"Kelsey Brunel."

"Ah. The daughter."

"I'm the ranch manager," Kelsey said with more calm than Elizabeth had ever heard. She had a feeling that calm was covering a volcano about to erupt.

"Yes—I recall something about your staying on. Temporarily." Jonas dismissed Kelsey with barely a shrug and turned to Elizabeth. "I hope you haven't let your emotions get in the way of your better judgment. I understand that you stonewalled several new work orders this morning."

So *now* he knew about them. Michael's network was quick.

"Since we have plans for a number of new excursions," Elizabeth said, "as I outlined in my reports several times, the horses are critical for our operations. Those orders were clearly in error." She shrugged, mimicking him. "These things happen."

His eyes flashed with the first sign of anger. "There won't be any need for them, your *ranch manager*, or most of the other help. We're shutting this down."

Kelsey uttered a curse.

Elizabeth expected it, but the blow hurt all the same. He had let her get this far, knowing this would destroy her credibility as a project head at best and ruin her reputation completely at worst. All for a profit? "When did you decide this?"

"When is not important. You and the rest of the crew need to be out by the end of the month."

"I don't think so."

"What are you talking about?" her father snapped. "Have you forgotten who I am?"

"No, I haven't forgotten. That's why I never believed you didn't know what was happening here." Elizabeth doubted anything she said would matter to him, but she needed to say it. "I've done everything for Sutton. I've taken every job you've handed me, and I've brought every project in on time."

"You're only as good as your last project, and this one has failed. Your own reports show that."

His words were hard, cruel, and bitterly cold, and Elizabeth almost flinched from the pain. She would not let him see how much she hurt.

Kelsey said, "You have no idea what you're talking about. Besides that, you're about to destroy something you might never get back."

"I don't need any advice from you." Jonas looked at Elizabeth. "Michael has a buyer ready—we won't lose any more money. In fact," he said, looking smug, "we'll make a bit of a profit, what with the write-offs on the lost revenues here."

"I don't think so, Dad," Elizabeth said softly.

"What did you say?" His eyes glinted like chips of stone. Hard, cold, and utterly without feeling.

"There won't be any sale of the Red Sky Ranch, because it's already been sold."

For the first time in her life, she saw her father caught off guard. He looked around as if for support, and she realized he was looking for Michael. The one he really counted on. The one who always had his ear. The one who had orchestrated all of this. The understanding hurt, but not as much as she expected.

He said, "Michael has—"

"Michael made a mistake when he hatched this little plan," Elizabeth said. "Were you always part of it, or did he just talk you into it after the fact?"

Her father's momentary hesitation told her what she needed to know. It didn't ease the pain—nothing ever would—but at least she knew he hadn't deliberately put her in the middle of Michael's scheme.

"I think you'd better explain what you're talking about," Jonas Sutton said.

"You thought Maguire Development was buying the Red Sky, didn't you," Elizabeth said.

He flushed. "How do you know—"

"It wasn't that hard when it became obvious someone was trying to derail the project—someone who knew every detail and exactly how to slow us down just enough. Michael needed more time—or should I say his *sister*, Julia Maguire, CEO of Maguire Development—needed more time to acquire the necessary funds to buy the ranch from Sutton. That was always the plan, wasn't it?"

"There's nothing underhanded about the legal sale of property," Jonas said.

"There is when Maguire's silent partners, Mayor Swigler and County Fire Commissioner Sherwood, have intentionally colluded to slow down the project."

Jonas paled and glanced around the room. "Michael's sister was willing to match our purchase price and add a percentage for all the work already done."

"Yes—so her development company could build a new bedroom community of townhouses for high-income buyers who want to get out of Phoenix." Elizabeth shook her head. "Unfortunately, Maguire's silent partners decided to pull out after my attorneys suggested to them we might need to review all the filings and permits pertaining to this project to sort out all the delays. Apparently, they decided not to invest after all. When the deal fell through, Julia Maguire wisely wanted to distance herself from the whole matter, too. She even convinced her brother Michael that the best way to handle the difficult situation was for him to find another buyer ASAP."

Elizabeth straightened. "That buyer is me." She looked at her watch. "I own the Red Sky Ranch as of twenty-two minutes ago. Oh, and don't worry, I offered exactly what Michael had intended to sell the ranch to his sister for. You won't lose anything at all."

Except me.

She glanced at Kelsey, who stiffened with surprise. *Just wait, give me time to explain,* she silently shouted. When Kelsey didn't bolt for the door, she drew a breath.

"Michael wouldn't sell to you," Jonas scoffed, but he looked uncertain.

"I never suggested I'd attempt legal action against the Wickenburg officials who colluded—such a nasty word—to derail this project, but apparently Michael's sister wasn't so sure." Elizabeth smiled. "She put in a good word for me to Michael after Olivia and I made a friendly call to express our concerns about her new partners. I might have mentioned I'd be happy to buy the ranch instead."

"Just what are you going to do out here in Podunk? You're not equipped to deal with the demands of *owning* anything."

"What I plan has nothing to do with you or Sutton Properties." Elizabeth took a breath, a deep breath that felt like freedom. "I quit."

"You can't quit," he exclaimed.

"Of course I can. I just did."

"You'll regret this," he said, standing abruptly. "When you fail at whatever this little plan of yours is, don't come to me to bail you out."

"If I fail, you'd be the last person I'd ask for help." Elizabeth lifted her chin, her gaze turning to Kelsey. "But I won't fail. I know exactly what I want, and what I'm doing."

Speechless at last, Jonas stalked to the door, yanked it open, and stormed off in the direction of the limo. A minute later the sound of screeching tires signaled his exit. Elizabeth sighed, sad and satisfied in equal measure. She'd won. She had everything she wanted. At least she hoped it was everything.

Kelsey said quietly, "So you own the Red Sky now."

"I—"

"Excuse me," Olivia said. "I have somewhere else to be, so I should go find out where that is."

She disappeared and Elizabeth took Kelsey's hand. "It's a bit complicated, but I can explain. Will you listen?"

Kelsey nodded. "I said I trusted you, and I do."

"Come sit down." Elizabeth led Kelsey to the bench seat along the wall. She'd been cautious her whole life, always following the rules, trying to be what her parents wanted her to be. This time she had followed her heart. In her mind's eye, she was standing once again on the starting block at the edge of the Olympic pool, ready to carve out her destiny. She took a deep breath and dove.

"Because of you, I've learned that being successful by my father's standards wasn't what I wanted. I think I tried for so long because I couldn't imagine anything else. I couldn't see myself in a world that wasn't Sutton ruled. My parents saw to that." She smiled and kissed Kelsey. "When I'm in your arms, I can see forever. I can see where I want to be, and what I want to do with my life."

"And that is?"

Elizabeth had asked for Kelsey's trust. She needed to trust her in return. "I want to spend my life with you, and I want that life to be here—on the ranch. I'll take care of the spa, and you do what you do best—run the ranch. I know that together, we can do anything."

"Partners," Kelsey said quietly. "How can we be partners when you own the ranch?"

"Olivia has another contract ready for signatures. If you sign, we'll be equal partners."

Kelsey stood and paced. "I don't have that kind of money, and I sure as hell won't take charity—especially not from you."

"You don't need cash. As far as I'm concerned, the assets of the ranch—including the land, the animals, and your experience in running it—are more than enough to offset any payments. But if the only way you'll be comfortable is with a buy-in, we'll work out a fair price and a long-term payment plan."

Kelsey stopped and regarded Elizabeth for so long, Elizabeth had the sinking feeling she'd made the worst mistake of her life. One she knew she would never recover from.

"You've been thinking about this for a long time," Kelsey said. "I would have told you sooner, but it took Olivia until just a few days ago to dig through all the paperwork and trace everything back to the mayor, the fire commissioner, and Michael's sister. Brinkman was getting kickbacks for keeping them all informed of our progress. I'm sorry."

"Don't be." Kelsey put her arms around her. "Why is Olivia the only one who calls you Ellie?"

"I've never liked it when my father used it," Elizabeth said slowly. "With him it was to make me feel small. It was about power. Olivia calls me that because she's the only one I'm certain loves me."

"I don't want to be just your business partner, Ellie." Kelsey cupped her chin and looked into her eyes. "I want us to be partners in every way. I love you. And yes, I want to live with you and make the Red Sky into something special. Something we make together— just like our lives. I want to be your partner in all the things that matter. I want to fall asleep beside you every night and watch the sunrise with you every morning. I love you, and I want you to stay. But only like that. Will you stay and be mine, always?"

Ellie kissed her, untroubled by the tears she couldn't hold back. She could trust Kelsey with her heart and her dreams. "I love you, too, and we'll be each other's forever."

About the Authors

In addition to editing over twenty LGBTQIA+ anthologies, RADCLYFFE has written over sixty-five romance and romantic intrigue novels, including a paranormal romance series, The Midnight Hunters, as L.L. Raand.

She is a three-time Lambda Literary Award winner in romance and erotica and received the Dr. James Duggins Outstanding Mid-Career Novelist Award from the Lambda Literary Foundation. A member of the Saints and Sinners Literary Hall of Fame, she is also an RWA/FF&P Prism Award winner for *Secrets in the Stone*, an RWA FTHRW Lories and RWA HODRW winner for *Firestorm*, an RWA Bean Pot winner for *Crossroads*, an RWA Laurel Wreath winner for *Blood Hunt*, a Book Buyers Best award winner for *Price of Honor* and *Secret Hearts*, and a 2023 Golden Crown Literary Award winner for *Perfect Rivalry*. She is also a featured author in the 2015 documentary film *Love Between the Covers*, from Blueberry Hill Productions. In 2019 she was recognized as a "Trailblazer of Romance" by the Romance Writers of America.

In 2004 she founded Bold Strokes Books, one of the world's largest independent LGBTQ publishing companies, and is the current president and publisher.

Find her at facebook.com/Radclyffe.BSB, follow her on Twitter @RadclyffeBSB, and visit her website at Radfic.com.

JULIE CANNON divides her time by being a corporate suit, a wife, mom, sister, friend, and writer. Julie and her wife have lived in at least a half a dozen states, traveled around the world, and have an unending supply of dedicated friends. And of course, the most important people in their lives are their three kids, #1, Dude, and the Divine Miss Em.

Among her numerous best-selling novels, *I Remember* won the Golden Crown Literary Society's award for Best Lesbian Romance.

Books Available From Bold Strokes Books

Coasting and Crashing by Ana Hartnett. Life comes easy to Emma Wilson until Lake Palmer shows up at Alder University and derails her every plan. (978-1-63679-511-9)

Every Beat of Her Heart by KC Richardson. Piper and Gillian have their own fears about falling in love, but will they be able to overcome those feelings once they learn each other's secrets? (978-1-63679-515-7)

Fire in the Sky Two women from different worlds have nothing in common and every reason to wish they'd never met—except for the attraction neither can deny. by Radclyffe and Julie Cannon. TK (978-1-63679-561-4)

Grave Consequences by Sandra Barret. A decade after necromancy became licensed and legalized, can Tamar and Maddy overcome the lingering prejudice against their kind and their growing attraction to each other to uncover a plot that threatens both their lives? (978-1-63679-467-9)

Haunted by Myth by Barbara Ann Wright. When ghost-hunter Chloe seeks an answer to the current spectral epidemic, all clues point to one very famous face: Helen of Troy, whose motives are more complicated than history suggests and whose charms few can resist. (978-1-63679-461-7)

Invisible by Anna Larner. When medical school dropout Phoebe Frink falls for the shy costume shop assistant Violet Unwin, everything about their love feels certain, but can the same be said about their future? (978-1-63679-469-3)

Like They Do in the Movies by Nan Campbell. Celebrity gossip writer Fran Underhill becomes Chelsea Cartwright's personal assistant with the aim of taking the popular actress down, but neither of them anticipates the clash of their attraction. (978-1-63679-525-6)

Limelight by Gun Brooke. Liberty Bell and Palmer Elliston loathe each other. They clash every week on the hottest new TV show, until Liberty starts to sing and the impossible happens. (978-1-63679-192-0)

Playing with Matches by Georgia Beers. To help save Cori's store and help Liz survive her ex's wedding, they strike a deal: a fake relationship, but just for one week. There's no way this will turn into the real deal. (978-1-63679-507-2)

The Memories of Marlie Rose by Morgan Lee Miller. Broadway legend Marlie Rose undergoes a procedure to erase all of her unwanted memories, but as she starts regretting her decision, she discovers that the only person who could help is the love she's trying to forget. (978-1-63679-347-4)

The Murders at Sugar Mill Farm by Ronica Black. A serial killer is on the loose in southern Louisiana, and it's up to three women to solve the case while carefully dancing around feelings for each other. (978-1-63679-455-6)

A Talent Ignited by Suzanne Lenoir. When Evelyne is abducted and Annika believes she has been abandoned, they must risk everything to find each other again. (978-1-63679-483-9)

All Things Beautiful by Alaina Erdell. Casey Norford only planned to learn to paint like her mentor, Leighton Vaughn, not sleep with her. (978-1-63679-479-2)

An Atlas to Forever by Krystina Rivers. Can Atlas, a difficult dog Ellie inherits after the death of her best friend, help the busy hopeless romantic find forever love with commitment-phobic animal behaviorist Hayden Brandt? (978-1-63679-451-8)

Bait and Witch by Clifford Mae Henderson. When Zeddi gets an unexpected inheritance from her client Mags, she discovers that Mags served as high priestess to a dwindling coven of old witches—who are positive that Mags was murdered. Zeddi owes it to her to uncover the truth. (978-1-63679-535-5)

Buried Secrets by Sheri Lewis Wohl. Tuesday and Addie, along with Tuesday's dog, Tripper, struggle to solve a twenty-five-year-old mystery while searching for love and redemption along the way. (978-1-63679-396-2)